THE
PARTY AT
NO.12

BOOKS BY KERRY WILKINSON

THE
PARTY AT
NO.12

KERRY WILKINSON

bookouture

Published by Bookouture in 2022

An imprint of Storyfire Ltd.
Carmelite House
50 Victoria Embankment
London EC4Y 0DZ

www.bookouture.com

ISBN: 978-1-80314-277-7
eBook ISBN: 978-1-80314-276-0

PROLOGUE

HANNAH

The sofa was a big bag of elbows, which was a problem for Hannah considering she was trying to sleep on it.

She wriggled one way, then the other, except the sofa wasn't the reason why she was awake. There was something else.

A low gasp seeped from the hallway that led to the bedrooms on one side of the unfamiliar house. Hannah heaved herself up, joints creaking, muscles complaining. Her younger sisters didn't know how good they had it. This sort of thing would all be theirs one day.

The breath echoed for the second time, perhaps the third, and Hannah stumbled towards it. Her throat was dry from the previous night's excess and she accidentally kicked a bottle across the floor as if to emphasise the point. There was a clunk as it thudded into the kitchen counter, spun in a circle, and then settled without breaking.

This time there was a call from the corridor, a woman's voice that sounded as scratchy as Hannah's felt.

'I think she's dead.'

Hannah paused mid-step, trying to figure out if she'd heard correctly. Light was beaming through the tall windows at the back of the living room, reflecting off the bright white walls. This place was like a show home, or something they'd knock together on one of those property shows. All style with little substance – which explained the sofa like a bag of elbows.

'Is someone there?'

The same voice reverberated along the hall again and Hannah followed it, squinting as the light dimmed down to a muddy grey.

Hannah's Aunt Dawn was at the end of the corridor, standing next to an open door. She turned between Hannah and whatever was beyond.

'She's not breathing,' Dawn said.

'Who?'

Hannah crept along the corridor, edging deeper into the darkness.

'She's blue,' Dawn whispered. 'Not blue, maybe grey...'

Hannah's aunt stepped to the side, allowing her free passage into the bedroom beyond.

'She's not moving,' Dawn added. 'I said her name but she won't reply.' There was another pause and then Dawn said it again: 'I think she's dead.'

PART 1
SLEEPOVER

ONE

SIXTEEN HOURS EARLIER

Dawn stretched her Tesco bag-for-life higher and rattled it up and down, making the bottles inside clank together. The jangling reminded Hannah of the psychopath who used to live next door. He'd get up at half-five every Tuesday and wheel his recycling bin down the driveway, waking half the neighbourhood. He couldn't put it out the night before, like a normal person. Or even in a mad panic when he heard the lorry screeching its way down the road. It *had* to be half-five.

Hannah was lost, thinking of that, when her aunt brought her back to the present.

'How many are we waiting on?' Dawn asked.

Hannah didn't bother to look up. 'Three,' she answered.

Dawn lowered her bag and glanced around the circle of women. 'How many's that?' she asked.

Hannah ignored the question. There were five of them standing on the pavement and, with three to come, it was hardly a complex algebraic equation. Some people talked for the sake of talking – and Aunt Dawn would make those people seem like the quiet, retiring type.

'Cold, isn't it?' Dawn added.

None of the other four women replied.

'They reckon it might snow tonight,' she continued, oblivious to the lack of interest, even though it was definitely cold.

Hannah pulled her jacket tighter around her shoulders and then glanced up, where she caught her sister's eye. Neither she nor Charlotte spoke but they didn't need to. The silent eye roll almost brought the gentlest of upward curves to her lips, not that Aunt Dawn noticed.

Hannah glanced away before she started giggling and, for a moment, it was like the old, old days with herself and Charlotte. Those times where they would have private jokes that could be told with the merest hint of a smirk. Hannah's mother said nothing – she'd had a lifetime of listening to her sister after all. The fifth member of the group, Hannah's youngest sister, Beth, also remained quiet.

Dawn remained oblivious. 'How long are we going to have to wait?' she added. 'I thought you said four? It's already five-past.'

She rattled her bag again and then, almost as if she'd summoned him, a man emerged from a few doors down and started along the street towards them. He was wearing jeans that were too tight, which meant he walked with something of a sideways gait, a bit like a constipated crab. His shirt was tight, too. Either he'd shrunk everything in the wash, or he was one of those blokes who confused moobs with pecs.

He tossed a set of keys from one hand to the other, dropped them, and then awkwardly picked them up from the ground, before acting as if it hadn't happened.

He eyed the semicircle of women, sniffed loudly and then wiped his nose with his sleeve. 'Which one of you is Hannah?' he asked.

Hannah raised a finger and offered a slim smile. The man had sounded friendly through his emails but he had the look of a bloke who'd stare at women on a train.

'I'm Jeff,' he said. 'The owner.'

Everyone turned to look up at the bungalow that loomed over them. There were three steps and then a short path that led towards the pristine white front door. An elegant, swirly '12' was chiselled into a sleek plaque attached to the wall.

Dawn chose that moment to rattle her bag once more. 'Wahey, let's get this party started!'

Jeff looked towards her and frowned as she lowered the bag. Charlotte huffed in annoyance, a sentiment that Hannah felt too.

'It's not that sort of party,' Hannah said quickly.

The owner was nervously scratching his neck. 'It's more of a *luxury* property,' he said. 'That's why it's on the *Luxury* Rentals website.'

Hannah glanced towards her mum, who picked up on the silent nudge. 'We won't be any trouble,' Hannah's mum said quickly. 'I'm Alison. This is my sister, Dawn, and these three are my daughters. It'll just be a few drinks. Family and close friends. Nothing crazy. I'm way too old for all that.'

She laughed at herself but it petered away almost instantly when nobody else joined in.

'My daughter's going travelling on Friday,' she added, with a nod towards Hannah. 'It's just her family and friends seeing her off. We won't be any trouble.'

Jeff eyed Dawn, who lowered her bag further and, for once, kept her mouth closed. He turned his attention to Hannah, looking her up and down and making her shiver for a reason that wasn't the cold.

'It's more of a dinner party,' Alison continued. 'Classy and upmarket.' She hoisted her small suitcase onto the bottom step, as if to say there was an expensive dress inside that would match her description. Hannah knew for a fact there wasn't anything of the sort within. It was more comfy pyjamas and a bottle of booze, like some sort of two-for-one desperation special at the cash and carry.

'The house looked lovely in the photos,' Hannah added, as she tapped her own suitcase. 'I brought board games!' She nudged Beth with her elbow. 'It was such a great find. My sister's friend lived here years ago.'

Jeff focused on Beth now, the youngest of the group. Beth stared past him, up towards the house.

'Who's your friend?' he asked.

'Lucy. Lucy Harris. She moved away.'

Jeff blinked with apparent surprise. 'Yeah, the previous owners *were* called Harris. The place was a wreck when I bought it...'

He tailed off and Beth offered a slim smile, though her gaze never left the house. Her arms remained wrapped around herself, her phone gripped tightly in her hand. Not engaging too much with a man like Jeff was a self-defence mechanism for young women who'd spent too much time on public transport. One minute, they were telling you to smile more; the next, they were calling you a bitch for not taking out your AirPods.

The silence hung awkwardly and, after a momentary glance towards Dawn and her bag of booze, Jeff nodded slightly and then turned back to the house. 'I'm only three doors down at number six, if there's trouble...' He passed the oversized bunch of keys from one hand to the other, carefully this time, and then headed up the stairs with the five women slotting in behind. At the end of the path, he unlocked the front door and then pushed it inwards, before holding it open and waiting for everyone to file past.

Hannah held her breath as she passed, tilting her head away from him, and pretending not to notice as he inhaled all too close to her hair.

When they were in, Jeff closed the door behind them and

then stood in front of it, holding his hands up to indicate the space beyond.

'I live three doors down,' he repeated. 'When this place went on the market, it needed a load of work. Took a couple of years to get it into shape but it's looking good now, isn't it?'

He stood, waiting for approval, and, though nobody gave it, it would have been impossible to disagree. Hannah scanned across the large, open space. There was a bright kitchen off to one side; all granite counter tops and bright white cupboard doors. Beyond that was an elaborate chandelier dangling over a dining table – and then a lounge at the rear of the room with a large U-shaped sofa. Past that was a tall bank of windows, beyond which was a lush green lawn. All of that had been in the photos on the Luxury Rentals website – but it was much more impressive in person. The sort of place featured in a mass-mailed interior design catalogue that would be dumped straight in the recycling.

Beth had taken a few steps into the open room and was looking up to the high ceilings, peering from side to side.

'Are the bedrooms still on both sides?' she asked.

'They are,' Jeff replied. 'But I bet this is all a bit different than the last time you saw it.'

Beth nodded in agreement. 'It's really nice,' she replied.

As the women started to spread out into the new space, Hannah watched Jeff, whose gaze was lingering on an unassuming Beth. Hannah's youngest sister had only recently turned eighteen and Jeff was likely three times her age.

'Is there anything else?'

Hannah's tone was deliberately stern and it was enough for Jeff to blink away from her sister.

'Not much,' Jeff replied. He indicated towards a door on the far side of the room, opposite the kitchen. There was a cupboard built into the wall, with a thick padlock latched through a bracket, sealing it closed. 'Don't worry about that,' he said. 'It's full of cleaning supplies – but, otherwise, you've got full run of the place. I think the fridge is empty but, if not, have whatever you want. Same for the cupboards.'

He hovered for a moment, perhaps waiting for any follow-ups. He turned between the women and then took half a step towards the front door, before stopping and poking a thumb towards the wall. 'I'm three doors down if you need anything. Don't worry about the time: just ring the bell.'

Nobody replied and there was an awkward moment before he turned and let himself out, clicking the front door into place behind him. Hannah waited a beat and then stepped towards it, latching the lock and then moving away.

'Is it just me, or...?'

Charlotte finished the thought. 'He's a creep,' she said.

At twenty-eight, Hannah was almost two years' older than Charlotte – although strangers had always confused which of them was the eldest. She had always assumed this was largely down to Charlotte's confidence and ability to take centre stage.

Charlotte broke into a smirk. 'How many doors down, is he?'

Hannah grinned back and the idea of the party suddenly didn't seem so bad after all. The house was far nicer than anything in which she'd ever lived – and everyone she cared about was going to be with her. They could chat, and drink, and laugh. Talk about the old days and the future days. A switch had been flicked and she was struggling to remember why she'd been hesitant about it all. Not everything had to be her idea. Being around her aunt was even entertaining when Charlotte was there to share the sideways glances.

Hannah didn't get a chance to reply to her sister, because Dawn hoisted her bag of bottles noisily onto the counter.

She huffed as she unzipped her jacket. 'Nosy so-and-so, isn't he? What's it got to do with him if we're having a few drinks?' She paused a moment and then added: 'Make sure you lock the windows tonight. He'll be back and peeping. I know that type.'

Alison didn't skip a beat: 'Half of your boyfriends were that sort.'

Dawn considered her sister for a moment before nodding along with a knowing grin. 'I need a new type.'

She started fiddling with one of the bottles from the bag just as Hannah noticed Charlotte edging towards one side of the living room, her rucksack in hand. Hannah realised what was about to happen a moment before it did.

'Bagsy the big room!'

Charlotte didn't wait for anyone to reply, instead bolting across the living room and into the corridor beyond. Beth wasn't too far behind and then, suddenly feeling half her age, Hannah was charging after her sisters. When she caught them, Charlotte was opening doors along the corridor. She poked her head into one at the end and then ducked back out. In all, there were three open doors and Charlotte nodded across to Beth.

'Are there three more on the other side?'

'One of them was being used as an office the last time I was here – but the ad said five bedrooms.'

Charlotte still had her bag in her hand and, for a moment, Hannah thought she was going to dart across to the other side of the house. There was no split level and, with the living room in the middle, there were three bedrooms on this side and two on the other.

As Charlotte dithered, Beth took a moment to check each of the rooms and then pointed towards the one by which Charlotte was standing.

'You should have that,' she said, nodding at Hannah. 'It's your party and there's an en suite in there.' She waved a hand towards the bedroom closest to the living room, near to where Hannah was standing. 'That's the biggest room, so Mum and Dawn can have that, I reckon – and then you can have this.' For the third choice, she nudged the door adjacent to the en suite and motioned towards Charlotte.

'What makes you think Mum wants to share with her sister?' Hannah asked.

Beth shrugged: 'The alternative is for one of them to share with one of us.'

Hannah didn't point out that another option was for two of *them* to share. Beth was so much younger, that she'd never had to share a room – and it was a long time since she and Charlotte had lived in the same house, let alone slept in the same room.

'Which one are you having?' Charlotte asked, not bothering to hide the hint of suspicion.

'The ad showed a box room on the other side,' Beth replied. 'Barely space for a single bed – but at least it's not the sofa. That's where the office used to be when Lucy lived here. I'll have that and then whoever gets here next can have the big room on that side. Last to arrive gets the sofa.'

Charlotte checked inside the room Beth had allocated and started to nod slowly. Hannah had a peep around the corner to see a double bed in the middle of a largely sparse room. The one Beth had offered her was around the same size – although there was an open doorway in the corner that gave a glimpse of the promised shower and toilet.

She could live with that and, as Beth had pointed out, it was *her* party. In a week, she'd be travelling and there wouldn't be too many en suites then. The only way the money would last as long as she hoped was if she stuck to hostels and one- or two-star hotels. Even that was a best-case scenario. She expected to sleep on the floors of friends she was yet to meet, and uncomfortable bus seats as she travelled from one place to the next.

With apparent agreement between the three sisters, Hannah dropped her case in her room; Charlotte put her bag in hers, and then they hovered in the corridor. It had been a long time since the three of them had been together like this, away from people Hannah still considered 'grown-ups'.

'Should be a good night,' Hannah said, hoping it would be. *Knowing* it would be.

Charlotte's reply was almost lost as she moved along the corridor – and when Hannah figured out what her sister had said: 'What could possibly go wrong?', she had no idea whether she was being sarcastic.

TWO

Hannah used the word 'biggest' three times in an attempt to convince her mum and aunt that they should share a room. In the end, neither of them seemed too bothered. Dawn giggled that it'd be like the old days, back when they were girls, although Hannah suspected the chirpy attitude was down to the open bottle of Prosecco on the counter.

After rooms had been allocated, Beth headed through to the corridor on the opposite side of the living room with her bag, so Hannah followed. The first door opened into a large room with two single beds and a window that faced next door's fence. The second door, at the end of the corridor, was concealing the promised box room. There was room for a single bed, a side table, and little else. Beth dropped her bag and then turned and shrugged at Hannah, as if to say 'told you so', even though it had been Charlotte who'd seemed sceptical of Beth's room choices.

'It's a big house,' Hannah said from the doorway. 'When were you last here?'

Beth edged around her sister, out of the room, and closed the door behind them. 'Ten years or so. Lucy had a birthday party for half the class and some of us stayed overnight. She moved away not long after that.'

'Why did she move?' Hannah asked.

'Not sure – but the house wasn't this nice back then. That weird guy must've spent a fortune doing it up.'

Their mother had drifted into the corridor from the main room. She was looking up and around, taking it in. 'It's like the Big Brother house.'

'Without the dickheads,' Hannah replied – although it was at the precise moment that Dawn's cackle echoed from the living room.

There was a degree of inevitability as they returned to the main area. Dawn was sitting by herself on a stool at the break-fast bar in the kitchen. She raised a near-empty glass and almost fell backwards off the seat as she cheered their arrival.

'Who wants a glass?' she called, refilling her own. 'Come on, Han, you'll be doing loads of this when you're travelling. Last one to pass out has to clean up!'

She cackled to herself as Hannah glanced across the room, looking for Charlotte, who wasn't there. 'It's really not that kind of night,' she said, uneasily.

Dawn scanned across Hannah and Alison, her features slip-ping into an undisguised frown. 'I thought it was a hen party-type thing?'

Hannah picked up the smaller suitcase that she'd left near the front door. 'I brought board games,' she said.

Dawn's eyes narrowed in confusion, as if she'd been asked to name the capital of a far-flung Pacific island. '*Board games?* I thought you were joking outside.'

'I thought we could order some pizza, eat a bit of ice cream, play some games and just... chat.'

It suddenly felt naive. Who played board games at a party?

Dawn snorted slightly, expecting a punchline. When it didn't come, she emptied her glass and then reached for the bottle to refill it. 'I didn't realise "quiet night" meant "*really* quiet night". I thought you meant "quiet" as in "just the one stripper".'

'It's Hannah's party,' Alison said, stretching a protective hand towards her daughter. 'The whole point is she can do what she wants with her friends and family. She goes away on Friday...'

There was a moment in which it seemed as if Dawn might argue with this, but instead she poured herself a full glass of Prosecco and then returned the bottle to the counter. That didn't stop Hannah from feeling self-conscious that board games might have been a bad idea. When her mum had suggested a send-off night in which she could do whatever she wanted, it was the first thing she'd thought of. She had been a big fan as a youngster but it was harder to find people with whom to play now she was grown up. Besides, it wasn't as if she thought the evening would be about games and *only* games. She was looking forward to the gossip and the chat; the laughs and a drink or two.

Any further complaints were headed off by the pleasant *ding-dong* of the doorbell. Hannah was only a step away and unlocked it, before pulling it open to reveal two women on the other side.

Janet was a friend of her mother's and had largely been invited so that Alison wasn't solely left with Dawn for the evening. Hannah figured that, with the three older women together, it would give her and her friends a little more space.

Janet and Alison had got pregnant at more or less the same time, which was why, as if it was destiny, their daughters became best friends. That was almost thirty years in the past – and yet here they all were, still together.

Sophie trailed her mum into the house, offering a beaming grin for Hannah. The friends hugged on the doorstep, before Hannah closed the door to shut out the freezing breeze.

'I can't believe you're going,' Sophie said.

'Not yet,' Hannah replied. 'I've got another six days.'

Sophie peered around the huge open space; up to the high ceilings and out towards the tall windows at the back. 'Nice house,' she said.

'If I worked until I'm a hundred, I might be able to afford a deposit on somewhere like this.'

Sophie laughed and snorted through her nose as she made her way inside and continued to look around, taking in the kitchen and the living room. 'How the other half live, huh? I'd kill to have a place this big.' She blinked back into the moment and then reached for Hannah. 'Why have you got to go? Let's just refuse to leave in the morning and we'll live here.'

'I wish.'

Janet was stepping from side to side anxiously but it was her daughter who expressed it for her. 'Mum needs a wee,' Sophie said.

Hannah pointed her across towards the side with the three bedrooms. As big as the house was, apart from the en suite, there was only one bathroom. If that didn't indicate a man had designed it, nothing would.

Janet hurried across and, with Dawn crossing to join her sister on the sofa, plus Charlotte and Beth out of sight, Hannah and Sophie were alone.

'We've reversed roles,' Sophie said. 'When I was a kid and we were going anywhere, Mum would always be on at me to go to the toilet before we left. If I needed to go at any point after that, she'd go on about how I should have taken my chance. Now, she can barely get down the road without needing a wee. She must go twice an hour, every hour.'

'Mum's the same,' Hannah replied. 'Like a pair of leaking taps.'

They sniggered quietly to themselves.

'You're going to have to share a room with your mum,'

Hannah said.

'Are you joking? She'll be up and weeing all night.'

'There's only one room left – but there are two beds in there. Mum's sharing with her sister. The last place is the sofa. The listing said it pulled out.'

Sophie let out a low sigh but Hannah quickly changed the subject.

'Where's Trent tonight?'

The reply came with a hint of a smile: 'With his dad.'

'Sounds like you've been waiting for a night away...'

The smile widened as Sophie reached into her bag and took out her phone. She skimmed a finger over the screen before offering it to Hannah. She'd loaded Instagram and there was a picture of Sophie with her husband and son. The three of them were standing shoulder to shoulder in front of a shiny red car, grinning at whoever was taking the photo, even though the focus was unquestionably the vehicle. It was the sort of thing someone puts online to show off a new car, under the guise of saying something nice about their family – #blessed, and all that.

'Thomas got it a few weeks back,' Sophie said. 'He's pretty proud of it. He's been getting Trent into cars – and it's all he talks about, even though he won't be able to drive for another ten years.'

Hannah handed back the phone. 'Remember when we were all into skiing at that age because the school took us to a dry slope? We spent about a month thinking we'd end up at the Olympics.'

'We only went twice, didn't we? Katherine grazed her cheek and then...'

Sophie tailed off. Hannah had forgotten the reason they'd stopped skiing – beyond the obvious reason that they were miles from any dry slopes and that there was almost no snow where they lived. Their friend had fallen over on their second visit, scuffing the skin on her face, and that was the last time they went.

It was almost as if Sophie knew what was still to come. She glanced around the room and then asked if everyone was there. Hannah forced herself not to turn away.

'Just one more,' she said.

Sophie opened her mouth but it took a second or two for the word to come. A second or two that were years in the making. Half a lifetime in the making.

'Katherine?'

Hannah nodded, not quite able to say 'yes'. And then, from nowhere, she was speaking quickly, all the words merging into one another. 'I ran into her in Morrisons the other day. I'd not seen her in a couple of months but she was right there and she'd heard I was going travelling. She asked if I wanted to go for a coffee to say goodbye and I ended up telling her about this.'

Sophie was blank at first, not entirely looking at Hannah but not quite looking past her. A couple of seconds passed in which Hannah pictured her friend grabbing her bag and turning to go. Then there was a blink and Sophie was looking at her properly again. 'I'm sure we can get along for one night.'

It felt like such a long time ago that Hannah, Sophie and Katherine had been an inseparable trio. Hannah tried to remember the last time the three of them had been in the same place together but the memory wasn't there. So much had happened between them that everything else was tainted.

The moment was lost as Janet emerged from the toilet, wringing her hands. She headed across to the sofas, where the other older women had settled. Sophie and Hannah watched them go and then Sophie sprang to life as she started opening and closing empty cupboards around the kitchen. 'Nice in here, isn't it?' she said.

As Sophie drifted around the space, Hannah had a proper look for the first time. There was a glimmering chrome toaster, with a matching kettle. One of the cupboards Sophie opened contained a posh blender and the one next to that had a coffee grinder, milk frother and espresso maker. It was a far cry from the dusty once-white kettle and out-of-date sugar packets in the hotel rooms where Hannah had stayed in the past. The more Hannah took everything in, the more the 'luxury' part of the Luxury Rentals website made sense.

As if mirroring her thoughts, Sophie finished opening and closing the cupboards. 'It's all so posh,' she said. 'Well, except *that*.' She pointed towards a ceramic dog sitting on the shelf closest to the living room. Compared to the tasteful minimalism of everything else, it was certainly out of place. Hannah wasn't great with dog breeds but it looked like some sort of Dalmatian with an oversized head. The sort of tat that would be left at the back of a charity shop for a decade or two.

Hannah was about to head across and examine it when Dawn called to them from the sofas. 'There's a drink here with your names on it!'

Sophie didn't need much in the way of persuading. She sailed across towards the sofas and settled in an empty spot, as Dawn poured a good third of a wine bottle into a glass for her. She repeated this, unasked, for Hannah and then stretched to offer the glass. Hannah wanted to keep a clearish head; largely because hangovers had become increasingly brutal as she'd moved through her twenties – but also because she wanted to remember this night. Figuring she'd make the drink last a good hour, Hannah headed across and took it. By the time that had happened, Sophie had already downed two large mouthfuls of hers.

Charlotte and Beth had drifted back from wherever they'd been, leaving seven of them milling around the central area of the house. Aunt Dawn was telling Sophie about some trip she'd been on a few months before, while Alison and Janet were in another corner laughing about something else. With Charlotte and Beth glued to their phones, Hannah started to worry she was the seventh wheel at her own party.

Keen to get started on what she'd planned for the night, she crossed to the large dining table and unpacked her *Ticket To Ride* game from the box, before separating out the pieces. Every card she removed felt sillier than the last. Britons never simply got together without it devolving into a competition to see who could drink the most. Perhaps Dawn was right and this should have been something closer to a hen do, even if that wasn't really her? There had been a lot of times in her life when she'd gone along with other people's plans. Those teenage nights in pubs and clubs, watching other people dance and snog and drink, while she would rather be home, warm, and in her pyjamas.

It was while Hannah was checking the game box was empty that she heard the gentle tap from the front of the house. Nobody else appeared to notice, so she crossed to the front door, which she unlocked and opened. A woman was standing on the top step, paying no attention to the house in front of her. Instead she was twisted sideways, neck craned, as she eyed the next-door property.

'Kath...?'

Katherine blinked to the front, where her features slipped into a slim smile as she noticed Hannah.

'Han... I was worried I had the wrong place but your message said number twelve. I'm glad I found it.'

In the rush of the supermarket the other day, both wrapped in coats and scarves, cheeks reddened by the outside cold, Hannah hadn't spent a lot of time taking in Katherine's appearance. As it was, out of their teenage trio along with Sophie, Katherine had unquestionably aged the best. The thought occurred to Hannah that Sophie had a child, while she'd had her own issues through her twenties. Meanwhile, Katherine was approaching her thirties unencumbered by children or ex-husbands. No wonder she had the sort of breezy youthful appearance that would likely get her IDed in an offy.

Katherine glanced back to the side and Hannah followed her stare towards the empty bay window of the adjacent house. 'What's up?' Hannah asked.

'I thought I saw someone there,' Katherine replied.

There was nobody in the window but the net curtain was bobbing from side to side, as if it had recently been dropped into place.

'It's probably a neighbourhood watch thing,' Hannah said.

Katherine turned back towards the house, though didn't acknowledge this. 'Is this yours?' she asked.

Hannah couldn't stop the pfft of laughter. 'I'm back living with Mum,' she said.

'When do you go travelling?'

'Friday.'

'Are those things connected?'

Hannah bit her lip. 'It's complicated,' she replied, wanting to change the subject and pushing the door open wider. 'Let's go inside.'

Katherine didn't seem to notice the moment of unease. She hoisted her small bag higher on her shoulder and continued into the house, leaving Hannah momentarily alone on the doorstep.

She almost followed her friend... *almost*, except the hairs on the back of her neck were tingling. She stopped and turned to where she was certain someone would be standing at the end of the path, watching her.

There was nobody there.

Hannah looked over the road, towards the row of anonymous, empty windows. She could feel eyes on her but had no idea where they were.

It was only as she turned back that she noticed the whispering flutter of a net curtain in the window of the house next door.

THREE

As Hannah was done closing the front door, Katherine was pacing her way towards the living room. Hannah could feel Sophie eyeing the pair of them over her wine glass from the sofas. Her stare was narrow and suspicious, though she said nothing.

Katherine and Dawn were the only pair without some sort of prior connection, so Hannah introduced them. Dawn reached for the wine bottle and let out an excited 'Are we all here now?' before realising the bottle was empty. 'I put some G&T cans in the fridge,' she added. 'There's more wine in there too.'

Katherine didn't seem too interested by this, while Sophie was still using her glass as something to partially hide behind. The rim hadn't left her lips since Katherine had entered. As best Hannah could tell, Katherine hadn't once looked at Sophie. Instead, the two women were pretending the other wasn't there.

Which was probably for the best.

Katherine shrugged off her coat and then turned, looking for a place to put it. Hannah led her away to a cupboard close to the front door, where she hung it with their own.

'I should've told you Sophie was coming,' Hannah said quietly.

'It's not a problem.'

'I wanted to see you before I left and—'

'It's fine.'

Katherine said it with a smile but there was steel, too.

'There are no bedrooms left,' Hannah said quickly. 'Mum's sharing with her sister and Sophie's in with her mum. I don't mind taking the floor if you want a bed, or the sofa pulls out.'

Katherine shook her head: 'I've slept on much worse surfaces than a sofa before.'

Hannah was still talking, wanting to explain the oversight. 'I'd not counted the rooms properly. It was all a bit impulsive when I saw you. I only realised about half an hour ago.'

Katherine batted away a yawn, which might have been fake, while ignoring the explanation. She turned back to the rest of the house. 'Beth's looking grown up,' she said, with a nod towards the sofa.

Beth was sitting in a corner, a little away from everyone else. She was thumbing her phone, not looking up.

'She must've been twelve or thirteen the last time I saw her,' Katherine added. 'Everyone grows up so fast.'

'Including us.'

'*Especially* us.'

Katherine took a few steps towards the dining table. 'I remember when you first got this.' She picked up some of the game cards and flicked through them, taking in the coloured trains. 'We played this loads. You, me and...' She tailed off, glancing towards the sofas and taking a breath. 'It's such a long time since I sat down and played a game. We loved this for about six weeks and then...' The words trickled away once more – but then she scraped out a chair and sat. 'Are we playing then?'

'That was the idea,' Hannah replied, grinning. She was a

teenager again – and, perhaps, that was why she'd brought the game in the first place. Hannah sat across from Katherine and then turned towards the sofas. 'Does anyone else want to play?' she asked.

Her mum was still talking to Janet and the pair looked up briefly, before her mother muttered, 'Maybe later.' That was, and had always been, Mum code for 'no'.

Charlotte and Beth were both on their phones, while Dawn was taking a particular interest in one of her fingernails. It was Sophie who stood, picking up her drink with her. She stepped around the coffee table and then crossed to the larger dining table, at which Katherine and Hannah were sitting. She sat, paying no attention to Katherine as she picked up and flicked through the cards in much the same way as her former friend had moments before.

'It's ages since we used to play this,' she said. 'We were *obsessed*. God, we were such *nerds*.'

She put the cards back down and then, without anyone else needing to say a word, Hannah finished setting up the game and they were away. For a moment they were teenagers again, sitting on Hannah's bedroom floor. It wasn't only board games and a couple of trips to the dry ski slope; there were the usual things as well. They talked about boys, their parents, and the other people in their school. They had sleepovers and got drunk on stolen vodka. They read magazines and listened to boy bands that now made Hannah pretend to cringe. She obviously still listened to them.

Back in the present, the mutterings between the three of them were all related to the game. They played and it really did feel as if they were their old teenage selves again. Hannah relaxed into the idea of how *pleasant* it all was. The evening was going about as well as she could have hoped.

She had a small sip of her drink and took a few moments to take everything in. Another week and she'd be somewhere else, thousands of miles away. These people, these voices, would be echoes.

Around them, Charlotte went out through the patio door to the rear of the house, probably to smoke a cigarette, and then returned not long after.

The three older women, Alison, Janet and Dawn, were happily chatting and drinking, although the bulk of the drinking was being done by Dawn. She was like a mum on a first night out, months after giving birth.

Beth was still sat looking at her phone, in an armchair a little away from the main sofas. She was the baby sister, the one with a different dad, born ten years after Charlotte. This had always made her something of a loner among family. Hannah thought about calling her over, asking if she wanted to join in, except it seemed silently clear that she was happy doing her own thing.

As Charlotte nipped out for another cigarette an hour or so later, Hannah ordered pizza for everyone. She then returned to the table, ready to continue the game. Conversation remained stunted but the upside was that it made it easier for Hannah to overhear the way her mum and aunt talked about her when they didn't realise she was close enough to hear.

It was Dawn who brought up the inevitable, with a slightly slurred: 'Don't you mind about the money?'

For a moment, Hannah thought her mum was going to ignore the question. It was the thing she'd not been brave enough herself to bring up, perhaps because she didn't want to know the answer. There was a soft, deliberate pause and then Alison replied with a clipped: 'What money?'

The tone was clear in that she didn't want to talk about it – but Dawn missed the obvious hint.

'Y'know what I'm talking about,' Dawn continued, 'the money that Richard's mum left the girls.'

Hannah risked a momentary glance towards Beth, who

was still staring at her phone. It might have been the way her finger seemed to have paused its swiping, or perhaps the way Beth was sitting a little straighter, but Hannah knew her sister was also listening. Sophie and Katherine had to be, too. Everybody was anticipating the reply, even though it wasn't clear whether Hannah's mother realised she was talking to the room.

'It's nothing to do with me,' Alison replied.

'But it's so much,' Dawn said.

'If my old mother-in-law wants to leave money to her grand-daughters in her will, that's her business.'

'But—' Dawn cut herself off and Hannah knew why. She was about to say the unsayable – but, even in her somewhat tipsy state, she realised she couldn't.

Beth had that different father, meaning she was no blood relation to Hannah and Charlotte's grandmother. Hannah had no issue with things being split between the three of them, instead of two. As far as she knew, Charlotte felt the same – but, to outsiders, it could seem odd.

Now the subject had been raised, Janet – Sophie's mum – wasn't about to leave questions unanswered. 'How much?' she asked.

'How much what?' Alison replied, failing to hide the annoyance.

Janet either didn't pick up the tone, or was too tipsy to care: 'How much money?'

Alison sighed and sipped her drink. She glanced up to the ceiling in the way she always peered up when she wanted something to go away. Hannah knew this look. It was the one her mother gave when queuing at the supermarket checkout. The one she perfected when parked outside somewhere waiting to pick up one or more of her daughters.

'Thirty thousand each,' Alison said.

Hannah stared at the board, feeling Sophie's eyes on her.

She'd told her friend she'd inherited some money – but not the amount.

Now it was in the open, Hannah's mother couldn't stop talking. 'That's what Hannah's using to go travelling,' she said. 'She's not happy at work and, after the divorce and moving back in with me and Beth, I think she wants to start again.'

It felt so blunt when spelled out in such a way. It was true, all of it, but Hannah still felt a stab of betrayal at hearing it laid out so forensically. Out of nothing, the unhappiness at her job and then the divorce felt entirely her fault.

She could feel Sophie and Katherine looking at her sideways, not making it obvious. The game had reached a standstill but nobody on the sofas appeared to have noticed.

'Is she coming back?' Dawn asked. There was no instant reply from Hannah's mum – and so Dawn continued talking. 'It's just you hear about these things, don't you? People go travelling, meet some boy somewhere – and then, before you know it, they're living in Thailand, or wherever.'

There was still no reply. Hannah glanced across to the sofas at the precise moment her mother looked up. They locked eyes for a moment and the silent answer was in her mother's stare. They *hadn't* talked about it but Hannah knew this was something her mum feared. The thought that Friday might not be a bye for now, but a bye for good.

Hannah had considered it, too. She wanted a new start, as her mum had said. If that meant travelling for a while and then returning home to find a new job, then so be it. If it meant bumbling her way across continents over the course of a few months, blowing through thirty grand, and finding a job or a life elsewhere, then she was open to that as well. Some parents seemed to delight in their children being in various places around the country, or the globe. It was a sign of their own successes if their kids were well-travelled. Others – like

Hannah's mum – simply wanted to see their children as often as possible.

Alison turned away, looking towards her own sister instead – and leaving Hannah in no doubt that her mother had known all along that she was being overheard.

'It's caused some tension,' Alison said. 'Not with me – but between the girls.' She spoke louder now, wanting everyone to hear. 'Beth's using her share for university; Charlotte's saving hers – but Han's spending hers on the trip. Beth says she's wasting it.'

At the second mention of her name, Beth glanced up from her phone and turned towards the older women on the sofas. 'That's *not* what I said,' she replied.

'I'm paraphrasing,' her mother replied.

'I didn't say "waste". I said there are lots of other things that so much money could be used for.'

Beth held her mother's eye for a moment and then looked back to her phone, not bothering to acknowledge Hannah. It was nothing Hannah hadn't known, of course. It felt like their mother was bringing it up to urge them to get over it.

At long last, Dawn seemingly picked up on the underlying hints and dropped the subject. Instead, she called towards Beth. 'I'm just waiting for the day our little Beth becomes the first Ford to go to uni.'

Beth didn't look up but it was impossible for Hannah to miss the gentle upturn in her youngest sister's lips. Nobody in their family had gone into higher education. With Beth months away from her A-level exams, plus her strong predicted grades and desire to go, she was almost certain to break that pattern.

A tiny niggle deep down inside Hannah wondered if this was the real reason she was going travelling. She was happy for Beth, or she thought she was. But perhaps she was jealous, too. If someone in a family became the first to do something, there was something implicit, something unsaid, about everyone else in that family. Travelling would be an escape, in more ways than one.

The sound of the doorbell offered a merciful relief from the building tension. Both Hannah and Beth sprang from their seats and hurried towards the front of the house. Hannah narrowly got there first – and swung open the door to reveal a young man on the other side holding onto a stack of pizza boxes. They had already been paid for and he started to hand them to Hannah before freezing momentarily as he looked past her.

'Beth...'

The delivery guy was in a red baseball cap, with a matching polo shirt. He had patchy bum fluff on his chin and dimply acne scars around his cheeks.

'Hi,' Beth replied, though Hannah could hear the surprised reluctance in her tone.

The young man passed the pizzas to Hannah, though he only had eyes for Beth. 'Do you live here?' he asked. 'It's a nice place. Really big.'

'It's not my house,' Beth replied quickly. She shuffled backwards, away from the door.

He continued trying to look towards Beth, although this time, it seemed as if he was trying to peer past her into the house. Hannah could feel the grease through the bottom of the pizza box and the heat was beginning to make her fingers tingle. She juggled the boxes inside and onto the kitchen counter, then returned with her purse, before offering a ten-pound note to the delivery driver. She said thanks and then closed the door, even though he hadn't left the top step.

When they were back inside, Hannah nodded back towards the door. 'Who was that?' she asked.

'Someone from school.'

'I think you have an admirer.'

'Ew.' Beth grinned and, for a moment, it felt as if there was a rare moment of connection between them. Hannah was about to ask a follow-up but the moment was gone almost as quickly as it arrived. Beth stepped past her and opened the top pizza box, before moving it to the side and checking the second, which she then picked up. 'Pizza's here,' she called to the room, stating the obvious.

It wasn't quite a rush from one side of the room to the other – but it did have a feel of the buffet opening at a wedding as the women do-si-doed around one another in an overly polite quick-step to the kitchen. Charlotte had reappeared from the garden, having missed the drama. She waited politely at the back as everyone else took a slice or three and then milled around, cradling paper plates.

There was still plenty left by the time Charlotte got to the front – but Hannah realised her mistake a moment before her sister opened the final box.

'There's meat on all these,' Charlotte said.

Hannah had a slice of pepperoni in her hand but put it down on a plate. 'I'm sorry,' she said. 'I ordered one each of the top six pizzas on the menu. I didn't even think...'

Charlotte pushed the final box away but everyone had stopped eating, sensing an argument. Charlotte had been vege-tarian since she was thirteen, a fact Hannah obviously knew. They had made very different choices in life. Hannah had got married and started a career: two things she no longer had. Charlotte had moved home and jobs roughly twice a year since leaving home at eighteen. Hannah relished stability, or she had, while Charlotte was always on the lookout for whatever was new. And, in the moment, Hannah ate meat, while her sister did not.

For a moment, it felt as if they might end up arguing like the old days when they shared a room. Their mother would storm up the stairs and make a series of broadly empty threats in an attempt to get them to stop shouting at one another. It was usually over something trivial but there were times when their running feud felt like the most important thing in Hannah's life.

They were older now.

Charlotte rolled her eyes, shook her head a fraction, and then headed back towards the patio doors and the garden beyond. A few seconds passed and nobody moved. It felt as if there was a general sense of relief that an argument had been averted.

Katherine shifted first. She put her plate on the counter and then took a couple of steps away. 'I'll make sure she's all right,' she said.

As soon as Katherine had left, Hannah's mum reached for another slice of pizza and then turned to Dawn. 'Just for once,' she said, loud enough for everyone to hear, 'it would be nice if all my daughters got on.'

FOUR

Hannah left it a couple of minutes and then quietly headed into the back garden herself. Katherine and Charlotte were standing away from the patio door, close to the fence and, as Hannah approached, they stopped talking. It might have been ego but Hannah felt sure they were talking about her.

Hannah had gone out primarily to apologise – except Charlotte batted it away as soon as she started talking. 'It's fine,' she said with a smile that Hannah realised she'd missed. Charlotte was standing with a cigarette expertly weighted between her fingers. Hannah had never smoked – but there was something about the way her sister did it that was undeniably stylish. Charlotte had an uncanny ability to do things well, while simultaneously looking as if she couldn't care less about whatever it was she was doing. Smoking was one of those things, even if Hannah couldn't quite identify precisely what her sister did differently to anyone else.

The three of them stood awkwardly for a few seconds and Hannah thought about returning inside. As far as she knew, Katherine and Charlotte weren't friends in any way other than that they knew each other through her. She wondered what they could have been talking about – but then Katherine spoke.

'I wish you'd said something about her being here...' She gave the merest of nods towards the house.

Hannah took a moment to think about how best to reply. 'I'm going away on Friday,' she said. 'I wanted to see both of you. If I said *you* were coming, I don't think Sophie would be here. And if I told you *Sophie* was coming, I didn't think you'd say yes.'

Katherine didn't respond immediately. She turned between the two sisters and then reached into her bra, from which she produced a roll-up out of a polythene packet. Unprompted, Charlotte took out a lighter to set it going and then, as Charlotte finished her cigarette, the two women passed the new one between them. The smell gave away that it wasn't tobacco within the Rizlas.

Charlotte took a deep drag and then passed back the rollie, while holding the smoke in her lungs. When she let it out, a series of rings drifted up into the air. Katherine took her turn and then offered it towards Hannah, who shook her head.

It was Charlotte to whom she replied: 'You know what Mum's like.'

Charlotte shrugged. 'You're almost thirty and you're about to go travelling the world. I think it's OK for you to smoke a bit of weed.'

Charlotte took another drag and then offered it to Hannah a second time. This time, even though she wasn't convinced she actually wanted it, Hannah accepted.

There was no way she was going to be able to hold the smoke in her mouth in the way Charlotte had, so she blew it out almost immediately. She had to clamp her mouth closed afterwards, biting her tongue and somehow managing not to cough.

She felt like a little girl, giving in to the peer pressure and joining in with her friends doing something they shouldn't. A vague, dreamy memory flittered around of shoplifting chocolate bars from a shop one time. She couldn't remember whether it was something with which she'd been involved, or if it had been on a TV show, or something like that.

The three of them each took puffs in rotation until it was done and Katherine stubbed out the remains on a fence post. Hannah moved as if to head back inside but neither of the other two joined her, so she stopped to wait.

'Why are you unhappy at work?' Katherine asked. The question was so blunt and out of nothing that Hannah could only blink back at her. 'Your mum said that's why you were going abroad.'

Hannah continued staring for a moment, before realising she should answer. 'I'd been working for the council since we left school – but I figured out about a year ago that I hated it.' She paused and then added: 'Nobody should have to deal with the public every day.'

That got a hint of a smile. 'Couldn't they have moved you sideways to something else?'

Hannah shook her head, wishing she still had the cigarette. 'I couldn't take any more answering phones, or replying to emails. I'd been doing it for too long. The stupidest people are the rudest people – and vice-versa. Then Grandma died... and we found out about the money.'

The final word came out quieter than the rest of the sentence, almost reluctantly. Neither Hannah nor Charlotte had been particularly close to their grandmother. They only seemed to see each other once or twice a year around Christmas – and if there was a wedding or a funeral. Hannah hadn't expected anything in her will.

Now the money had been brought up, Katherine took the opportunity. 'Is Beth really mad about you going travelling?'

Hannah glanced to Charlotte and then away again. As far as she knew, Charlotte didn't know about any arguments. They weren't the sort of sisters who'd message back and forth each day and only saw each other in passing if Charlotte visited their mother's house.

'I don't think she's mad at me,' Hannah replied. 'There wasn't an argument. Beth said she thought using the money to go travelling was a waste but that was it.' She paused and then added: 'We're both living at home and I think that's a big part of it.'

Hannah glanced to Charlotte again, who didn't say that Beth was lucky to be getting anything, considering she was no relation to their grandmother. Hannah wondered if Charlotte thought it, as she had occasionally. She didn't *want* to think it. She understood that it would have been unfair to leave something to two sisters and not the third, regardless of genetics. But, given that, Beth could've at least been a little less judgey about the way Hannah chose to spend her share.

Katherine twisted slightly on the spot, wrapping her arms around her front. It was chilly now the cigarettes had disappeared. 'Are you looking forward to Friday?' she asked.

'Sort of,' Hannah replied. 'Not the journey to the airport, the waiting, the flying, the cramped seats and all that. Everything after that. The new places.' She paused and then added: 'The people...'

'I've often thought about travelling,' Katherine said with a shrug. 'It's not as if there's much here for me. Just work and volunteering and...' She tailed off and then added: 'I've been off for a week and done almost nothing.'

'What do you do?' Charlotte asked.

'Waitress at a coffee bar.'

'Which one?'

'The Grind. Do you know it?'

Charlotte nodded along. 'I work round the corner at Tortilla.'

Katherine laughed at this. 'I always wondered how they

decided to name it. They spent a day brainstorming anything that sounds Mexican – and Tortilla is what they came up with.'

Charlotte smiled back. 'I wouldn't be surprised.'

They talked for a couple more minutes, figuring out that, as well as working so near to one another, they also lived in flats a few streets away. Hannah listened in, not feeling as if there was anything she could add.

She'd known Katherine since primary school – but, already by that point, Katherine had been through a lot. Her parents had died in a car crash when she'd been two or three and she had been raised by foster parents.

Sophie, Katherine and Hannah were a tight trio of friends through school. Then everything had happened between Sophie and Katherine and the three had gone off in different directions. Hannah had spent time with both of them at various points in the ten years or so since – but, similarly, she could go months while barely talking to either.

She'd been closest to Katherine four or five years back, in their early twenties, when Katherine's foster parents had passed away. Hannah went to the funeral and there had been a couple of weeks in which they'd seen one another every day. It hadn't lasted, with it becoming every couple of days, and then once or twice a week. Their lives had drifted in different directions.

Hannah sometimes wondered if she was the problem. She watched Charlotte and Katherine effortlessly chatting as if *they* were the old friends. Katherine was playing with a small, simple silver heart pendant that hung around her neck and Hannah couldn't avoid thinking about why she'd never been able to be as comfortable with new people.

There was a flicker of movement from beyond the fence, perhaps a curtain from the next-door house, but the glare meant Hannah couldn't see anyone. When she focused back on the conversation of which she wasn't a part, Katherine was saying something about a recent date with a guy from work. Charlotte wanted details but Katherine said that nothing had come of it – and that there was nobody waiting at home for her. She squirmed a little and Charlotte replied that she knew the feeling – and then they were comparing their jobs. Charlotte had the drunker customers but Katherine had the yummy mummies and their phalanx of prams. They gently teased one another about who had it worse.

The sense of being left out continued to grow and then Hannah really did turn back to the house, saying she was going in. It was cold and she thought they might follow – but Katherine and Charlotte seemed set.

'Are you coming back to the game?' Hannah asked, talking to Katherine.

Katherine deferred to Charlotte: 'Why don't you join in?'

'Not really my thing,' Charlotte replied.

'It's fun – and this is probably the only time you'll ever have to play...?'

If Hannah had asked, she doubted her sister would've been persuaded – but because Katherine was seemingly her new best friend, she could see Charlotte's reluctance beginning to waver.

'Fine,' she said, talking to Hannah now. 'Just give us two minutes out here to finish up and we'll be in.'

Hannah had already nodded and was on her way to the door when she wondered what it was they were finishing up.

FIVE

Hannah wasn't sure what had changed while she'd been out back but, within fifteen minutes of her returning to the house, all eight women were sitting around the newly crowded dining table, poring over the board game. She thought her mum might've said something to everyone inside, asking them to come together on Hannah's last proper night with them.

Dawn was struggling with the rules but it didn't particularly matter because the game was a sideshow to a conversation in which all of them were participating. They talked about where Hannah was flying from and to, then it was onto various travel mishaps. Sophie once got stuck on the tarmac in Alicante for almost eight hours when her plane broke down; Dawn once locked herself in the toilets at Amsterdam and missed her flight – a fact that didn't surprise anyone.

Hannah told them how her flights were free as long as she continued to travel in one direction around the planet. She planned to be away for around nine months and then back for Christmas. She couldn't meet her mother's eye as she said this. It was a plan, but they both knew a plan wasn't a promise.

The game continued slowly – and it was when Hannah

passed a card towards Katherine at her side that she noticed her friend's hand twitching. Every few seconds it was as if she was being electrocuted because her thumb and half her hand would jump. Nobody else had seemingly noticed and, when Hannah whispered to ask if she was all right, Katherine nodded and then started to giggle to herself.

The pattern continued for a few minutes more. Conversation swerved across subjects, with people talking over one another as their tipsiness increased. On one side, Hannah had a snickering, drunk Sophie; on the other, she had a giggling, twitchy Katherine.

The game had been largely forgotten at the expense of drink and slurred chat when Sophie placed a piece on the board to block Katherine. Hannah saw the momentary hesitation in Sophie's hand as she put it down – but she did it nonetheless. Sophie and Katherine had barely acknowledged one another all night but there was a subtle shift in the atmosphere. Or, perhaps, it wasn't so subtle.

Katherine straightened in her chair. Her eyes were wide and unblinking, with sweat pooling in a V at the front of her top. For perhaps the first time that night, she properly turned to take in Sophie.

'It's not the first time you've stolen from me. This really is like the old days.'

In the garden, Katherine had been relaxed and calm – but not now.

'What does that mean?' Sophie replied.

Hannah started to speak but Katherine's sigh was louder. Everybody else was silent, with Dawn's glass frozen halfway towards her mouth.

'Go on,' Sophie said harshly. 'What does that mean?' Her hard tone wasn't enough to mask the way she slurred the words.

'It's called breathing,' Katherine replied, being deliberately antagonising.

'Do you really want to do this again?'

Sophie was staring at Katherine, who was now avoiding the gaze and gaping towards the empty corner of the room. There was no reply – and then Hannah's mum took charge: 'Perhaps we should finish the game?' she said.

Time stopped. Hannah knew there was a chance things could explode but she'd hoped everything could be forgotten for a few hours.

Everything hung still and then Dawn's hand unfroze as she gulped yet more wine. Play continued in silence for a couple of minutes but the damage had been done and the easy conversation of moments before was gone.

It was Hannah's turn to draw a card when Katherine shunted back her chair with a loud scrape that echoed around the high ceilings. She muttered something that might have been 'toilet' and then stumbled around the table, in the direction of the bathroom.

For a moment after she'd left, everyone seemed to stare after her, wondering if there was more to come. It was Sophie who spoke – and this time her words weren't slurred. She spoke mainly to Dawn, the person who had no reason to know about Sophie and Katherine's past.

'For the record, Thomas – my husband – *used* to be Katherine's boyfriend. They broke up and then *we* got together about eight months later.' She paused for a sip of her drink and then added: 'I didn't *steal* her boyfriend, it just happened. We were teenagers and she's never let it go.'

Janet reached forward and touched her daughter on her arm. She offered a gentle smile when Sophie turned to her. 'You don't have to explain,' she said. 'Everyone knows you didn't do anything wrong.'

'So why is it still a problem ten years later? We got married years ago – and Trent's almost eight. It's not as if Thomas wants her back and I doubt she'd want that anyway. We were kids!'

'Why'd you send the message then?'

Everyone was looking at Sophie, whose only reply was to stare at the table. She mumbled: 'I said sorry for that' but then the silence settled.

It was not long after Trent was born that someone had posted a Facebook photo of their old class. They were all seven or eight and lined up in two awkward rows ahead of their Christmas play. Hannah, Katherine and Sophie had all been shepherds and were standing as a trio. One of their old, old friends had posted an innocuous comment, wondering what had happened to them. Katherine had posted a reply that was equally innocuous – and then Sophie had replied to that with a stone-cold 'I wish you were dead'.

Later, Sophie said she had been struggling with post-natal depression, which was probably true. But for almost two days, the comment had sat for everyone to see until Sophie deleted it. By then, it had been screengrabbed and passed around various WhatsApp groups. It was probably in other places too. It would still be out there now.

Dawn was looking around, hoping someone would fill her in, although nobody did.

'You know I didn't mean that,' Sophie added quietly.

'Blah, blah, blah, blah, blah.'

Katherine clapped a single hand together, mimicking a mouth as Hannah wondered what had gone on between her and Katherine outside. This felt like a different Katherine, perhaps a different person entirely. There was no way she could ask without everyone overhearing.

As they regrouped, Dawn asked if anyone wanted anything more to drink and then her eyes widened as she stared towards the kitchen. Hannah followed her gaze, and it felt like everyone else was doing the same, as they turned to see Katherine standing on top of the kitchen counter. She was bare-footed, with sweat making her face glisten as she giggled to herself.

Hannah stood and took a hesitant step towards the kitchen. 'Are you all right?' she asked.

Katherine continued laughing as she stretched towards the chandelier that hung between the kitchen and the living room. She was on tiptoes. Things were simultaneously happening in slow motion and at twice the speed.

'Let's go to the roof,' Katherine said, dreamily.

'I think—'

Hannah didn't finish the thought, let alone the sentence, because Katherine leapt from the counter, grabbing for the chandelier and clasping onto the light fitting as she swung across the room.

Katherine cheered herself and there was a second in which it felt as if everything would be all right.

And then it wasn't.

Hannah wasn't sure whether Katherine let go, or if gravity got the better of her – but, in a blink, her friend was hurtling towards the floor. She landed on the back of her neck, slamming into the tiles with a wince-inducing, echoing, *thunk*.

She lifted her head a fraction, inhaled a rasping, wheezing breath – and then slumped lifelessly onto the ground.

SIX

Nobody moved – and then *everybody* moved. Hannah got to Katherine first, narrowly avoiding the pooling body of red that was seeping from her friend's head. Katherine opened her eyes and rolled from her side onto her back as she groaned to herself. The groan quickly became a giggle.

'Again...'

Hannah wasn't sure if it was a question or an intention as it sounded like both.

There was a cut across the top of Katherine's right eye, another on her chin, and scuffs along both of the arms she was trying to use to push herself up.

'Are you OK?' Hannah asked, unsure what else to say.

Katherine nodded vigorously. She was sitting now, with smears of blood across the bright tiles, and more on her face. 'That didn't go to plan,' she said, cradling her left arm across her front.

'Is your arm all right?'

'It's a bit floppy.'

Katherine chuckled to herself and let the arm droop uselessly.

'You might've broken it,' Hannah said.

'Nah…'

Hannah started looking towards her mum. It was still an instinct, despite being nearly thirty. She realised everyone was standing in a semicircle behind her. 'Someone should call an ambulance,' she said.

'No,' Katherine said. 'I'm fine.' She lifted her arm as if to prove the point – and managed to keep it in place without assistance this time. 'Just a bump.'

Katherine moved quickly, almost jumping to her feet, as she strode between the watching crowd and headed for the sofas. She raised her top over her head and dropped it on the ground, before plopping into the chair and starting to examine herself.

Hannah joined her and could instantly see the marks across Katherine's upper right arm, shoulder and collarbone. The skin had turned a dark red and would likely be a purply-black by morning.

'Are you sure you're all right?' Hannah asked.

Katherine scratched manically at her arms. 'Just tired. Or not tired.' There was a second as her eyes clouded and then: 'We should go out!'

'I'm not sure that's a good idea.'

Hannah's mum's handbag had long been bottomlessly full of useful things – and she appeared at Hannah's side with a box of plasters, a tube of antibacterial cream and a blister packet of paracetamol tablets.

'This might help,' she whispered.

'I still think we should call an ambulance,' Hannah replied.

Her mum was reaching for her phone. 'I'll do it—'

Katherine was shaking her head. 'No. I'll leave if you call one. Just let me sit here. You go play.'

Hannah had forgotten the game – and was in no mood to continue. It felt as if a balloon had popped.

'Katherine.' Hannah's mum was talking in her firm and decisive motherly voice. 'You really should—'

'No!' Katherine was glaring and there was a long silence as Hannah and her mum exchanged a look. If Katherine didn't want an ambulance, could they force her?

'At least let me help clean you up,' Hannah said.

Katherine didn't say 'yes', but she didn't say 'no', either. Hannah checked her over, finding a cut at the back of her head, into which Katherine's hair was already matting. There were the cuts above her eye and on her chin – but, other than that, everything else seemed to be scuffs and bumps.

Hannah dabbed at the cuts, cleaning them as best she could and then covering them with plasters. The one in Katherine's hair was harder to manage. The bleeding had stopped and Hannah gently freed the hairs that were starting to stick in the forming scab. They really should call an ambulance, especially for a head injury, but she didn't want Katherine to disappear off if she heard the sirens or saw the blue lights.

When Hannah had finished as best she could, she left Katherine on the sofa with a bottle of water and then turned to the rest of the room. Sophie was sitting by herself at the dining table, with the pile of game cards in front of her. Alison, Janet and Dawn were on the far side of the sofa, saying nothing, although it was clear they'd been watching Hannah clean up Katherine. Beth was nowhere in sight – but Charlotte was in the kitchen, drinking a glass of water next to the sink. As she finished, she ran the tap and filled the glass again.

Hannah joined her, leaning on the fridge and looking up towards the chandelier that was, mercifully, still attached to the ceiling.

'What did you do outside?' Hannah asked.

Charlotte answered almost before the question was over. 'When?'

'You know when. After I came inside and you said you had to finish up. We'd already finished smoking. What was there to finish?'

Charlotte held the glass to her mouth and sipped at the top before angling herself away. 'Nothing,' she said.

'I've known Katherine most of my life – and she's never done anything like this before.'

Charlotte was defensive now. 'I don't know why you're asking me.'

'I think you do.'

'Get lost, Han.'

It wasn't said harshly – but it was clear she wasn't going to talk about it any further. Hannah hovered for a moment, trying to come up with something more persuasive to say. When nothing occurred, she was on her way back towards the sofa when she noticed that, although someone had made an attempt at wiping up the blood from the floor, there was still a reddy-black tinge to the cream tiles where Katherine had fallen.

Hannah made a move towards it but never got as far.

'I'll sort that,' Hannah's mum said, as she pushed herself up from the sofa.

The atmosphere was sober and sombre, with Sophie packing away the game and nobody else speaking. Katherine was awake on the sofa, though she was hugging her knees to her chest and staring into nothingness.

Hannah's mother began opening cupboards around the sink, then poked her head back up and looked towards Hannah. 'There's only washing-up liquid under here.'

Hannah nodded towards the cupboard off to the side. 'The owner said something about cleaning supplies being locked in there.'

It was padlocked and, after trying it just in case, Hannah's mum pulled out a plastic bowl from under the sink. She squirted some liquid soap inside and then started to run the warm water.

Which was when the doorbell chimed.

SEVEN

It felt as if time had stopped. Nobody moved – and the only sound was the running water. Hannah realised everybody, including her mother, was looking towards her, perhaps because she was closest to the door.

The bell chimed a second time and Hannah found herself drifting across the room until she was at the door. The room suddenly felt hot and sweat was forming around the base of her neck. She scratched at it before realising what she was doing. Everything was going wrong.

She'd never been great with figuring out ages but Hannah guessed the man at the door was in his sixties. He had round glasses and a sleeveless paisley vest over a regular jumper. The sort of man who could easily be spotted hanging around train platforms. As Hannah opened the door wider, he looked over his glasses at her and then took a small step forward, as if he was about to let himself in.

'Can I help you?' Hannah asked, blocking the way. There was an accidental politeness that came from her mother drumming manners into her as she grew up.

The man cleared his throat and angled himself to the side,

trying to look around her. 'I live next door,' he said. He pointed towards the house in which Hannah had seen curtains twitching at both the front and the back. He didn't need to say anything more because she knew immediately he was one of those neighbourhood watch types. The sort who'd take down the number plates of anyone who parked outside his house, or gossiped to his put-upon other half about how some woman over the road had a bloke over, so she must be having an affair. 'I heard a noise,' he added.

'What sort of noise?'

'A big sort of... bang, I suppose.'

Hannah eyed him unmovingly. 'OK...'

'It sounded like it came from here.'

Hannah edged forward, making the man move backwards, away from the door frame. She pulled the door closed a fraction behind her. 'I didn't hear anything.'

He pushed onto his tiptoes, trying to peer over her shoulder. 'Have you got a party going on in there, or something?'

Hannah hit him with her best smile. Yes, politeness had been instilled into her – but she could do obstinate as well as anyone. 'Something,' she said.

He wasn't remotely put off. 'It's just people are always coming and going. Different people each weekend. You never know who's going to be in there.' He paused to clear his throat once more. 'Do you know the owner?'

'Not personally,' Hannah said.

She could have replied with anything because the man had stopped listening. He was looking along the street, towards the door from where the owner had emerged hours before.

'He's a tricky fellow to get a hold of,' the man continued. 'I know he lives there – and I've tried to talk to him about the comings and goings but he doesn't listen. He ran away the last time I saw him...'

The man tailed off, still staring along the street. Hannah

could understand the feeling of wanting to run away if the alternative was having this man talk at her.

Hannah edged back into the door frame. 'Anyway...'

The man turned and took her in once more. 'I hope everything's all right. It was quite a bang. Are you sure you didn't hear anything?'

'Not even a gentle bump.'

'Hmm...' The man scratched his chin. 'It's just—'

He didn't get any further, because there was a gust of movement and then Hannah's mother appeared at her side. 'Is there a problem?' she asked. Her tone was very much *not* the polite one she'd taught Hannah. Practise what you preach, and all that.

The man's body language changed instantly as he was faced with someone close to his own age. He straightened his back and then his collar. 'I heard a bang and—'

Alison stepped neatly backwards through the door, taking Hannah with her. 'You've got the wrong house.'

The man was halfway through a word when the door was closed in his face by Hannah's mum. She clipped the latch into place and then stepped away.

'People like that can never stop sticking their noses in,' she said. 'Best tell them to get lost right at the beginning.'

'You used to tell me to use "please" and "thank you" at all times.' That's what she remembered, anyway.

She had the briefest thought that maybe her instinct to lie and deflect when asked questions could have come from her mother as well... but Alison was already striding back towards the middle of the room, and Hannah pushed the thought away as she replied over her shoulder: 'I used to say a lot of things.'

In the time she'd been on the doorstep, Hannah noticed that the bowl of soapy water was now next to the bloodstain. A pair of sponges were on the ground at its side and her mum hunched next to it, grunting as she went down in stages.

'I'll do it,' Hannah said.

Katherine called, '*I'll* do it' from the sofas – although she didn't move.

Hannah crouched next to her mother and, together, they looked across towards the sofas. 'Do you think she's all right?' Hannah whispered.

'She was talking to herself while you were at the door.'

'I've never seen her like this. She was always the sensible one.'

'Well, we've all been drinking...'

Hannah's mother said this as if it was an explanation or a revelation. Except Katherine had hardly drunk anything – and, even if she had, trying to swing from a chandelier was quite the extreme reaction.

Alison moved on instantly, as if everything was settled. She reached for a tub of bicarbonate of soda, which she said had been in one of the cupboards, and then dusted it across the sticky floor. She waited a few seconds and then drizzled vinegar across, letting the powder bubble. A minute or so later and she scrubbed everything away, then squeezed the sponge into the bowl.

'That'll do,' she said, pushing herself up until she was standing.

Hannah picked up the bowl and then emptied it down the sink.

Back on the sofas, the evening had well and truly petered out. Everyone, including Dawn, had given up on the drinking and all eight of them were making the U-shaped sofa feel small. Katherine was staring at the wall, Charlotte was staring at her phone, and everyone else was sitting in an uncomfortable hush.

It wasn't how Hannah had pictured this evening going, even though none of this was her idea. Her mum said Beth had suggested this, even though Beth now seemed reluctant about the entire thing. Hannah suspected it was actually her mother's idea – and that having all her daughters around her for the last time in a long time was more important to her than anyone else.

Hannah yawned first – and then everyone did. The infection travelled in waves, around the circle in both directions until it felt as if they were all trying to outdo one another.

Surprisingly, it was Dawn who first suggested it might be time for bed. She stretched high and yawned long and loud without covering her mouth, then said she was turning in for the night. She waved a vague cheerio to everyone and then stumbled across towards the bedrooms by herself.

At this, Katherine started trying to figure out how to pull out the sofa bed, even though Beth was sitting on it.

Charlotte went to bed next, giving the vaguest of 'goodnights' and then hurrying towards the bedrooms. Janet and Alison stood together – with Sophie telling her mother she'd follow soon after. Alison insisted on checking Katherine's wounds one more time, although her offer of calling an ambulance was again turned down.

After they were gone, there was only Hannah, Katherine, Sophie and a curled-up Beth remaining. The clock on the wall was suddenly ticking noisily, like a steady drip of a tap. Hannah wanted to go to bed, too – but it was her party and she felt as if she should probably be the last to go.

For a few minutes there was nothing except the *tick-tick-ticking* of the clock. Hannah found herself counting each one, trying to think of something to say. Aside from Beth, this was the first time she, Sophie and Katherine had been alone together in ten years.

It was Sophie who couldn't take it any longer. She had her knees hugged to her chest and she spoke quietly. 'I didn't want this,' she said. It felt as if she was talking directly to Katherine, even though the 'this' wasn't defined.

'I shouldn't have invited you both,' Hannah said.

There was no answer. Katherine continued to stare at the

wall, her eyelids twitching. Sophie was watching Katherine and it felt as if she was willing her to talk.

In the end, when no reply came, she turned to Hannah instead. 'Are you going because of Paul?'

It was another blunt question. The booze had lowered their inhibitions and all subjects were on the table now.

'Not *only* him,' Hannah said.

It was probably a mix of the alcohol and the shock of Katherine's fall – but the mention of her ex-husband had suddenly brought those thoughts of him back to the front of her mind.

'You never really explained why you were divorcing...'

It was an undeniable piece of fishing but Sophie was right in that Hannah had never gone into it with her. She'd never particularly gone into it with anyone – and that included Paul.

She'd known within months of marrying him that it wasn't going to work. She'd fallen into the small-town mindset of the Four Gets. Get a partner. Get married. Get pregnant. Get a house.

Not necessarily in that order.

After that came live out the next four or five decades... except Hannah had become self-aware before reaching the third step.

Paul didn't understand why she wanted more than the Four Gets – and she didn't understand why he wanted *only* the Four Gets.

Hannah thought about answering Sophie's implied question – except, even in her slightly inebriated state, and even with everything that had happened that evening, she knew she couldn't. Since they'd left school at the same time, with broadly the same qualifications, Sophie had got the boyfriend, the marriage, the child and the house. How could Hannah tell her that the things Sophie had were the same things driving her away?

Time passed and then: 'It wasn't his fault,' Hannah said quietly. 'We just weren't compatible.'

Sophie opened her mouth to reply but then she closed it again. Katherine wasn't saying anything but she'd twisted a little to face Hannah and was listening. Beth was doing the same, although she was pretending not to.

'I saw Paul with his new girlfriend when I was filling up the car a month or so before Christmas,' Hannah added.

'You never said,' Sophie replied.

Hannah hadn't told anyone – and Paul hadn't seen her at the time. She wondered why she'd kept it to herself until now.

'I think I knew then that I wanted to go away,' Hannah said. 'They were asking for redundancies at work and I thought "Why not?". I got a bit of money from that – and then the inheritance.'

Hannah was talking to Beth at this point, wanting her younger sister to understand why she was using the money in the way she was. Beth wouldn't meet her eye and Hannah understood. It was difficult to explain to an eighteen-year-old what it was like to be stuck in a job going nowhere and a marriage that wasn't much better. All that in the town where you'd grown up. Beth's share was going towards tuition fees and living costs: worthy things to make her life better. Except Hannah's was *also* going to make her life better – just in a different way.

She didn't necessarily expect a reply from Beth – but she certainly didn't expect one from Sophie.

'There is a lot you could do with thirty thousand,' Sophie said. 'Well, thirty thousand *plus* your redundancy...'

Hannah knew she should stay quiet. They wouldn't be talking like this if they were sober.

'Like what?' There was an edge to Hannah's reply – and it wasn't accidental.

'Use it as a deposit for a flat or a house. Or go back to uni yourself.'

'Experiencing the world *is* an education,' Hannah said, frustrated. 'Just not the sort that people bang on about. You mix with different people and cultures. You have to plan where and when you're next going to eat, or clean your clothes. Where you're going to sleep each night. You have to make friends with people who might not speak the same language as you. Every skill you might need for life can be learnt – it's just that you don't get a piece of paper at the end.'

It sounded rehearsed, because it was. Hannah felt as if she'd been practising this sort of speech in her mind for months. She'd expected criticism that hadn't come in any serious way – but now, on the brink of leaving, here it was from the person who was probably her best friend.

Nobody replied and Hannah couldn't figure out if it was because she had a point, or if her point was so ridiculous that nobody wanted to say so.

Beth reacted first – by standing, stretching high, and saying she was going to bed. Hannah watched her disappear into the corridor and then, moments later, there was the soft click of a door.

It was as if that spurred Sophie into action – because she stood a moment later, did a similar sort of stretch to the ceiling as Beth had done, and then said she was going to bed as well. She added: 'Mum will be out like a light already,' as she headed in the same direction as Beth. She hadn't acknowledged Katherine – but they hadn't exchanged cross words either. All it had taken was a catastrophic fall and a possible head injury for civility to settle.

Hannah and Katherine sat quietly for a few seconds, listening to the creaks and clicks of the house. It sounded as if somebody was walking on the floor above, even though it was a giant bungalow. Hannah didn't realise Katherine was paying attention but, when she looked across to the other side of the sofa, Katherine was peering up towards the ceiling.

'Burglars,' Katherine said, with a croakily dramatic flair.

'More likely the wind,' Hannah replied.

Katherine didn't miss a beat: 'You should go enjoy yourself.'

It took Hannah a moment to realise her friend was talking about the trip, not the roof.

'You're doing the right thing,' Katherine added. She was sounding as coherent as she had since coming in from the back a couple of hours before. 'That's the difference between us and Soph. We want to live our lives and she wants the paper to say she has.'

Hannah didn't reply. She didn't think the criticism was entirely true, although it wasn't completely wrong either.

'Are you feeling all right?' Hannah asked.

Katherine touched the back of her head and checked her fingers for blood, although it seemed to be clear. 'I think so.'

There was a calm quiet between them, a moment of peace. Hannah felt a yawn rippling through her as her eyelids suddenly felt heavy. She stood. 'There are sheets and blankets in the ottoman,' she said, indicating the padded box at the side of the sofa. 'Will you be OK?'

'Of course.'

'See you in the morning then,' Hannah said.

'Night.'

Hannah headed out of the living room, into the corridor that led to half the bedrooms. She crept along, not wanting to wake anyone who might already be sleeping, and it was only when she was outside the door to the en-suite bedroom that she noticed the ceramic dog sitting on a shelf three-quarters of the way up the wall. It matched the one from the living room in its tackiness and she wondered why the owner had bothered with a pair when one was bad enough.

Perhaps it was the gloominess, but the corridor looked

cheaper than it appeared under brighter lights. There was wood panelling across the lower half of the wall that felt thin and lightweight. If it wasn't for the newer white paint, it could be the set of a 1970s TV show.

Hannah ran a hand across it, thinking the house summed up the evening as whole. All seemed well – except there were problems underneath. Perhaps it summed up *her* as a whole, which meant, of all the options, this probably was the send-off she deserved.

She turned and paced back to the living room, where Katherine was still sitting. Looking at the marks on her friend's arms and her still-hazy expression, Hannah made a decision.

'You should take the bed.' Hannah pointed a finger towards the side of the house. 'I'm supposed to have the en suite, but you have it. It's much better if you're not feeling well in the night.'

Katherine shook her head and curled her legs tighter underneath herself. 'The sofa feels comfortable.' She finished the sentence with a yawn and a gentle smile.

'Take the bed,' Hannah said. 'I'd rather sleep here.'

Katherine started to say no but then she smiled gently and lifted herself up. She was a little unsteady as Hannah helped her into the corridor and then towards the bedroom.

'Thank you for inviting me,' Katherine said.

'Maybe we'll all be friends again one day and we'll laugh about this?' Hannah could hear the helpless hopelessness in her voice. She didn't know if she even meant it herself.

It might have been the dim bedroom light but the bruises on Katherine's face didn't seem as vibrant as they had before. She gave something of a smile in return.

'Maybe.'

EIGHT

ZACK, TWENTY-TWO HOURS EARLIER

Zack rolled onto his side, blinked at the gentle winter sun that was pouring through his curtains, and took in the girl who was sleeping at his side. It only took him three seconds to realise that watching somebody else sleep was both cliched and deeply weird. Also, a bit boring.

He rolled back the other way and slipped off the bed, before tiptoeing across the chilly floor into the bathroom.

The problem with living in a flat that had one main room and one small bathroom was that it was impossible to get much in the way of privacy. That was all well and good seeing that he lived alone. But, when he had visitors, much less *overnight* visitors, it meant he had to use the toilet with the delicate finesse of a tightrope walker edging across fishing wire that was stretched between a pair of skyscrapers.

Afterwards, Zack headed back into the main room and across to the kitchenette. He filled the kettle and flicked it on, then opened the fridge to survey its contents. By any measure, it was a disappointing collection of what could barely be called food.

'What are we having?'

Zack jolted backwards, catching his head on the corner of the fridge door.

'Oops.' When he turned, Katherine was staring at him with a not very apologetic smile on her face. 'There's a door there,' she said.

'I noticed.'

'Why'd you smash your head on it then?'

Zack rubbed a spot close to the crown of his head, realising as he did so that it didn't particularly hurt.

'I don't suppose there's any chance of sympathy...' he replied.

'That depends on what there is to eat.'

Zack swung the fridge door open for her to see. Katherine leaned in and looked from side to side. She was in a large T-shirt that came down to her thighs and shivered, then wrapped her arms around her front.

'Bread, no milk, one egg, four tomatoes and Marmite.' She closed the door. 'I don't know why half that stuff's in the fridge.'

Zack opened the cupboard next to the fridge. 'There's some beans in here. We could have that on toast.'

'I've had worse breakfasts.'

'Do you want it in bed?'

Katherine looked across the room towards the bed in the corner. 'I've never understood breakfast in bed. Let's eat on the sofa. Who wants toast crumbs in their bum crack?'

Zack took the bread out of the fridge, then the beans from the cupboard. 'I suppose it depends on how messy an eater you are.'

'Why risk a toasty bum?'

Katherine laughed at herself and there was a second in which they looked at one another and Zack knew this wasn't a one-night thing.

'I'll take a coffee if there's one going,' Katherine said.

'I only have instant.'

Katherine held his eye for a second and then snorted. 'Wait till I tell Linda that her golden barista boy is actually into instant.'

'If you did that, you'd have to explain how you know…'

The grin remained on Katherine's face, even though they both knew neither of them was going to tell their boss at The Grind about their new-found out-of-work activities.

Katherine did a lap of the flat, not that there was a lot to see. She stopped at regular intervals to take a closer look at the photos Zack had decorating the place. While she did that, he set about toasting the bread underneath the grill and warming the beans on the hob. He also scooped instant coffee into a pair of mugs and waited for the kettle to boil. It wasn't gourmet but it would do.

He also watched her, of course. The T-shirt was large and shapeless and yet she was perfect in it. She fingered the silver pendant around her neck and continued checking out the bits and pieces dotted around the room.

When the food and coffee was ready, they sat side by side on the sofa and ate off their laps. The scrape of knives and forks was the soundtrack as they munched their way through the impromptu breakfast. If Katherine minded his lack of planning, then she said nothing as she moved on to her coffee and pressed back into the sofa.

'I've got to go out later,' she said.

'For your volunteering thing?'

'No.'

She paused to sip her drink and Zack had to stop himself from saying that he wished she didn't have to go out. They weren't due back at work until Monday, so they could have spent the entire weekend together, just as they had the previous few days. Until the previous evening, they had been at her flat – which was a lot tidier than his.

'Not volunteering,' she added. 'One of my friends is going

travelling. She inherited some money and there's a leaving party. It's a friends and family thing.'

'Where's the party?'

'Some house on the other side of town. It's not hers but she texted me the address. It's an overnight thing, like an old-fashioned sleepover.'

Zack took this in, realising it meant they wouldn't be able to see one another for the best part of a day – or more. It was corny and, in many ways, pathetic – but he had no idea what he'd do with her gone. This was the first Friday night they'd spent together, yet he struggled to remember what he'd done the previous weekend.

As if picking up on this, or perhaps because she felt the same, Katherine smiled kindly. 'It should all be done by lunchtime tomorrow. You can pick me up and we'll do something on Sunday before work on Monday.' She nodded towards the fridge. 'Maybe get some food in before then.'

It was a simple reply and yet the request to get in more food implied that she was happy to return. That the few days they'd spent together, away from work, wasn't an end but perhaps a beginning.

'Do you want dropping off?'

Katherine glanced up to the clock on the wall above the TV. 'Only if you can drop me home first,' she said. 'I need to change.' She reached for his empty plate and put it on top of hers, ready to carry to the sink. 'I'll text you when we're done tomorrow.'

'Promise?'

'Cross my heart.'

NINE

HANNAH, NOW

'She's not moving,' Dawn said. There was another pause and then: 'I think she's dead.'

Hannah stepped past her aunt, into the bedroom. A door opened behind her and she twisted to see her mother emerging into the corridor, bare-footed in a dressing gown.

'I think she's dead,' Dawn repeated.

Alison was battling a yawn, not understanding. 'Who?'

Hannah turned away from them, back into the room again. There were more clicks of doors behind, more footsteps, more yawns, more voices. Hannah ignored them all and stepped forward, alone.

Lying on the bed, her skin a bluey-grey, was Katherine. She was on her back, eyes open, as if staring at a spot on the ceiling. Hannah looked up, though there was nothing there. She edged forward, alert for any movement, a faintest hint of her chest rising or falling.

Nothing moved.

From behind, Dawn was talking. Of course she was. 'I wondered what time we had to leave. I was looking to see who was up.'

Hannah continued to stare, unsure what to do. Her body was tingling and, when she finally found herself gasping for air, she realised she hadn't breathed for a while.

From nowhere, there was a hand on her shoulder. Her mum slotted in at her side and they stood together for a moment, until Alison stepped forward. She held her fingers to the other woman's wrist, waited, tried the other one – and then slowly closed Katherine's eyes.

'She's gone,' she said softly.

Hannah reached forward and took her friend's hand. It was cold and clammy, like a piece of fruit that had recently been in the fridge. She pulled away, although her gaze never wavered.

'I don't understand,' Hannah said.

Her mum reached forward once more and pulled the sheet that was covering Katherine's body higher, until it was over her face. When that was done, she backed out of the room, shooing Hannah ahead of her. She pulled the door behind them although didn't quite close it, which was when Hannah realised everyone had massed in the corridor. Charlotte was staring at the floor, while Beth was blinking with tiredness. Janet and Sophie seemed confused, while Dawn was horror-struck. Everyone was half-dressed in varying combinations of pyjamas and nighties. Nobody was speaking.

'What do we do?' Hannah asked.

'What's happened?' Sophie replied.

Alison scanned them all. 'Katherine's dead.'

It felt as if everybody gasped at the same time. Hannah could feel it in her chest, as if they'd sucked the air out of her.

It might have been Sophie who spoke but Hannah wasn't sure. Someone said: 'I'll call an ambulance,' although nobody moved. Somebody else replied, saying that calling an ambulance would do no good for someone who was already dead – and then there was a brief back and forth about whether the police should be called.

Hannah hadn't registered who was speaking – but it was Charlotte who talked over them with a firm 'No.'

It was somehow both soft, as if she was talking to herself, and yet loud enough to be heard over the top of the other voices. Everyone stopped and looked towards her, including Hannah. Charlotte made sure she had eye contact with her oldest sister before continuing.

'If you call an ambulance, or the police,' she said, 'they'll do an autopsy.'

Hannah stared back at Charlotte but her younger sister turned away now. 'OK...'

'There'll be stuff in her system,' Charlotte said.

The pause went on for what felt like an age. Hannah didn't want to ask the question but, in the end, it became clear nobody else wanted to either.

'What stuff?' Hannah asked.

Charlotte took her time to reply. She wriggled on the spot, like a young girl, not the fully grown woman she was.

'What stuff?' It was their mother who asked this time. That mix of steel and fury that they grew up knowing all too well.

'Molly,' she said quietly and then, louder: 'MDMA.'

Their mother turned to Hannah, as if she was some sort of expert on the subject. 'Is that ecstasy?'

'Yes,' Hannah said. She wasn't an expert but she knew that much.

Charlotte continued, unprompted. 'We took a tablet each in the back garden last night.'

Their mother stood incredulously for a moment and then she pointed towards the back. '*This* garden?'

Hannah knew where this would go. Her mum would increasingly ask for clarification on obvious points until, in the end, when everything was revealed, she'd go off the deep end.

Not that the situation didn't warrant it.

'Yes,' Charlotte said.

'Last night... as in *last* night?'

'Yes.'

It probably explained some of Katherine's erratic behaviour, with the twitching and the swinging from the lampshade.

Hannah could hear her mother breathing loudly through her nose. She was trying to calm herself. The explosion would come another time but, for now, she was trying to think around the problem.

'There's no reason for them to think she got any of that stuff from you.'

Hannah felt her sister's stare flick towards her again, though she didn't meet it this time. As if everything beyond the door wasn't bad enough, it was about to get a lot worse on this side.

Charlotte continued staring and Hannah knew she was hoping she would say it for her.

Hannah waited until it became clear her sister was never going to say the words. 'Charlotte's on probation,' Hannah said.

There was a long silence in which Hannah felt as if everyone was staring at her. It was as if she was making the admission about herself.

Her mother's reply was loud and clipped, the fury bubbling close to the surface. 'What? *Why?* What for? Probation?! Who? Not *my* Charlotte?'

It was a lot of questions, though it was immediately clear from the way she shrank away that Charlotte had no intention of answering.

The assembled crowd weren't looking to Charlotte anyway, they were looking to Hannah. 'For dealing,' Hannah said. It was too much, too quickly. A second ago she'd been looking at the dead body of one of her oldest friends, now she was spilling her sister's biggest secret to their mother. It felt as if it was *her* secret and, in a way, it was.

She stared at her sister, who had her eyes on the floor.

'*Dealing?*' Their mum's reply rattled back with the all-too familiar steel and fury. With no immediate clarification, she added a harsh: 'Dealing *what*?'

'Ecstasy.'

Their mother bobbed on the spot, unsure at which daughter she should be looking, like a bull about to charge into an arena.

'It's not as bad as it sounds,' Charlotte said, quietly.

Hannah had been waiting for her sister to do the talking but, the moment she spoke, it was clear she should have kept her mouth shut. Not that Charlotte noticed. Their mother's face puffed with redness as her middle daughter continued to talk.

'I had some pills and shared them with a friend,' Charlotte continued. 'I didn't know her dad is a police officer. One thing led to another and...'

She didn't finish because she didn't need to. Trying to minimise it and then following with an immediate 'I had some pills' was the perfect combination to set off their mother like Mentos in a Coke bottle.

Not that Hannah blamed her. When she had found out, she'd felt more resigned than angry. As if she perhaps knew something like that was inevitable. She wondered what that said about her and her relationship with her sister.

When their mother replied, Hannah was surprised at how level her voice was, even though every word was spoken through clenched teeth.

'How did you keep it from me?'

'I'm not a kid, Mum, I—'

Charlotte finally shut up, having managed to say way too much and nowhere near enough.

Their mother spun to Hannah – and it was like they were children again. Charlotte would get into trouble at school, or at some club, and Hannah would end up being asked why she hadn't stopped it.

'You *knew*?' It wasn't really a question. It sounded far more like a threat.

Hannah knew there was no point in replying, so she looked away, and along the corridor instead. It was unclear at whom their mother was more angry.

With everyone on the brink of exploding, Charlotte finally got to her point. 'If you call the police and they find MDMA in Katherine's system, and they know I was here, it's not going to take a genius to put two and two together.' There was a momentary pause and then: 'I'll go to prison.'

She let this sit and nobody dared reply – or, perhaps, nobody knew what to say. Hannah certainly didn't. It felt as if everyone was looking to everyone else, hoping that one of them might have a solution. Worse still, on the other side of the door, her childhood friend lay underneath a sheet.

It was Janet who eventually broke the impasse. She turned between the women and finally settled on Charlotte. 'I don't understand,' she said. 'Did she have a bad reaction, or something?'

'That's what the autopsy would be for,' Hannah replied, trying not to make it sound as if she was talking to a child.

Janet nodded along, although Hannah wasn't entirely sure the other woman got it. The authorities wouldn't be able to understand why Katherine was dead unless there was an autopsy – but, if there was an autopsy, the drugs in her system would be discovered. That would probably get Charlotte in trouble and, worse still, if something about the drug had killed her, Charlotte could be in *serious* trouble.

'Why are you fine?' Janet said, looking back to Charlotte. 'If she had a bad reaction, wouldn't you have had one too?'

Charlotte shrugged, though it was more a way of saying she didn't know than anything dismissive. 'Some people react badly. Sometimes the pills can be made with different ingredients...'

The silence descended again and all Hannah could picture was Katherine's lifeless eyes staring at the ceiling until her mother had closed them.

She didn't know what to do.

'What did I always tell you about drugs?'

Hannah's mum had that tone of a disappointed parent. She scanned across her daughters as if one of them had knocked over an ornament they'd been told to keep away from. If it wasn't so serious, the fact she was speaking to them like thirteen-year-olds would be funny.

'Why's she in there?'

Hannah blinked up towards Beth. Her youngest sister looked between her and the closed bedroom door. 'I thought she was sleeping on the sofa...?'

As Beth pointed this out, Hannah felt as if everyone else was realising this at the same time.

'She was awake on the sofa and sweating badly,' Hannah said. 'I told her we should swap, so she could be near the bathroom. Forced her, really. I slept on the sofa. I didn't think she'd...'

Hannah couldn't quite finish the sentence. She'd known that something wasn't quite right with Katherine but she couldn't have expected *this*.

'It's not only the drugs.' Beth was speaking again. She was the youngest of the eight... of the *seven* – and yet there was an assuredness about her. 'Didn't you see her before Mum pulled the sheet over her? She's covered in bruises. There's that cut on her head. It looks like she's been beaten up.'

When Hannah had been in the room with Katherine's unmoving body, none of this had occurred to her. She'd been focused on the overall horror. Of the sense of loss, waste and confusion.

Except Beth was right.

'But she fell.' Janet was speaking again, turning between the circle of women with her arms out, palms up. 'We all saw her fall. She wasn't feeling well. We should call the police and tell them that.'

Hannah was about to reply – but her mother got in first. '*We* know she fell – but it won't look like that. We're in a house with no stairs, so how can we explain that she fell so hard, it caused all those bruises.'

'But she fell from the chandelier! We all saw it.'

Janet was getting louder, as if this was the most obvious thing in the world. That annoying condescension of an older woman arguing with a trainee cashier.

When Hannah's mother replied, her tone was calm and measured. So calm that it sent chills along Hannah's back.

'It sounds like a lie,' she said. '*I* know it happened – and we all saw it – but it *sounds* made up, especially when you consider there's drugs in her system. And we never called for an ambulance. It's like we came up with it to cover something else that happened.'

'But nothing else happened!'

Nobody bothered to answer Janet this time. Even her daughter, Sophie, took a small sidestep away, as if to indicate that she herself wasn't misunderstanding the dilemma.

'Maybe it was the hit to her head,' Hannah said quietly, wanting to convince herself. 'Some sort of internal bleeding. Nothing to do with the drugs?'

'They'd still be in her system,' Charlotte replied. 'I'd still be in trouble.'

The truth was almost irrelevant because their mother was right. It sounded like a lie. Maybe Charlotte would be in trouble, or maybe she wouldn't.

It wasn't only Charlotte who was worried about how things would seem. 'People will know our past,' Sophie said quietly, talking to her mum.

'Whose past?'

'Me and Katherine. People will know that Thomas used to be her boyfriend and then he married me. They'll know we fell out. They'll see all the bruises and wonder what really happened.'

'But nothing *really* happened,' Janet replied.

Sophie was angry now, shouting at her mother with a frustration Hannah felt. 'I know, Mum! I *know* nothing really happened but you're not looking at it as someone outside the house. It *looks* like someone beat her up and the person most likely to do that is me.'

Janet opened her mouth to say something but then closed it again.

Hannah couldn't look anyone in the eye. In barely a few minutes, she'd shifted from the horror of discovering her friend's body to whatever this was.

Except, deep down, she knew what this was.

Hannah looked to her mother, feeling like a little girl again. She wanted somebody to do something to make it all go away – or, better yet, to go back to how it was a day before.

Dawn had been quiet for perhaps the longest time since arriving in the house – but, for once, she said what they were all thinking.

'What do we do?'

TEN

ZACK

Zack snatched his phone from the arm of the chair for what felt like the hundredth time that morning. He'd felt the gentle hint of a vibration but, when the screen lit up, there was nothing there except the time. He unlocked it and checked his messages just in case – but there was nothing new. It was another phantom notification, like all the others.

He was waiting for the text from Katherine, telling him she was ready to be picked up. It was early but, from what little Katherine had said about the going-away party, it hadn't sounded as if she planned to spend too much time there. He thought they might be able to get brunch and then spend the afternoon and evening together, before they went back to work in the morning.

They'd have to arrive at the coffee shop separately, of course. With the politics of who got what shifts, it wouldn't be a good time to go public with their relationship – although, if Katherine wanted to say something, he wasn't going to deny it.

He picked up his phone again but it was another ghost notification. He kept the phone in his hand this time, before making his decision.

Five minutes later, he was dressed and in his car. Instead of sitting in his flat and waiting for her text, he'd drive towards the house where he'd dropped her off. When she messaged him for the pick-up, he'd only be a few minutes away. It wasn't quite *full* stalker, maybe 10 per cent stalker. Something in that region. Perhaps the low teens.

Frost clung to the verges and low bushes and the roads were quiet as Zack drove across town. There were a few cars parked outside the old church and a couple of vehicles in the almost empty Tesco car park. Other than that, there was a general air of desertedness about the town. This was the earliest he'd been up on a Sunday for months and there had been the odd weekend where he'd have not long been in bed by this time.

As Zack neared the spot where he'd dropped off Katherine, he realised he couldn't quite remember where she'd got out of the car. The house was on the opposite side of town from where he lived, which took fifteen minutes with the traffic lights and 20 mph limits around the schools, even though they were closed. She had directed him the day before but, now he was on his own, all the streets looked the same and she hadn't mentioned the house number.

There were terraced two-storey houses along both sides of the road, with cars parked nose to tail and no apparent gaps to park. Even as he drove slowly, looking for the right place, Zack noticed the handmade 'NO PARKING' signs in practically every window. It was that sort of area – but it didn't feel like the place he'd dropped off Katherine the night before. He probably should have paid more attention.

The first thing he recognised was a coffee shop that sat on a corner opposite a petrol station. It was called Grounds and Katherine had asked if he'd heard of it considering they worked in a place called The Grind across town. He hadn't – and it had only been a few seconds after that she'd asked him to drop her off. He'd waited on the corner, watching where she went before pulling away.

Zack continued past the shop and pulled into a space on the side of the road. There were fewer houses, as well as a hotch-potch of designs. Some properties were three-storey town-houses, others two, and a few were posh bungalows. Some had small front yards, others had cars parked on driveways. He'd only been in the area less than a day ago – but the light was fading then and everything seemed different in the crisp sunlight of the morning.

After turning off the engine, Zack checked his phone, wondering if Katherine had messaged while he'd been driving.

She hadn't – and he thought about taking the initiative and messaging her instead. He almost did but he didn't want to be too needy, too forward. Nobody liked that.

He was sure it would only be a matter of time before she got in contact. Until then, he'd wait.

ELEVEN

HANNAH

As everyone looked to everyone else, hoping there was a solution that didn't involve the unthinkable, Hannah felt as if she was floating. She could see everyone from above, watching their reactions as they each hoped for a solution that none of them could think of. If not that, that somebody would say the thing nobody wanted to.

Janet left the circle first. She mumbled something about needing the toilet and drifted along the corridor, then locked herself in the bathroom. Hannah figured she wouldn't be out anytime soon, not that she blamed her.

Somebody's phone started beeping from beyond a door – and both Dawn and Sophie claimed it was theirs, even though Hannah knew it was her mum's because of the tone. Charlotte didn't bother to make up a reason for leaving, she simply slipped through the nearest door, into the room in which she'd been sleeping. Hannah didn't necessarily blame her for wanting to get away. When Beth said that she needed a glass of water, and headed off towards the kitchen, it left only Hannah and her mother standing outside the bedroom door beyond which Katherine lay.

Hannah's mother didn't speak, not at first. Instead she stretched and pulled the bedroom door until it clicked fully closed.

That was all it took because the decision had been made. Hannah wanted to say that she didn't agree and that there had to be another way – but she couldn't think of anything. Certainly not one that wouldn't lead to a chance of Charlotte sitting in court, or Sophie. Was calling the police now worth that gamble? Perhaps they'd believe everything that had happened the night before. They'd all have the same story, after all – and it would be the truth.

Except none of them knew how Katherine had died. If it was the hit on the head, it really did look like someone had beaten her up. There was that stupid old 'I wish you were dead' Facebook message from Sophie. Then the drugs would be found in her system from the post-mortem. If it was something to do with the drugs themselves, Charlotte was probably right in that she'd be the person they looked at first. She had the prior conviction and actually had shared with Katherine.

What was the alternative? When Dawn had asked what they should do, she was really asking whether they should. Whether they *could*. They were all thinking the same thing.

It was inconceivable – and yet, with a simple closing of the door, the finality of it all had been conceived.

Hannah followed her mother into the living room, where they waited until everyone else had run out of excuses and re-gathered. Some were sitting, some standing. Beth was clasping a glass of water, while Charlotte had her phone in her hand.

Charlotte started with 'I just—' but she was cut off by her mother.

'I don't want to hear a single word from you.' Alison's tone was so sharp that Hannah winced and took a small step away. She'd seen her mother angry but never like this. This was an adult situation and yet, suddenly, their mother was in charge and everyone else was a passive child, ready to do what they were told.

'Who knew Katherine was here?' Alison asked. She sounded like a strict schoolteacher, asking a class for the answer to something she'd written on the board.

Hannah realised her mum was looking to her – but Hannah looked across to Charlotte.

'She said something out back, didn't she?' Hannah replied. 'Something about nobody waiting at home for her.'

Charlotte's eyes were wide, which left Hannah wondering whether she'd taken anything more that morning. After everything that had happened, she wouldn't have been surprised.

'*Well?*' It was their mother who was pushing for the answer.

'Something like that,' Charlotte said, her head bowed. 'I remember her saying nobody was waiting for her... I don't remember properly.'

'But did anyone know she was here?'

'Not that she said to me,' Hannah replied.

'Does she still live alone?'

'Yes.'

Dawn chose that moment to speak up: 'She might've told her mum and dad.'

Hannah shook her head. 'Her parents died when she was young. Her foster parents died a few years ago. I was at the funeral. She doesn't have any brothers or sisters, aunts or uncles, or anything like that.'

Dawn squinted towards Hannah, her forehead wrinkled with a mix of confusion and, probably, hangover. 'No family at all?'

Hannah risked a glance at Sophie, who immediately turned away. '*We* used to be her family.'

Dawn looked between Hannah and Sophie and then went quiet. Hannah felt a strange mix of déjà vu and something dreamlike. A memory of the night before, through a sleepy haze.

She was on the sofa and someone was up, crossing the living room. Was it Sophie? Did it happen at all?

She blinked away the thought as she realised her mum was talking again. 'Is there anything on her Facebook? That sort of thing?'

Hannah picked up her phone from the coffee table. She flicked between a couple of apps and then looked up to realise everyone was watching her.

'She's not been on Facebook for about eighteen months,' Hannah said. 'Her last post was about the Tories and she's not put up anything since. She's on Instagram but it's either photos of coffee, or dogs sitting outside the shop where she works. I can't see anything she's posted anywhere for a month.' She paused and then added: 'Katherine's always kept to herself.'

Hannah thought on it for a second. Is that all her friend's life had become? She should have been there for her, inviting Katherine over and asking what she was up to. That's what a proper friend would have done. She felt blank, as if she was staring at an endless white of nothing. It was hard to understand everything.

Katherine was dead.

Her friend was dead.

Nobody spoke and then: 'She got here late,' Hannah's mum said. 'It was after we'd met the owner and it was more or less dark.'

'You can't be suggesting...' Janet was finally getting it. She didn't finish the sentence because Hannah's mum talked over her.

'How did she get here?'

Hannah looked to Charlotte, who wasn't catching her eye. 'I don't know,' she said.

Nobody spoke up to offer anything different.

'Did she drive?'

'She failed her test a couple of times ages ago – and gave up learning after that. She used buses, trains and taxis to get around. Either that, or she walked.'

'Could someone have given her a lift? Or she got an Uber, something like that?'

'I don't know,' Hannah replied. 'If she did, she never said. When I opened the door, she was already on the step.'

Her mother thought on this for a moment and then added: 'Did anyone take any photos last night?'

It took a couple of seconds but everyone was suddenly on their phones at once. There was a series of mumbled 'no' replies, then Sophie clarified 'nothing with her'. Hannah had one photo that contained her and Katherine standing together next to the fridge. It was a selfie with them both smiling for the camera. She deleted it, then went into the deleted photos folder and erased it from there, too. A little voice inside told her she'd done it too quickly, too callously. She forced it down and away, not wanting to hear it. Not believing herself capable of what was to come.

'Nothing with Katherine,' Hannah said, and it sounded almost like an apology.

Janet was the only person who'd not been checking her phone. She was staring at Alison, arms folded across her front. 'You can't be suggesting—'

'Did the neighbour see her when he was at the door?'

Hannah's mum was talking to her again, though it took Hannah a moment to realise she meant the man who'd complained about the crashing sound.

'I don't see how he could've done,' Hannah replied. 'There were a few curtain twitches at the back and front.'

Alison turned to Charlotte: 'Did you notice anyone watching you at the back?'

'No.'

Their mother considered this for a couple of seconds, seemingly trying to think of any other angles.

Hannah had a sense of what would be coming in the end. Her stomach was gurgling with an emptiness that wasn't only related to food.

'Who else might she have told about this?'

Alison was looking to Hannah again, wanting answers about the impossible.

'I don't know,' Hannah said.

'Does she have a boyfriend?'

'No. She said something about a date but said nothing came of it. It didn't sound like a big deal.'

Hannah looked to Charlotte, who had also been there. She wanted confirmation that didn't come.

'What about friends? Workmates?'

'I don't know, Mum.'

'When did you invite her?'

'Wednesday. I saw her in Morrisons and thought she'd say no...'

Her mum nodded at this. It had left less than three days for her to have told someone.

Janet chose that moment to repeat, 'You can't be suggesting —' but Alison didn't ignore her this time.

'Will you shut up!'

The snapped reply was so harsh, so fiery, that Janet almost fell off the sofa. She grabbed the armrest and stopped herself, then curled her legs underneath and stared out towards the back of the house. Sophie said nothing to defend her mother.

'She's been off work.' It was Charlotte who spoke and there was something haunted in her voice. Not haunted... *frightened*. Hannah stared at her sister, knowing she'd never seen her in such a way. Charlotte was always confident and sure of herself – but not now. She was rocking from side to side, her fists clenched.

'What did you say?' their mother asked.

'When we were out the back, she said she'd been off work

since Wednesday. If Han only invited her on Wednesday, she wouldn't have been back to work since then.'

Their mum thought on this for a few more seconds, before: 'She might've messaged someone...'

'Maybe,' Hannah replied.

'Her phone must be here.'

Nobody moved – and then Alison clapped her hands, back to being that mother who used to ferry them to clubs and classes with a ruthless efficiency.

'Well,' she said, 'let's find it.'

TWELVE

Hannah got to the door of the en-suite bedroom before anyone else – not that there had been any sort of race. She waited outside and took a breath, not wanting to go inside but knowing she needed to.

Beth was suddenly at her side. 'Mum told me to come in with you.'

'You don't have to.'

Beth replied with a tight-lipped, humourless smile. She was so young to be caught up in all this, with a life ahead of her. Hannah was glad for the company, though the biggest part of her wished it was Sophie. In another reality the pair of them, with Katherine, would have taken their friendship into adult-hood. They'd catch up a couple of times a week over coffee or wine and their days would be peppered with back-and-forth three-way WhatsApp messages.

With the thought in her mind, Hannah almost ached for it. If the trio had remained close, perhaps she'd never have married Paul. Perhaps she'd never have trapped herself in a career she didn't want. Perhaps she'd never have felt the need to go travelling. And then, most of all, perhaps none of this would ever have happened.

It wasn't Sophie with her, though – and they'd not had that sort of relationship in a long time. It was her youngest sister.

'You should go,' Hannah said.

'Go where?'

'Home, or to a friend's. Anywhere that's away from this.'

Beth sounded resigned when she replied. 'It's a bit late now...'

The thing that hurt Hannah the most, at least in the moment, was that it felt like her sister's age of innocence was over. It was naive, of course – Beth was eighteen and almost nobody of that age was a delicate flower. And yet this was so much worse than getting drunk while underage, or any of the other sorts of things teenagers got up to. There'd be no going back from whatever happened next.

It wasn't that which hurt Hannah the most, of course.

Hannah opened the door and edged inside. A part of her hoped Katherine would be sitting up, awake and wondering what all the fuss was about.

She wasn't.

She was exactly where Hannah's mother had left her: prone on the bed and covered with the sheet.

They were in the room to look for a phone but Hannah couldn't help herself. She gently pulled back the sheet and stared at her friend's unmoving features. It was hard to know why she did it, other than curiosity.

'I've never seen a dead body...'

It was Beth who spoke.

Hannah blinked around to look at her and then turned back to Katherine. It could have gone without saying. Hannah had never seen a dead body, either. It was somehow both better and worse than she could have believed. There was none of the gore or horror that went with something she might have seen on television – and yet that made it worse. If there had been something grim like a stab wound, or blood, or anything obvious, it would explain why she was dead. But there was none of that. If it wasn't for the lack of movement, Katherine could have been sleeping. Her skin had a hint of glisten to it and there was a morbid serenity about her.

'What do you think happened?' Beth had spoken again, echoing Hannah's thoughts.

Hannah leaned in looking for any sign around Katherine's mouth that she might have choked on her own saliva or vomit – but there was nothing. 'I don't know,' she replied. 'Ecstasy makes your heart beat faster – so maybe a heart attack, or something like that?'

Hannah reached for the sheet and re-covered Katherine, unable to look any longer. She wanted to know the truth, except that would bring a barely imaginable amount of trouble to everyone she cared about. Whatever she did next would be wrong.

As she tried to push away those thoughts, Hannah dropped to her knees and looked around the bottom of the bed, trying to spot Katherine's phone. Under her current bed, at her mum's house, there was unpacked luggage, bags and boxes full of things she'd taken when she left the house she shared with Paul. Here, there was nothing. She swished her hand across the carpet but there was only fabric. Beth was opening and closing drawers of the side unit but shrugged towards Hannah as she stood.

'Nothing,' she said.

Hannah checked the bathroom, although the only thing there was her own toiletry bag. She tried to remember whether Katherine had taken anything with her when they swapped rooms last night, though it was all fuzzy.

Back in the main bedroom, Beth was holding a small black bag.

'This was under the other pillow,' she said, pointing towards the one that wasn't covered with a sheet. Hannah had no chance to reply before her sister started removing the contents one by one. There was a ten-pound note, a hairbrush and tie, a key, and a receipt dated two months before from the coffee shop where Katherine worked.

No phone.

Hannah was about to say that the phone was probably in the living room when Beth crossed and crouched close to the door. She muttered something to herself and then stood and peered closely at something in her hand before offering it to Hannah. 'Do you think this is hers?'

Hannah took what turned out to be a thin gold ring from her sister's palm. It was a plain band which was slightly flattened and misshapen. The sort of cheap, costume jewellery that might've come from a market stall.

Hannah twisted it between her thumb and forefinger. 'It's not mine,' she said.

The two women both looked towards the bed and then turned away again. Hannah took the bag from her sister and dropped the ring into it, before they both exited and closed the door.

The living room was a hive of people opening and closing things. Dawn was on her hands and knees trying to get a hand underneath the sofa, while Charlotte was in the kitchen with Sophie. Everybody stopped and looked towards Hannah, who shook her head.

'It's not in there.'

Janet was the only person not doing anything. She was standing in the corner, arms folded with disapproval, like a presenter who's just had to apologise for a guest swearing on live television.

Hannah was about to head out to the back of the house to look, when the obvious solution dawned on her. The confusion and trauma of the morning had left her thoughts muddier than usual, as she took out her phone and called Katherine's number. A few seconds later, Dawn bounced backwards, away from where she was sitting, as something started to buzz.

Hannah stepped across to the sofa on which she had been sleeping barely an hour before. She fumbled with the cushions, remembering how uncomfortable it had been to sleep on, and figuring it was such a nothing thing by which to have been bothered.

She found the phone in between two cushions, almost hidden down the back. The case was scuffed, the screen scratched. Hannah was used to her own phone and this felt heavy and small in her hand. It was a few years old: the sort of thing her mum had.

As Hannah held up the phone, the lock screen illuminated to show a single message, saying there was one missed call – from her.

Hannah's mother moved across the room as everybody stood and watched. 'Is there anything on there?' she asked.

'Only the call from me.'

'What about messages?'

'Nothing overnight. I don't know the passcode to check before that.'

Sophie had been in the kitchen but she was now closer to the living room. 'You might...' she said.

Hannah was momentarily confused. She looked to the phone's lock screen and then back up again. Then, from nowhere, she knew what Sophie was talking about. They had been twelve or thirteen when someone from the local NatWest had come into school to give a talk about personal finance. There must have been some sort of dodgy kickback going on because, afterwards, students were encouraged to sign up for accounts at the bank where he worked. There were forms to fill in and, when it came to select a PIN, Hannah, Katherine and

Sophie had all entered the same. They thought they were being so clever when they amalgamated their various door numbers from the time and came up with nine (Sophie), nineteen (Katherine), nine (Hannah). Two and a half decades later and Hannah's bank PIN was *still* 9199.

She typed the numbers into Katherine's device and, after a millisecond in which it felt as if everything had stopped, the screen unlocked.

It happened so unexpectedly that Hannah fumbled the phone and almost dropped it.

'Did it work?' Sophie asked.

Hannah didn't reply, not properly, she simply gave a short nod. Her unlock code was also 9199. Were they all so predictable? So locked into their teenage lives?

Nobody else seemed to know what they were talking about – but that was part of growing up so closely to another person. Things could be understood with only a word or two. Sometimes, it didn't even take that. A glance or a touch could send a person spiralling back to a memory thought lost.

Katherine's home screen was so tidy and minimal that Hannah couldn't believe somebody operated in such a way. Hannah had apps spread across five different screens, arranged as only she would understand. Katherine had everything on a single page, each app sorted meticulously into named folders.

Hannah was unsure what to do at first – but then tapped to the 'people' folder, where she found 'messages'.

It felt wrong because it *was* wrong. Hannah knew that but there was an invisible pressure from her mother standing nearby.

Hannah's messages were depressingly empty. There was something from somebody named 'Zack' that was sent earlier in the week, asking where Katherine was – but that had gone without reply. Hannah's own messages, giving details of the house and party, were there – as were some from Katherine's boss, mentioning shift details. There were names Hannah didn't recognise and a couple she did – but none from the past week.

Hannah held the button to turn off the phone and then put it into Katherine's bag, which was now on the coffee table.

'What was in there?'

It took Hannah a few seconds to reply to her mum's question. There was a near overwhelming sadness about how lonely Katherine appeared to be. Hannah was hardly a party animal but she'd have a string of messages from various people throughout more or less any day. She should have made more of an effort to be a better friend but now it would forever be too late.

'Nothing,' Hannah said.

And then her mother took control, in the way mums can. Alison spoke to the entire room as if they were all her children, laying out precisely what was going to happen and giving no option for dissent.

'Don't tell anyone Katherine was here,' she said. 'If any of us need to talk about her, we do it in person. No texts, Facebook, WhatsApp, no emails, no calls. Assume anything you type is going to be read. If anyone asks what happened last night, talk about whatever you want. The house, the pizza, the games – everything except Katherine.'

Hannah had once seen a car turn left, straight into the cyclist who was already there. She'd known what was going to happen a second or so before it actually did and yet she'd been unable to do anything. She was feeling that same creeping sense of dread. Things were out of her control.

Not only that, her mum was speaking so clearly, in a way that felt calculated and rehearsed, that Hannah couldn't ignore the niggle of fear that was beginning to crease through her.

She wanted to say something but she couldn't. There was

only one voice of anything close to dissent: 'What are you going to do?' Janet asked.

Not for the first time, Alison ignored her.

'Katherine might have told someone she was coming – and, if she did, then she never arrived. Hannah invited her but she didn't show and none of us saw her. If she got on a bus to come here, or an Uber, or a taxi, then she never reached the door.'

'But—'

Janet tried to interrupt but Alison spoke over her. 'At some point, someone will notice she isn't going to work, or answering her door. The police will come to ask at least some of us questions. If they do, then we all say the same thing: Katherine was never here and we didn't see her.'

She paused and looked around the room, trying to catch everyone's stare, even momentarily. Hannah couldn't look her mother directly in the eye, although she noticed that her mum spent an extra second or two waiting for Janet's attention.

'We all say the same thing,' she repeated.

The lack of enthusiastic replies wasn't surprising – but nobody spoke up to say anything different. The seven of them were going to be locked into the darkest of pacts and Hannah knew this was the last chance to speak out. She'd never been afraid to question her mother and they'd had a series of raging rows when Hannah had been a teenager. They'd argued about everything from bedtimes to what Hannah was allowed to watch on television. She'd known precisely how far she could push her mother before it was too much. She'd walk the line but rarely cross it. She was older now, an adult in her own right. If ever was the time to speak out, it was now.

Except she couldn't. Her mother was right. There was a choice: they agree to do this together, or either her sister or her oldest friend could go to prison. Was it worth the risk to do the right thing?

People were staring at the floor, scratching their arms,

playing with their hair. Anything that meant not having to look at one another.

'What are we going to do?' Hannah asked.

'With what?' her mum replied.

'With the body.'

THIRTEEN

ZACK

Zack did a few laps of the block, parking in different spots and fiddling with his phone until he wasn't sure what else to do. The sun continued to rise and it was a little before noon when he settled at a table in the window of Grounds. It gave him a clear view along the road towards where Katherine had gone after he'd dropped her off. He wasn't sure which house she'd gone into – although there was a large bungalow, with steps at the front, about six or seven doors down. As she had disappeared into the gloom, he thought it might have been to that house.

It was pathetic, he knew that. Possibly up to around 30 per cent stalkerish – but he didn't have anything better to do. Once Katherine had said he could pick her up, he'd planned the day around that. And now... nothing.

Zack kept half an eye on the bungalow but there wasn't much in the way of movement from people or traffic. It felt as if everyone was still sleeping: either that, or this was one of the streets where the owners lived elsewhere. He kept hearing how rich people were buying up houses in town as investments.

Grounds was a lot quieter than the coffee shop in which

Zack worked. The lack of custom here probably explained why his place didn't open on Sundays. The town didn't get much in the way of tourists, let alone in February. Most of the custom where he worked came from people working nearby, older people, or mums meeting up.

Zack watched the server take orders on a pad, from which she ripped off the top page and passed it to the young man who was making drinks behind her. It was impossible not to picture Katherine handing orders to him. This couple had something stunted about the way they interacted. She would shove the piece of paper onto the counter at his side and he'd immediately move it out of his way. It was as if they were trying to annoy one another. Zack wondered if he and Katherine had any sort of method that made it obvious there was more between them than just workmates. It had been a slow thing that happened over a couple of months. Smiles here, inadvertent touches of the hand or arm there.

It had taken a while to get to the place in which they'd been the past few days.

As Zack waited for Katherine, the clock on the wall ticked past twelve – and he decided it was time to text. He tapped out – and deleted – a few variations, before settling on a simple: 'Hope you've had fun. Want picking up?'

After sending, he sat with his phone in his hand, hoping a reply would come back instantly. It took him a minute or so to realise that there was only a single tick and that the message hadn't been received at the other end. He had full reception but there were dead reception spots in the town. Katherine could be staying in a house like that and he hadn't heard anything since dropping her off. They weren't officially boyfriend-girlfriend, so he didn't know if that was something to worry about.

Zack was distracted by the server calling his name. He picked up his drink and returned to his table by the window. As he did that an older man slotted in at the adjacent table and unfolded a paper across the space. It was one of those with too many pages, plus pullouts that go all over the floor. Zack's dad used to get a similar paper every weekend. He'd read the sport and everything else would go in the bin.

Perhaps because he realised Zack was watching, the man nodded towards him in the way people did when they didn't recognise the person looking at them.

'Everything all right?' the man asked.

'Do you live round here?' Zack replied.

The man lowered the paper and nodded towards the street beyond, where Katherine had headed the night before. 'About five minutes that way.'

'Do you know the bungalow with the steps?' Zack asked.

The man put down his paper and lifted his glasses so they were resting on his forehead. He leaned in and squinted down the street. For a moment, Zack thought he was going to be told to mind his own business.

'It was run-down for a while,' the man said. 'Was on the market for a couple of years. Someone's done it up but I don't know anyone who lives there, if that's what you're asking.' He motioned to pick up the paper but didn't. 'I think my neighbour said it was a party house, or something like that. People rent it for a night, or a weekend.' The man examined Zack for a moment, looking him up and down, or as much as he could considering Zack was sitting at a table. 'Why d'you want to know?'

'Just curious,' Zack replied.

The man continued to look at him for a couple of seconds, wanting more, before deciding it wasn't going to come. He picked up the sport section of the paper and started to read.

Zack turned back towards the house with the steps. He checked the message he'd sent Katherine, although there was still only a single tick. Zack rarely used his phone to actually call anyone – but he pressed the dial button and held the device to his ear.

He waited. And waited. Then he noticed that his phone had gone back to the home screen without even ringing.

PART 2
ACCIDENT

FOURTEEN

HANNAH

Hannah felt as if she'd not spoken all day. Her throat was dry, her lips sore and cracking. Hours had passed since her Aunt Dawn had woken her up with the shout, or scream, or whatever it was. Hannah couldn't really remember because the day had passed as if she'd been watching it through a Vaseline-smeared lens. For the first time she could remember, she'd done everything her mum had told her to without question.

It was dark again now and the creeping night was cold and cloying. She was sitting in the passenger seat as her mother drove. Heat spewed from the vents, though that didn't stop the regular shivers from teasing across Hannah's body. Whenever she'd heard someone say that something felt like a dream, it had seemed a cliché... until now. Everything from waking up until being in the car really did feel like something she was seeing, not experiencing.

She had already done things she never thought she would. Her mum had driven the car into the back alley behind the bungalow and, while the others had gone out the front, making as much noise as possible, Hannah, Charlotte and her mother had carried Katherine's body out to the car as quickly as they could.

She now knew why something was called 'dead weight'. Katherine must have been nine or ten stone at most, and yet it was like lifting the actual car as Hannah helped carry her towards it.

The fact her mother had mentioned that the others should go out via the front, and then hang around on the street making noise, was worrying to Hannah. Not because it *wasn't* a clever way of covering what they were doing at the back – but because it was.

Her mum had always been a 'spring into action' sort. A doer, not a talker. When Hannah was five or six, there was a boy at the end of the street who used to pick on her. He'd call her 'piggy' and make oink noises whenever he saw her. When Hannah's mother found out, there was no debate over what should happen. Instead, she marched along the road, banged on the boy's door and told his dad that he better stop his son bullying her daughter, or else. Hannah never found out what the 'or else' might entail – but the boy never oinked at her again. There was another time when Hannah's maths teacher had called her 'stupid' in front of the class and, after finding this out, her mum had a finger-pointing, voice-raised, full-on row with the woman on the school playground.

Those moments stuck in Hannah's mind as she continued to sit silently in the passenger seat while her mother drove. The wipers flashed back and forth, though it was more because of the mist than any rain. They were on country lanes with high hedges, shadowed verges and no lights. Her mum was driving below the speed limit, probably because of the conditions, although Hannah also thought she didn't want to risk being pulled over for speeding, no matter how unlikely that seemed.

As the car bumped over a pothole, there was a gentle *thunk* from the boot that neither of them acknowledged, even though there was no way to miss the sound. At every stage of the day, it felt as if a line had been crossed. That nothing would ever be the same. Then they'd cross another line and it would somehow feel worse.

When her mum spoke, Hannah had to stop herself from jumping too openly. It was the first words either of them had exchanged since getting into the car. After sitting at home, in her room, all afternoon, it was strange to hear someone's actual voice.

'Do you think Janet and Sophie will stay quiet?' her mother asked.

Hannah didn't reply right away. Anything she might have wanted to say was stuck in her dry throat.

'They're the only ones outside the family,' her mum added. 'Dawn will shut up, so will Beth. Charlotte definitely will, seeing as this is all for her.'

Hannah wanted to say that she didn't know, except it wasn't what her mum wanted to hear. Her voice was croaky at first and she had to restart her sentence to get it all out.

'I think so,' she said, hesitantly. 'Sophie seemed worried that this could be blamed on her.' A pause. 'I don't know about her mum but she'd want to protect Sophie.' A pause. 'I only invited her for you...'

It sounded a little more accusatory than she meant, even though it was true. Dawn and Janet were there because, otherwise, her mum would've been left as the odd-one-out among the group of younger women. Hannah had never understood the sort of mothers and daughters who claimed to be best friends. It was weird. *Really* weird. Friends were supposed to be one thing and family another.

The night was cold but the silence was colder. Hannah wanted to say something but couldn't quite bring herself to actually form the words. She opened her mouth a few times and a sentence felt close, although it never came out.

The road eventually widened as they passed through a small village, though it was gone almost as soon as Hannah had realised they were back with civilisation. It was as they passed a sign pointing towards the police headquarters, eight miles from wherever it was they were, that Hannah finally managed to get her words out.

'Do you *really* think this is the right thing to do...?' There was no immediate answer and she added: 'It just... doesn't feel like it.'

Hannah waited as her mum eased off the accelerator and they went through a four-way junction. The road bent up and around a ridge, then down the other side, where a small stream was trickling across the carriageway. It was dark. It was quiet. No answer came.

And then it did.

Her mum was quieter now, less decisive. 'Sometimes there are only wrong choices,' she said. 'We can't bring her back.'

'Katherine,' Hannah said. 'Her name's Katherine.'

Hannah felt her mother take a breath. 'If we tell anyone, your sister would be in trouble. We all would be. If we were going to tell someone, it would have had to be this morning.'

It would have been easy for Hannah to say that the reason nobody had spoken out that morning was because her mother had taken control. The window to act had come and gone so quickly that Katherine's body was already wrapped and in the car boot before the full enormity had fallen. The body had spent most of the day in there, parked outside the house, until her mum had called her downstairs after dark, and said it was time to act.

'It's not like *I* want this,' Hannah's mum said – and it was as if she was reading her daughter's thoughts. 'Somebody had to take charge to protect your sister. It would be different if Katherine had family, or a husband, or kids, or...'

She tailed off, perhaps realising how bad it sounded. That

the value of another person was whether they had others in their life.

Hannah didn't reply. Perhaps her mum was correct in that someone had to take charge. It wasn't as if anybody else wanted to make the tough decisions. That's what parents were supposed to do, wasn't it? And maybe, instead of being a horrific act of callousness, it was one of love? One of protection? It wasn't about Katherine, it was about looking after Charlotte, the way any parent would look out for their child. Their mother would have done this to keep any of her daughters safe. Janet was doing the same for Sophie.

Their silence wasn't that of guilt, it was that of love.

Hannah repeated that silently to herself as the darkened hedges whirred by. She had to tell herself that, because what else was there? If it wasn't love, it had to be...

The car slowed and Hannah's mother indicated to take a turn onto yet another dark, narrow lane. They'd not passed a car in a good fifteen or twenty minutes. The only light was that of the full beams spraying across the tarmac and the hedges. Hannah realised she'd got into the car unquestioningly, on a sort of autopilot for obeying her mother.

'Where are we going?' she asked.

'Somewhere I know.'

There was no elaboration and Hannah felt like a child again. *Are we there yet?* she thought, although she didn't say.

Hannah's mum continued to drive along the empty, dark lanes. Ten minutes passed, maybe more, until she eventually turned onto a gravelly track. Small stones pinged and fizzed under the car until they rolled to a halt in a small car park. There were no other cars and no lights. A low rotting wooden fence ringed the area, with a mud-coated blue portaloo in the corner.

'Where are we?' Hannah asked.

'It's the back entrance for the nature reserve,' her mum

replied. She stretched into the back seat and picked up a coat, into which she started to wriggle her shoulders. 'Jason brought me here a couple of times.'

Hannah wondered if the mention of Beth's father was to simply state the fact, or to shut her up. Jason was her mum's second husband – and there had always been an awkward relationship between him and both Charlotte and Hannah. They wanted *their* dad and yet, when they were both under ten, their mother left *their* dad for another man.

They had never really talked about it much as a mother and daughter. Hannah was too young at the time and, when she was old enough, she was past caring and used to her mum and dad being divorced. She had never called Jason 'Dad', mainly because she knew how much he wanted her to. Perhaps that was why it felt as if he never cared about them?

Hannah wondered if divorce ran in their family. Her mother had two and she had one. Still, without Jason, there would be no Beth – so not everything about her mum's second marriage was bad news.

'He brought me here when we were close to finishing it,' her mum said, without prompting. It felt as if she was thinking out loud. 'I don't know what he thought it would change. He kept talking about "fresh air", as if that would make everything better. It didn't, obviously.'

Hannah's mum had finished contorting her body into the jacket and she pressed against the backrest of the driver's seat while making no motion to get out of the car. Hannah wondered if there was more to come.

Her own dad – and their family of four along with Charlotte – had never been particularly outdoorsy. They weren't the sort for long walks to country pubs to sit in front of a fire and eat a roast. She didn't even realise that sort of life existed until she was grown up and away from home.

'Why here?' Hannah asked, even though she feared the answer.

'Jason and I hadn't been getting on. We were walking through these empty trails together and neither of us were talking. It was October or November and there was mud everywhere. I was wearing the wrong shoes and my gym trainers were covered in mud. There was hardly anybody else here. It was cold and windy and, when we'd been walking for about twenty minutes, it started to spot with rain. There was all this undergrowth and little boggy ponds and I remember walking next to him, where all I could think was that it would be a really good place to dump a body.'

Hannah was holding her breath, not wanting to hear any more. Nobody wanted to think of their parents in such a way.

'It wasn't a serious thing,' her mother added. 'I'd probably been watching some crime show on TV the night before. One of those random thoughts. You're standing at a bus stop and there's that moment where you think about pushing someone in front of it.'

'Mum—'

She turned to face Hannah. 'You're never going to do it but everybody has those thoughts.' She paused. 'Don't you...?'

'I don't know, Mum.'

They sat in the same positions for a few moments. Hannah wanted to be anywhere that wasn't in the car. She continued avoiding the sideways stare until her mum turned away and clicked open the driver's door. She muttered something that might've been 'come on' – and Hannah reacted by opening her own door and joining her mum at the back of the car.

Hannah kept thinking that another car would pull into the car park. A part of her yearned for it, wanting an out from what was about to happen. Instead, her mum opened the boot and, without needing a word to be spoken between them, they lifted out Katherine's sheet-wrapped body.

It was heavier than Hannah remembered from earlier, although that might have been because there were only two of them now. Hannah didn't know why her mum had chosen her specifically for this, other than that she was the oldest. Or, perhaps, some sort of morbid idea around Katherine being *her* friend. She didn't know if it was worse to be a part of this or to be sitting in her room at her mum's house, wondering what was going on.

Between them, they carried Katherine's body across the crunchy gravel onto a dark dirt path. There were no lights and only a gloomy moon trying to glimmer through gathering clouds. They walked for two or three minutes at a time, before their aching arms got the better of them and they had to rest. Hannah's forearms and biceps burned. Her shoulders were fire. She'd not had such a workout in years, if ever – but the pain – *this* pain – was deserved.

'There's some sort of swamp around here...'

They were the first words Hannah's mother had said since the car. Her breath twisted up into the air and disappeared.

'When I was here with Jason, some guy had dropped their phone. He went in to get it but the water was up to his chin. Jason and three other blokes heaved him out. It's much deeper than it looks.'

Hannah didn't reply. The path was tacky and each step felt as if it might be the one where the mud gripped her shoe tightly enough to pull it off.

They continued to walk and Hannah lost count of the number of times they'd stopped until her mum finally said, 'I think it's here.'

The path was marshy and the faint moonlight was shimmering from the bog on either side. Trees sprouted high from the mud, with narrow branches swaying in the breeze, like a series of flappy-armed giants.

'I don't want to do this,' Hannah said.

For a second, just a second, she decided she wanted no more of whatever was going to happen.

Except she did it anyway.

It was out of love. It had to be.

Without another dissenting word, she followed her mother's lead as they carried Katherine's body off the path and across a makeshift trail of sticks and stones that led deeper into the trees. Twigs cracked and the undergrowth rustled with critters and birds.

The two of them rested on the solid roots of a towering, ancient tree and then continued. Minutes passed and then Hannah's mum said, 'Here.'

They were on a mound of mud on the edge of a moss-coated pond that stretched out towards another bank of trees. Any further and they'd have been in the water.

Hannah's mother crouched as they placed the body on the ground. There would be no turning back after this but Hannah felt unable to stop what was happening. She was watching herself again, watching herself do the worst thing she'd ever done.

Except she couldn't watch any longer. She turned her back and stared up at the twisting, gnarling branches, before closing her eyes. She heard the slurp of the mud and the accepting, gentle splosh of the water. Her mother grunted and wheezed with effort, taking on the final, dreadful, deed herself. She was doing it for her family, Hannah knew that, but it didn't make things feel any better.

A minute or so passed and then: 'Let's go.'

Hannah felt the brush of her mother's arms against hers and she opened her eyes to watch her heading back in the direction from which they had, presumably, come. It all looked the same to Hannah – mud and sticks; trees and water.

She only realised she hadn't moved when her mum stopped

and turned back. Her face was washed with the greying light of a barely-there moon.

'I put some towels in the car,' Hannah's mum said. 'Let's dry off and then head home for a shower.'

Hannah turned between her mother and the bog behind. There was no sign of the sheet, or Katherine – and everything looked the same anyway. Even if it were daytime, she doubted she'd be able to re-find the place.

Her mother's voice echoed through the bristling dampness. 'It's time to go,' she said, more firmly this time.

A second passed and then, once again, Hannah did as she was told.

FIFTEEN

The first car Hannah saw on the drive home came when they'd already been on the road for ten minutes. They were well away from the nature reserve and heading through a village when they had to pull onto the verge to let a little Toyota pass in the opposite direction. The other car flashed their lights as a thank you and then Hannah's mum eased back onto the road.

Hannah hadn't spoken a word. Her thoughts were a mess of how much had happened during the day, of how far she'd lowered herself. She vaguely remembered some sort of famous quote about a crisis showing a person who they really are. She couldn't fight the increasingly grim sense that she was a person who said nothing up front. A person who went along with an ever-increasing display of horrors.

Her mother continued driving. The village had a short row of houses that dipped down towards a bridge. After that was a small shop, with the lights off and blinds down. No need for metal shutters and expensive CCTV systems in a place like this. There were a few dim orange street lights lining the road, with televisions blinking through open curtains. After the shop were more stone houses as the road rose up out of the village once more. Hannah had missed the 'Welcome To'-sign and wasn't sure where they were. The houses started to thin and they were almost out the back of the village when her mum abruptly steered the car over to the side of the road without indicating. They were in between a pair of street lights, cloaked by the shadows, next to a low wall.

'What are you doing?' Hannah asked, although the question went unanswered.

Her mum pulled up on the handbrake and turned off the headlights. She left the engine idling as she unclipped her seatbelt and twisted to reach onto the back seat. When she turned back, Katherine's overnight bag was in her hand.

She moved quickly, as if this was planned all along. She ducked out of the car, leaving the door open, and strode around the front until she was next to a wheelie bin that had been left out for a morning pick-up. She lifted the lid and dropped in the bag, then returned to the back of the car, where she clicked open the boot and grabbed the black bin bag that Hannah knew was full of the clothes and shoes they'd been wearing in the house that morning. That was swiftly dispatched into the bin on top of Katherine's bag – and then, it was as if none of it had happened. Hannah's mum slotted back into the car, closed the door, clipped in her seatbelt, turned on the headlights, and set off again.

Hannah watched everything play out without a word. It wasn't a stranger doing all this, it was her mother. There had been no hesitation, no reluctance. Her mum had always been into crime books and dramas and Hannah wondered if that had led to whatever this had been.

Her mum continued driving out of the village and through the winding country lanes on the route back to her house. Hannah closed her eyes for much of it, focusing on the hum of the engine and letting the bumpy surface jolt her back and forth against the seatbelt. It hurt more when she wasn't expecting it and that's what she wanted.

She knew the journey was almost over as the roads smoothed out and then there were the four speed bumps on the road that ran perpendicular to where her mum lived. Where *she* now lived. After Hannah's own divorce, she'd moved back into her mum's house, which was a situation that suited nobody. Hannah hated the lack of space and privacy, compared to what she'd been used to since leaving home as a nineteen-year-old. Beth hated it because there was somebody else in her space, another person with whom she had to share the bathroom and kitchen. Hannah's mum acted as if it was all fine, and perhaps it was, but she had her own routine of Slimming World twice a week, Zumba at the community centre, plus TV shows she would watch religiously. It always felt as if they were tripping over each other's feet – which was one more reason why Hannah had decided to get away from everything.

Her trip...

It was supposed to have been the focus of why they'd all met the night before. It was five days away – and yet, as her mum pulled onto the driveway, it was the first time she'd thought about it since the night before.

Could she really go now? Simply fly away and forget everything? Perhaps it would be for the best if she did...?

Her mum parked the car on the driveway and then opened the garage door. There were too many boxes inside for a car to fit, though Hannah had never questioned why her mum chose to enter the house this way, rather than through the front door. She was beginning to realise that there were a lot of things she didn't question.

Once the large garage door had been locked into place, her mum crossed and stood next to the door that led into the kitchen. Hannah was about to follow her inside, except that she stopped. Hannah knew what her mum was going to say a moment before she did, almost as if they were reading one another's minds.

'I'm not proud of this,' Alison said. 'It's important that you know that I'd do this to protect you as well as Charlotte.' A pause. 'For Beth, too. For any of you. It's not about Katherine, it's about you three.'

Perhaps it was true, it probably was, but Hannah wasn't sure that it felt like an act of love any longer. Perhaps it never had. The lies a person told to themselves were stronger than anything ever told to anyone else.

They waited on the step for a moment, looking to each other but seemingly neither knowing what to say next. Hannah certainly didn't know. It didn't make any of this feel better.

After those few seconds, her mum turned and led the way into the house. There was the usual muffled sound of Beth's music creeping down the stairs. She spent a lot of time in her room, which wasn't something Hannah could talk much about, considering she'd been the same at that age. She might not have heard her mum and sister arrive home but, either way, Beth didn't come out of her room or down the stairs.

'Do you want something to eat?' It took Hannah a moment to realise her mum was talking to her. 'I was going to have some toast but I don't mind making you something more.'

'I'm not hungry,' Hannah replied.

They stood a metre or so apart at the bottom of the stairs but it might as well have been acres. Something was broken between them that Hannah doubted could ever be healed.

She waited a second and then turned and headed up the stairs to where the music seeping from Beth's room was getting steadily louder. Hannah's mum had moved twice since Hannah had left home and, in this house, Beth had the biggest of the bedrooms. With their mother taking the one marginally smaller, Hannah had the smallest 'guest' room that was little more than an oversized cupboard.

Hannah had been through a couple of flats with Paul before they got their own house. Then came the divorce and the return to living with Mum. It was home but it wasn't really.

She pushed her way into the bedroom, although the door couldn't open fully because the bed was in the way. Once inside, Beth's music was louder through the separating wall. Hannah didn't recognise it, which wasn't a surprise. Every generation perplexed the next with their music choices.

The curtains were open and the room was clouded in a hazy grey blue. Hannah didn't bother with the light, instead sitting on the bed and listening to the autotuned din from the other side of the wall.

Much of the stuff she'd taken from the house shared with Paul was in the garage downstairs. She had managed to squeeze a couple of suitcases under the bed, along with a bag-for-life full of things she couldn't quite bear to be without. She found herself delving into the bag. There was her passport and paper part of her driving licence, her old work lanyard, gig tickets and a cinema stub from her first date with Paul. Most of it was things she didn't need and wouldn't look through – except she couldn't quite force herself to throw any of it away.

Underneath those was the photo she knew she'd kept. It had been taken on a school trip when she'd been twelve or thirteen. Her English class had gone to the Barbican on a musty coach. The girls had commandeered the back seat, leaving the boys to claim they didn't want it anyway. That had turned a three-hour journey there into one of Hannah's best moments at school. She couldn't remember a single thing they had talked about on that trip – but she remembered laughing the whole time. Those three hours passed in the clicking of fingers – and the actual theatre was a nuisance that got in the way of the journey back. That sense of happiness was something that had never left.

It was all distilled down to a single photo, taken by someone Hannah couldn't remember, at a time when none of them knew it was being captured. She was sitting in the back right seat, with Katherine at her side and Sophie in the middle seat. There were two other girls in the other chairs and all five of them were laughing at something Hannah couldn't recall. They were all in school uniform, their ties loose and skirts short. None of them were posing, or pretending. This was what friendship actually was.

Katherine looked so young, they all did. Hannah stared at the unmoving image of her friend, absorbing the joy in her face and not knowing what could come next.

It was an accident, Hannah told herself. Charlotte had been reckless with the pills but anyone could have had a bad reaction. If not that, it was something to do with the way she'd hit her head from the fall. Hannah had done her best to help out by switching beds and letting Katherine have the one with the bathroom. If someone had found her earlier and called an ambulance, it might have been different. But, by the time Dawn had gone poking around the hallway, it was too late. They'd all slept through the opportunity to save Katherine.

Next door, one song moved onto the next, though the only reason Hannah knew it was different was because a man's voice had become a woman's. Beth had a dreadful taste in music. Kids today, and all that.

Not my fault, Hannah told herself. *Not my fault.*

She knew she'd be telling herself this for weeks, for months. Perhaps forever.

Not my fault.

At first she thought the *ding-dong* was part of Beth's music. It took her a moment to realise that there was somebody at the door and she put down the bag and opened the bedroom door. She took a step onto the landing, straining to listen to whatever might be going on downstairs. She and Charlotte had both been like this as kids. The moment somebody came to the door, they'd be trying to listen in to either find out if it was someone for them, or if there was some gossip they could overhear.

Hannah supposed she'd never quite grown out of it, though Beth's music made it impossible to hear anything other than a stifled back and forth between her mum and whoever was at the door. She couldn't make out the voices, let alone contort herself to see who was there, but Hannah remained where she was at the top of the stairs. Something about the timing had her on edge.

She waited as the voices continued and then it came.

'Han...?'

Her mum sounded hesitant, although it might not have been apparent to someone who didn't know her.

Hannah headed down the stairs, where she was met by her mother at the bottom. Her mum angled her body towards the front door, speaking deliberately enough so that whoever was there could also hear.

'There's a man here for you,' she said.

Hannah peered around the corner, out towards the front of the house where a young man in a baseball cap stood with his hands in his pockets. He smiled politely, though Hannah had no idea who he was.

'This is Zack,' her mum added. 'He says he's looking for Katherine...'

SIXTEEN

Hannah's mum disappeared through the door into the kitchen and, though she pulled it closed behind her, Hannah suspected she remained on the other side, trying to listen in.

The man at the door was likely a few years younger than Hannah, though it was hard to tell for sure. He had a babyish face that was offset with dark stubble which matched his brown eyes. The sort of guy who could be anywhere from twenty to late-thirties and who got IDed if he tried to buy booze at Tesco. His cap was pulled down tight, though tufts of dark hair poked out around his ears. Hannah wondered if he might be someone from their school but, if he was, she couldn't place him.

'I wasn't sure if this was the right address,' the man said. He angled himself to the side, taking in the hallway past Hannah, who now stood in front of him. 'You might not know me but I'm Zack. I work with Katherine and we went out a few times.'

Zack stopped for a moment, straightening himself and burying his hands deeper into his pockets. His breath steamed high above him.

'Did you invite Katherine to a party last night?' he added. 'Some sort of night in because you're going travelling?'

Hannah stared blankly at him, not because she didn't know what he was talking about – but because he was so spot on. She felt him staring as she tried to think of an answer. Her mum had said something back at the house about the police and their stories and...

'We ran into each other at Morrisons a few days ago,' Hannah said. 'She was ahead of me in the self-checkout and we had a bit of a catch-up after we paid.'

She was speaking quickly, aware she was giving too much information. Hannah pictured Katherine saying goodbye afterwards and then heading out the double doors. She almost said that, too – except it had even less relevance.

'I'm going travelling on Friday,' she added, still talking too quickly. 'We had a little get-together last night. Nothing massive, just a few drinks and some board games. I texted Katherine the details and she said she was going to come.'

A breath. No lies had been told so far, until...

'She never showed up,' Hannah added. 'We were expecting her but nothing.'

Zack's eyes narrowed and Hannah felt as if he was staring into her soul. Had she spoken too confidently? Did it sound rehearsed? Had she made too much eye contact? Too little?

It was like Zack was doing some sort of Derren Brown mind trick, where he could know whether she was telling the truth.

'I dropped her off...' he said.

Hannah felt something ebb through her that she'd never felt before. A sense of control slipping, of absolute dread.

'Where did you drop her off?' she asked.

Hannah's neck was tingling. Arms too. Perhaps it was all of her?

'At the end of the street, opposite the coffee shop. She pointed along to a house with steps at the front.'

Hannah tried not to react. He was talking about where they'd been.

'She stayed at mine the night before,' Zack added. 'She told me about the party and we'd gone to the house via her flat, so she could get changed. She was running a bit late and...'

He tailed off and Hannah realised the thing that he *hadn't* said. It felt like a dangerous question. 'Did you see her go into the house...?'

Zack straightened, finally taking his eyes away from Hannah and sighing up towards the ceiling. 'No...'

He sounded wistful and regretful – but only for a moment.

'Was that the house?'

Hannah thought about lying – though not for long. It would be too easy to discover the truth. 'Yes,' she said. 'There were seven of us there. I was waiting for Katherine to arrive but the doorbell never went and she never texted. I assumed she changed her mind.'

It was out there now: not the truth but a story with a lot of truthful elements. Her lack of panic had surprised even her. She wouldn't have thought Zack's sudden appearance would leave her calm and yet... here she was. Perhaps her mother's ruthlessness had been passed down?

Zack sighed again and started to stumble over whatever he was trying to say. He rested a hand on the door frame and leaned onto it. 'She never called for a lift this morning. She said she would but I never heard from her. She's not answering her phone or replying to texts and she's not at her flat.'

He sounded exhausted, as if he'd spent the day driving around looking for Katherine – which Hannah realised he probably had.

'Are you going out with her...?'

Hannah pictured being with Katherine and Charlotte at the back of the house, where Katherine had said she'd had a date with someone from work. She must have been talking about Zack, except she'd said something along the lines of it not going anywhere. Hannah couldn't remember the exact phrase. There was also the unreplied text he'd sent to her.

'Sort of,' Zack replied. 'I guess we never called it that...' He puffed out another breath and then added: 'We were both off work the last few days. We spent every day together.'

It took Hannah a moment to process this. The fact they had been together explained why there were no messages between the pair on Katherine's phone. There'd be no need if they were *with* one another. She also had an inkling of why Katherine might have played it down in the garden. Spending a few days in a row with a person must have felt intense, especially with it seemingly being a new relationship. She likely didn't want to jinx anything by talking about it. Hannah and Paul had been like that at one time. They'd spend whole weekends in bed together and then go off to their respective jobs and lives and not mention it to anybody else. It took about six weeks until they were ready to tell people.

Hannah blinked back to the moment and realised that Zack was staring at her. A few seconds must have passed with her zoned out.

'I don't suppose you have a key to her flat?' he asked.

Hannah shook her head. 'Sorry, it's just... we're not that close any more. We were friends at school and I guess things have drifted since then...' She waited a moment and then added another 'sorry', that was entirely genuine.

Zack stepped backwards and forwards, suddenly anxious. He took his hands out of his pockets and tugged at his cap, before blowing into his palms.

'I'm wondering if I should call the police and report her missing...?'

It felt like a question and left Hannah unsure what to say. When her mother had laid out everything that morning, she'd said the police would likely ask questions at some point.

Hannah coughed as she fumbled for the words. The cold air raced into her lungs, filling her nostrils and leaving her gasping.

'Has she ever gone missing before...?' Zack asked.

The question left Hannah somewhat bewildered. 'I don't think so,' she said. 'Definitely not when we were at school. I don't know about after that.'

Zack nodded again, although it felt like something had changed in the way he was holding himself. Hannah couldn't quite figure out what it was, although it might have been something as simple as his hands now being out of his pockets. He seemed more imposing and a few inches taller than she had first thought.

'Who was with you last night?'

Hannah answered without question, as if she'd been compelled: 'My mum, my aunt, my two sisters, my friend, Sophie, and her mum.'

She wondered if the name 'Sophie' might mean something to him, given that Sophie and Katherine had fallen out so badly. If it did, then he had a terrific poker face as nothing changed in his features. He continued to watch her, giving it the Derren Brown eyes again.

A second or two passed and then he stepped away from the door, nodding slightly. 'Can I give you my number?' he asked. 'If you hear anything, will you let me know?'

'Of course.'

Hannah fumbled with her phone, struggling to unlock it with the wrong passcode and picturing herself typing those numbers into Katherine's device. She got there in the end but her thumbs felt bloated and she couldn't hit the right keys. As Zack read his number, she said it back to him a digit at a time but it took four or five attempts to get it into her contacts properly. He said that she could text him, so that he'd have her number – and Hannah did it without question. She'd done so much of that in the past day that she wondered if she'd ever have another independent thought again.

Zack held his phone up when they were finished, as if signifying the deed was done, then he stuffed it into his jacket pocket. She didn't particularly want him to have her number, especially as he knew where she lived, though it was a bit late now.

'You will text me, won't you?' he asked. 'If you hear from her, I mean.'

'Of course,' Hannah repeated.

Zack half turned to go and then twisted back again. 'I just...' Another sigh. 'She was right there. Right at the house. If she didn't go inside, then where did she go?'

Hannah looked at him and desperately wanted to suggest something plausible. In the end, all she could manage was a slim smile that she hoped was consoling.

'I wish I knew,' she said.

SEVENTEEN

ZACK, MONDAY

Zack texted the coffee shop manager to say he wasn't feeling well and then sat staring partly at his phone but mainly at the road where he'd dropped off Katherine. It was supposed to be his and Katherine's first day back at The Grind but he couldn't face being there without her. He couldn't face *not knowing* what had happened after he'd driven away a day and half before.

He got an almost immediate reply, saying not to worry, then he sat and waited. He watched as residents left their houses and headed off to work, or to take their kids to school. He only realised almost an hour had passed when he received a message back from his manager to say that Katherine hadn't turned up. Unless he was really, *really* ill, she wondered if he could show up for the late morning rush.

Zack hadn't told anyone that he and Katherine had been spending time together away from work, mainly because he didn't want to jinx anything. He wondered if his manager knew. She must have spotted those glances between them that lasted a fraction too long, even if she hadn't said anything. Zack wondered what she was thinking now, given neither of them had turned up for work. Did she think they were together? That they were holed up somewhere, skiving off?

He read the message one more time and then pocketed the phone.

Nothing out of the ordinary had happened on the street while he'd been parked. If anything, *he* was the oddity. He'd been sitting in his car watching the mundanity of everyday life for more than an hour. If he wasn't careful, someone would call the police on him.

To avoid that, he got out of the car and tucked his hands into his jacket pockets. There were crunchy patches of frost on the sides of the pavement, where people hadn't been walking.

He stepped along the street and, for the first time, stopped outside the house with the steps. It looked cleaner and newer than those around it, as if it had been renovated at some point recently. That's what the guy in the café had said the day before. It was big but, unless there was a basement, it only appeared to have one storey. The sort of place that could be deceptive because there was so much room at the back. If this was a new estate, they'd have crammed three or four boxy red-bricks onto it.

Hannah had told him they had seven people staying in this house and he could see why they'd hired it for a night. It wouldn't be expensive in February, the road was quiet – and there would be plenty of space for whatever they had planned.

Zack was as sure as he could be that Hannah had been lying the night before. Or, at least, lying about some of what had happened. She said Katherine hadn't turned up at the house but there was a strange mix of her sounding too confident and over-rehearsed, while simultaneously trying to mask a sense of panic. Her breathing had quickened when she'd talked of Katherine and he couldn't get over the sense that she didn't seem surprised. If he'd had plans with someone, who hadn't turned up – and he'd later found out that person was missing, he would definitely be blindsided by it. Hannah hadn't. She had taken in the news with barely a blink.

And if she really was lying, it meant Katherine *had* been in this house on Saturday and something *had* happened to her. The problem was that the other people who'd been at the party were seemingly either members of Hannah's family, or a close friend of hers. He didn't know any of them, let alone how to approach finding out what might have happened.

At the absolute least, Katherine had been missing for a full day. The police would be an option, especially as she had no family to report her missing, but it still seemed like a nuclear option. If she was to turn up having gone off to do something by herself for a day, he'd be the idiot who thought their relationship was something it wasn't.

As Zack stared up, there was a flicker of movement from the house next door. A man was standing in the window, looking down towards him and apparently caught between backing away and continuing to stare. Zack offered a half wave of acknowledgement, which seemingly made up the other man's mind. A moment later and he was in the doorway. He wore round glasses, with a sleeveless jumper over a regular one.

'Can I help you?' he called.

Zack had moved along the pavement, so that he was standing in front of the neighbour's house. They were at opposite ends of the path. Zack pointed towards the house with the steps.

'My girlfriend was due to be at some sort of party here on Saturday but she never came home.'

Zack had to fight the internal wince at the word 'girlfriend'. If Katherine was, then they'd never quite got around to admitting it to one another. On the other hand, aside from a few hours here and there, they'd spent almost four days together until he'd dropped her off here. They'd slept at one another's flats and it felt so natural and normal.

Either way, the neighbour was suddenly interested. He closed the door behind him and walked along the path until he was at Zack's side. Together, they looked up at the adjacent house.

'There was one hell of a noise,' he said. 'Enormous. I went round to see what was going on and there was this woman who said she'd not heard anything. Then they closed the door on me.'

Zack found himself eyeing the man, wondering if this could be true. Except, why wouldn't it be?

'Did the noise come from here?' he asked, nodding at the house.

'I heard it through the wall. Right on the other side. Couldn't have come from anywhere else.' The man pointed to a house with a green door that was further along the street in the direction of the coffee shop. 'The owner lives down there – Jeff something – not that he answers the door, of course. He rents this place out at the weekends and there's always something. I've been down there a few times to complain about the noise. I think he hides when he sees me.'

It took Zack a moment to take it all in. He tried to remain calm, even though a voice inside was screaming at him. 'What sort of noise was it?' he asked.

'A bang. A really *big* bang, as if somebody had dropped something heavy.'

'And you knocked on the door?'

'Of course. I thought a meteor had hit.'

It was a clear exaggeration – but the man sounded interested as well.

Zack fished into his jacket pocket for his phone. He flipped through the photos until he found one of Katherine. He'd taken it in the coffee shop when she was on the way to the kitchen while balancing two stacks of plates and a tower of mugs, like some sort of talent-show contestant. She was grinning at him, her tongue out.

'Did you see her?'

Zack turned the screen so the man could see it. He lifted his glasses and squinted over the top, before lowering them again and leaning in closer. There was a moment in which Zack felt sure he was about to say he had – but then the man angled away and shook his head.

'I don't think so.' He lifted his glasses again. 'Maybe. I think it was all women in there but she wasn't the one who answered the door. Right rude woman, that was.' He puffed up his chest, on a roll. 'Not the first time, of course. I have to knock on the door most weekends to tell them to keep it down. I've been on to the council and all sorts. The owner's a wrong 'un, too. Caused a right scene a while back, with his girlfriend or his wife. Right there, it was.'

He pointed to a spot a little along the street, in front of the house with the green door.

'She was throwing things at him, telling him she never wanted to see him again. It only stopped when the police turned up. Was a right palaver.'

Zack almost laughed. He didn't think he'd ever heard anyone use the word 'palaver' outside of TV. Not that any of it was funny.

'What did the council say when you complained?'

'Pah. Nothing. Told me to keep a diary of all the noise. Fat lot of good all that did. I talked to some of the other neighbours and ended up with the owner's phone number, not that he ever answers. Wouldn't surprise me if he's blocked my number. I leave messages but he never replies.'

The man threw a hand up in the air and made a 'pfft' sound with his lips. Zack had the sense that, even if his neighbours were perfect, he'd find something to complain about. That didn't mean he was wrong about this, though. It also didn't mean he'd not heard that bang on Saturday night.

'Can you give me the number?' Zack asked.

'What number?'

'The owner's. Maybe he'll take *my* call?'

The man turned and looked Zack up and down for the first time. Whatever he saw was seemingly enough to convince him. 'Fine,' he said, 'I'll give you mine as well – and if you hear anything from him, you make sure you let me know. I'll put it in the diary.' He took a step back towards his house and mumbled something about his phone, then stopped halfway along the path. 'Did you say your girlfriend's missing?'

'Yes.'

The man frowned and shook his head gently. 'I honestly wouldn't be surprised by anything that happens in that house.'

EIGHTEEN

HANNAH

Hannah pulled her jacket tighter, wishing she'd worn an extra layer. The bench next to the duck pond had no surrounding trees and it had to be a few degrees colder than it had been when she was walking to the park. The water was still and even the ducks couldn't be arsed with this sort of weather. They'd either sodded off south, or were hiding somewhere much warmer. Hannah didn't blame them one bit.

Sophie slotted onto the bench next to her and it was as if they were rubbish spies in a dodgy movie.

'Thanks for coming,' Sophie said. 'Your mum said not to mention anything in a text and I didn't know if it was all right to call.'

'I don't think anybody's listening into our calls.'

Sophie started to say something but Hannah didn't wait to hear her out. She stood and took a step away from the bench.

'Let's walk,' she said. 'It's too cold sitting still.'

There were no arguments from Sophie and the two women walked side by side on the path that looped around the park.

Sophie spoke in a whispered hiss, as if worried that they'd

be overheard, despite the emptiness of the park. 'What if it comes back to me?' she said.

'What if *what* comes back to you?'

'Katherine. Someone's going to notice she's missing sooner or later. What if people think *I'm* involved? People are going to know about Thomas leaving her for me.'

'It was ten years ago.'

'But people will remember! Then there was that stupid Facebook post. I've seen the screengrabs people kept. I've been awake all night, thinking about it. Someone will tell the police and they'll be round.' She paused, then added: 'I don't wish she was dead. I *never* wished that. I didn't mean it. I wasn't well. The doctor said...'

She tailed off but Sophie sounded panicked in a way Hannah had only heard her once or twice before. Hannah was suddenly fourteen years old, waiting outside the newsagent as Sophie scuttled outside with half a dozen magazines crammed into the inside of her jacket. 'I think he saw me,' she'd hissed then, talking about the shop owner. They'd bolted along an alley, deeper into the estate where they both lived at the time.

'I've got to think of Trent,' Sophie added, talking about her son and returning Hannah to the present. 'He's only a kid. It's not like he's done anything wrong – and neither have I.'

'Nobody's linking anything back to you,' Hannah said, as she told herself that everything had happened out of love for Charlotte. It was getting harder and harder to believe that.

Sophie huffed a long sigh of annoyance, which merged into a yawn that she tried to flap away. She must be worried because they weren't the sort of friends to have these mid-morning meetings, let alone in a freezing park.

Hannah was worried, too.

'Someone called Zack came to the house last night,' she said. 'He dropped Katherine off on Saturday night. I don't know how he got my details – I forgot to ask. It must've been off Katherine.'

Sophie had stopped on the path. She put a hand on Hannah's arm and almost spun her around.

'What do you mean "dropped her off"?'

'I don't think he saw her going into the house. He said he dropped her at the end of the road. I stuck to the story, saying she never got there.'

Sophie hesitated for a second, her brows almost meeting in the middle of her head. 'Who is he?'

'I think it's someone she works with. She said something about a date that didn't go anywhere and I think it's him. He said they'd spent a few days together. I don't know if they're going out properly.'

Hannah took a step away, continuing on the route and Sophie again slotted in at her side. The park was deserted, with the only sound that of screaming children drifting from the primary-school playground somewhere on the far side. It must be break time.

Sophie was back to hissed whispers: 'Did he believe you?'

'I don't know. He didn't wait around and said something about going to the police.'

Sophie stopped and grabbed at Hannah's arm. 'What did you say?'

Hannah started to reply and then realised that she hadn't said anything. Zack had mentioned going to the police as some sort of question and she'd more or less ignored it. She suddenly realised how dodgy it must have looked to him. If someone's friend goes missing, they'd *want* the police involved.

'Han...?'

She'd been lost in those thoughts for a few seconds but Sophie brought her back to the park.

'Nothing,' Hannah replied. 'What could I say? It sounded

like he was going anyway. We knew someone would notice her missing sooner or later.'

Sophie didn't seem to have anything to say to that. They continued walking along the path as a man with a dog cut diagonally across the grass. His dog bounded ahead, tongue flapping, chasing a ball with joyous abandon. The man shuffled after the dog and there was something about the way he moved that stirred another memory for Hannah. It had first popped into her mind the morning before – but there'd been so much happening in the house that it had arrived and disappeared in an instant.

'Did you hear anyone moving around?' Hannah asked.

'When?'

'Saturday night... well, Sunday morning, I guess. After I swapped beds with Katherine, I was sleeping on the sofa and I vaguely remember somebody shuffling around the kitchen. I thought I might have been dreaming.'

Sophie's pace slowed a fraction. 'I didn't hear anyone. Mum would've made a load of noise if she was up and about.'

It had only been a stride or three but Sophie re-upped her pace, probably not realising she'd slowed. She continued talking, moving from one thought to the next.

'What did you do last night with, um... you know...'

Hannah knew she was talking about Katherine's body. It was a natural thing to wonder, considering how they'd all been involved. She thought about saying she didn't know, as if everything that happened once they left the house was on her mother and out of her control.

'It's probably best you don't know,' she replied.

Sophie started to say something but then stopped. Further up the path, the dog raced across, still chasing the ball. The owner was busy trying to light a cigarette as he continued to shuffle after the dog.

'I never thought I'd end up involved in something like this,' Sophie said. The urgency was gone from her voice and she sounded as if she was apologising for something. Perhaps she was. Perhaps they all should be. 'It happens to other people,' she added. 'You see and hear things, or there are TV shows, and you think the people who do things like this are all bad. You think they're bad people. Then you're in the middle of it and everything looks terrible, even though it's all innocent.' She paused for breath. 'Sort of innocent.'

Hannah couldn't reply. It was everything she'd been thinking: how the barely comprehensible had somehow become real. Three days ago, she'd have been certain of knowing where the line between good and bad lay – but, now, she wasn't sure.

Sophie wasn't done speaking: 'Did you sleep last night?'

'Not much.'

'Me neither. Thomas said I kept turning over in the night. He asked if something was wrong. He specifically talked about the party and whether something had happened. I tried to play it all down, saying that we had a few drinks and played cards, that sort of thing. Blamed it all on a hangover.'

'Did he believe you?'

Sophie's phone beeped and she stopped for a moment to wriggle it out of her bag. She checked the screen, shook her head a fraction and then returned it without comment. They continued walking, although they were close to the gates near the school and the screeching made it difficult to hear one another.

'Probably – but I don't know how long I can keep it going. How are you supposed to act normal when everything *isn't* normal? I had to force myself to eat a Weetabix this morning, because that's what I do every other breakfast.'

Hannah had no idea how to reply because the feelings Sophie was describing were again her own. At least she had the luxury of sharing a house with people in the same situation as she was. Sophie lived with her husband and son.

'I just keep seeing her body in that bed,' Sophie said. 'She was so grey. I've never seen a dead body before and—'

She cut herself off as a woman with a pushchair entered through the park gates. They exchanged smiles and nods and then continued walking in opposite directions.

'I just want it all to go away,' Sophie added, quieter this time.

'I do, too.'

'It's easy for you. You're going away on Friday. You're literally getting away from here. What am I supposed to do?'

Hannah tried to think of something comforting to say but nothing came. The truth was, she couldn't wait to be on that plane – and Friday couldn't come quickly enough.

NINETEEN

ZACK

Zack checked his phone, where there were two new messages from his manager. The first asked how he was doing and the second had a whiff of desperation as it asked if he might make it in for noon. Zack replied with a quick 'Sorry, not feeling well' and then put it back in his pocket.

He had tried calling the owner of the house but only got a voicemail where a terse man's voice told him to leave a message. He'd returned to his car near the coffee shop and then changed his mind about driving away. Now he was standing at the end of the path that led to the house with the green door. He was fairly sure this was the house the neighbour had pointed towards when mentioning the owner – but, even if it wasn't, he could try the ones on either side.

There was no doorbell, so Zack knocked on the glass and waited. Because of the way the neighbour had said he couldn't get an answer, Zack didn't expect much. Almost immediately, there were footsteps from the other side of the door and then the sliding of a chain before the door popped open.

Considering the neighbour had offered tales of shouted arguments on the street and apparently debauched house parties, Zack was expecting somebody who wasn't a relatively normal-looking man. The homeowner's clothes were a bit tight and he'd pushed his hair forward to cover a receding hairline – but Zack saw worse fashion crimes every day of the week when he was working.

The man blinked up at him. 'Are you the meter reader?' he asked.

Zack was on the back foot for a moment. 'Huh?'

'The meter reader's due. I thought...'

'I'm looking for someone named Jeff,' Zack replied.

The man took a half-step back and frowned. 'I'm Jeff.'

Zack poked a thumb towards the house with the steps a few doors down. 'Do you own that place?'

The frown deepened: 'Who's asking?'

'My girlfriend was supposed to be at a party there on Saturday. I dropped her off and I've not seen her since. Someone told me you were the owner and—'

Zack stopped, took his phone out of his pocket and found the photo of Katherine balancing all the plates.

'—I was wondering if you've seen her.'

Zack held up the phone for Jeff to see, not giving him much of an option of whether to look. The man angled away a fraction but couldn't avoid it.

Jeff looked at the screen, then at Zack, then the screen, and then finally back to Zack. 'Who did you say you were?'

'I'm Zack and this is my girlfriend, Katherine.'

Jeff pulled a face somewhere between exhausted and annoyed. The sort of face Zack knew from when he didn't want any extra jobs dumped on him at work.

'Don't know her,' Jeff said.

'Did you see any of the people at the house on Saturday?'

Jeff had a hand on the door, apparently ready to close it, although he didn't. 'Some of them. I gave them the keys and let them in. Hannah-something was the main one.'

Zack spoke quickly, not wanting to give Jeff a chance to shut down the conversation. 'Can I see the house?' he said. 'I know it's a big ask but I was wondering if something of Katherine's might have been left...?'

'Why don't you ask Hannah-something what happened to your girlfriend?'

'I did – and she said she doesn't know. Nobody seems to. I could go to the police but—'

The man straightened at the mention of police, interrupting Zack without saying a word. There was a moment of silence and then:

'I haven't got long,' Jeff said. 'The meter man's coming by soon and I've already missed him last week. Dunno what you're hoping to find, though. I've already been in and cleaned up since they left.'

'Oh.' Zack found himself sinking lower. 'It's probably nothing but I figured I'd ask ahead of going to the police.'

Jeff seemed wiser to this second mention of the authorities, managing not to react. Instead, he opened a small cabinet close to the door and fished out a large set of keys that he tossed from one hand to the other.

'Let's be quick,' he said.

Moments later, they were at the top of the stairs of the house three doors down and Jeff was using the wrong key to try to get in. He muttered something to himself that Zack didn't catch – and then he tried a different key, before shoving open the front door. He stood to the side, letting Zack enter ahead of him.

It didn't take Zack long to realise why the house would've been hired for a small party. There was a huge open-plan living room, with a large U-shaped sofa. The high ceiling and windows at the back gave everything a show-home appeal. It was the sort of place Zack would be afraid to spend any time in, because everything was so white and clean that he'd be worried about getting it dirty.

Zack moved further into the room as Jeff closed the door behind them.

'It's a nice place,' Zack said, almost without thinking. He'd been brought up to be polite when it came to new people and new things.

'I had it all refitted,' Jeff replied. 'New floor, new surfaces, new paint. I bought a bunch of new appliances – which works against me.'

Zack turned to see that Jeff had moved into the kitchen. He opened a cupboard and closed it.

'What do you mean?' Zack asked.

Jeff glanced across to an ugly ceramic dog on a shelf close to his shoulder. 'I think your friends stole some things when they left yesterday.'

Zack didn't bother to correct him in that they weren't *his* friends. 'What did they steal?'

'A coffee grinder and a blender. I try to market the place as luxury and thought people might want it for dinner parties, that sort of thing. I guess I made a mistake...'

Jeff tailed off, although it all had the air of a person who'd made this argument in his own head many times in the past. Zack wondered why he was telling him this, although he wanted to keep him on side in case he needed his help at some point.

'Why do you think they stole it?' he asked.

Jeff blinked, probably surprised that someone was taking the complaint on board. 'I double-checked the place on Saturday morning and they were definitely here. When I cleaned up yesterday afternoon, they were gone. I think your friends might have taken a sheet, too – although I'm not sure about that. The bedding's in the washer at the moment.'

Zack wondered why the owner hadn't simply *asked*

Hannah about the apparently stolen items. Even if he'd noticed after she, her family and friends had left, then he surely had her details? He was obviously annoyed, though in a way that sounded as if he wasn't going to do anything about it. There was something not quite right about Jeff and his attitude, although Zack wasn't going to push it.

'Can I have a quick look around?' he asked. 'I won't move anything or make a mess.'

Jeff shrugged. 'As long as you're quick.'

Zack moved swiftly around the house. Everything was on a single level, with bedrooms on either side of the main room. It was bigger than it looked from the outside, though the more time he spent looking from bedroom to bedroom, the more it all felt a bit soulless. Everything was plain and, aside from the odd ceramic dog, there was nothing to stop it looking like an advert for a Boxing Day sale.

He was back in the main room when he realised it felt like a house, not a home. The sort of place that would be in the news every now and then because some rich kid had rented it and then thrown a party for a hundred other rich kids. There'd be a mound of beer bottles in one corner and vomit across the pavement outside.

Zack also couldn't find anything remotely related to Katherine, or anybody else. When the owner said it had been cleaned, he meant it.

Jeff was checking his phone as Zack re-entered the main space. He glanced up and then eyed his watch. 'Find what you were looking for?'

'Not really.'

Jeff shrugged dismissively. 'I'm sure she'll show up. You sure she hasn't got some other lad on the go? If you want my advice, you're better off without 'em. Women are all the same in my book.'

He laughed to himself as Zack ignored the remark and

edged towards the door. Jeff didn't appear to notice that he was the only one who found himself funny.

It was as Zack caught his foot on the edge of a rug that he noticed the spot on the ground. The tiles were white and bright, except for a small patch of reddy-brown that had stained a corner around the grouting. He crouched and looked more closely, then touched it. When he removed his finger, there was nothing on it.

'What've you found?' Jeff asked.

'Not sure. Do you know if this was here before?'

Jeff left his phone on the counter and crossed the room until he was at Zack's side. He grumbled as he bent over to take a closer look, then licked his fingers before trying to wipe away the blemish. When he pulled away, the stain remained unmoved.

'I don't remember seeing it before,' he said. 'But I don't usually go around looking at the floor. Could be anything.'

The owner didn't seem too bothered and he stepped away towards the sofas, where he started to plump a cushion. As he was doing that, Zack noticed something glimmering underneath the edge of the rug. He knew what it was the moment he saw it, though he barely had time to examine it before Jeff turned. As quickly as he'd spotted it, Zack stuffed it into his sleeve and pushed himself up.

'Are we done?' Jeff asked.

'I think so.'

The owner led the way across to the kitchen, where he reached under the counter and picked up a stack of pizza boxes marked 'Mario's' on the side. He muttered something about 'recycling' and then balanced them on the crook of his arm as he opened the front door.

'No need for the police then, I guess,' he said.

'Huh?'

'There's no sign she was here, is there? Your friends must've been right.'

Zack mumbled something close to agreement. 'Thanks for showing me around,' he said.

The cold bit hard as Zack exited onto the top step. Pinpricks stabbed at his cheeks as he tried to catch his breath. Jeff was oblivious as he locked the front door and then silently shooed Zack down to the street. He muttered something about hoping he hadn't missed the man who was coming to read his meter – and then hurried along, while tossing the keys from one hand to the other.

Zack headed back to his car and, as soon as he slammed the driver's door, the windows started to steam. His heart raced as he pulled his hand out from his sleeve to reveal the item that had been partly hidden under the edge of the rug. He knew what it was when he'd seen it – and, as he ran his fingers across the cool metal, he wondered what it meant.

In his palm sat Katherine's silver heart pendant.

TWENTY

HANNAH

As Hannah blustered her way back into the house, she hadn't realised her mum would be waiting in the kitchen for her. Or, perhaps, not *for* her – although it felt like it. Hannah hadn't even taken her coat off when her mother asked what Sophie had wanted.

'Not much,' Hannah replied. 'She hadn't slept well and I think she wanted a chat. It's not like she can talk to Thomas about what happened.'

Her mum frowned, though didn't say anything – which, in many ways, made it worse. Hannah suddenly felt that once-familiar teenage spikiness.

'I'm almost thirty, Mum. I don't need to tell you every time I talk to my friends.'

Hannah's mother eyed her for a second, though didn't reply. It was probably for the best, else they'd be back in the realms of loud discussions about what could and couldn't be done under her roof.

'She's in there,' Hannah's mum said, nodding towards the living room.

There was a second in which Hannah thought she meant

Katherine. A second in which she'd blocked the horror of the day before. 'Who?'

There was no answer. Instead, Alison stood and led the way into the living room, where Charlotte was waiting for them on the sofa. Her back was stooped, her head bowed, as she stared at the floor. She didn't bother to look up as Hannah sat next to her on the sofa, as their mother took the armchair.

Hannah assumed Beth was at college, which was why their mother had chosen now to arrange whatever this was going to be.

Hannah touched her sister's shoulder, though there was no reaction. 'How are you doing?' she asked.

'How d'you think?'

Hannah didn't need to answer that, so she tried something else: 'What are you doing here?'

Their mother replied before Charlotte could: 'I asked her to come round.'

Charlotte snorted at this: '"Asked" is an interesting way of putting it.' She sat up straighter and turned to Hannah. '"Demanded" is more like it.'

Their mother's reply flashed like the snap of a whip. 'You're lucky it was me doing the asking, considering what you did.'

'Give it a rest, Mum,' Charlotte said.

Hannah pressed backwards on the sofa, getting out of the line of fire. It had been a long time since they'd had a full-on family row.

'Tell me about your probation,' their mother asked.

In everything that had happened over the past day or so, Hannah had forgotten that their mum didn't know the full details of what had happened with Charlotte. At least that explained why this was happening now. It was straight out of her mum's parenting handbook. First, deal with the crisis; second, go mental at whoever caused it.

The one thing both sisters knew was that there was little point in arguing.

Charlotte sighed and dipped her head again as Hannah shuffled in her seat: 'Do you need me here for—'

'Sit!'

Hannah straightened herself. Not only was there little point in arguing, there was even less point in trying to escape.

'Don't think I've forgotten that you were in on it,' her mum added, before focusing back on Charlotte.

It was a bit rich, considering they were all 'in on' something far, far worse.

'What do you want to know?' Charlotte asked.

'Why you're on probation, for one.'

Charlotte sighed and sagged a little lower. She continued to look at the floor as she spoke, her hair dangling around her face. 'I told you,' she said. 'I bought some pills off a friend. It was like anything: the more you buy, the cheaper the price. I had a bunch left over, so sold them on to one of my *other* friends. What I didn't know was that her dad is a detective. Some sort of sergeant. She'd left the pills under her mattress and he'd gone snooping because he's a psychopath, or something like that.'

Even Hannah had to admit that Charlotte was talking like a spoiled teenager, not a woman in her mid-twenties. Not that she dared say anything.

'What happened then?' her mother asked.

'What do you think? Her dad went ape and she told him she got the pills off me. They got a search warrant for my flat and pulled everything apart.'

'What did they find?'

Charlotte sighed again and sat back on the sofa, tugging her hair away from her face and wrapping it into a ponytail with the tie from her wrist.

The reply was sharp with annoyance. 'Drugs, Mum. They found drugs.'

'What drugs?'

'Why does it matter?'

'Because the only reason everything happened this weekend is because of you – and the least you can do is tell me what you've done.'

Hannah tried to avoid looking in anything like the direction of either her mum or sister. She focused at a spot on the wall above the television and watched that. It felt safer.

'Some weed and a small bag of pills.'

'Ecstasy?'

Charlotte's only reply was a slight raise of the eyebrows but it was seemingly enough.

'What then?' their mum asked.

'I was arrested and charged with possession with intent to supply. It's not like I could deny it. The solicitor reckoned most charges like this are dismissed. He was surprised it got to court, until I told him about my friend's dad. He hoped they'd go for a conditional discharge because it was obvious I'm not a real dealer – but they gave me community service with probation.'

There was a pause and, when their mother didn't fill it, Charlotte nodded towards Hannah.

'Han was there for support.'

That instantly changed the mood as their mother spun to rain down her fire and fury upon daughter number one.

Before she could, Charlotte quickly added: 'It's not Han's fault. I asked her to come and she did.'

Their mother hesitated, as if not quite sure which of her daughters should be first in line for both barrels.

'How did I not know any of this?' she asked.

Charlotte shrugged. 'Because I didn't tell you. There was hardly anyone in court, so it didn't end up on Facebook, or in the papers. I got on and did my hours. It was mainly picking up litter – and that was it. I have to see my probation officer every fortnight.'

Their mother chewed angrily on this. 'How much longer?'

'Three months or so.'

'What else?'

Charlotte bit her bottom lip and started twiddling a strand of hair around her finger. 'Nothing, really. The solicitor said I'd be banned from the US if I ever wanted to go – but that it shouldn't affect anything else as long as there's no reoffending.'

It was their mother's turn to huff out a breath. 'You've made a mess of that, haven't you?'

Charlotte didn't reply. 'Mess' was an understatement.

Before any of them could say anything more, Hannah's phone started to buzz. She had already checked the screen to see 'Unknown' ringing before realising it wasn't a good time to answer. Under her mother's disapproving eye, she returned the phone to the arm of the sofa and the call rang off. For a few moments, she wondered if the inquisition was over – then her mum picked up where she'd left off.

'If you went through *all that*. If you're *on probation*, what were you doing with *more pills*?'

Charlotte stared towards the other side of the room, her head resting against the back of the sofa. She looked exhausted. 'You wouldn't understand.'

'You're right – I *don't* understand.'

It wasn't a question and Charlotte didn't seem to have an answer anyway. For the first time, Hannah wondered if she should have done more to keep a closer eye on her sister. She had assumed the community service and probation would be a wake-up call but it clearly wasn't. If she had spent more time checking in with Charlotte, making sure she was clean and well, then none of this would have happened. Instead, she'd been more focused on herself, more interested in escaping.

There was an impasse and then their mother drew herself up taller in the seat. 'I've never been more disappointed in you.'

Hannah knew it was a mistake the moment it was said. She

felt Charlotte stirring at her side and there was only going to be one outcome after that. In the exact way their mother had, Charlotte pushed herself up taller in the seat. She turned and faced their mum for the first time and practically spat the reply.

'Maybe if you hadn't walked out on Dad when we were kids, it wouldn't have happened. Jason only ever had eyes for Beth – because she was his. He never cared for Hannah and me. You did that to us – and then you left him, too. You leave everyone, Mum. We are who we are 'cos that's how you made us.'

Hannah didn't dare move. She didn't want to be drawn into any of this and yet there was a nugget of truth in that their mum had left their dad for Jason and he was only interested in Beth as she was biologically his. Hannah and Charlotte had each other and they had their friends. What they didn't have was two parents looking out for them.

Whether all that had an effect on Charlotte's choices as an adult was unclear – and Hannah wasn't brave enough to question any of it.

The bitterness of Charlotte's words had an immediate effect on their mother, who reeled back into the seat, open-mouthed. 'That's not true,' she said.

Hannah felt Charlotte looking to her, wanting support. Their mother was doing the same, each wanting a verdict on who was right.

'I wouldn't say Jason *only* had eyes for Beth,' Hannah said, choosing her words, 'but it was different with her – and *he* was different with us.'

There were tears in the corners of their mother's eyes: 'Are you saying I put him before you?'

Charlotte answered immediately, drily and savagely. A trick learned from their mother: 'Yes, Mum. That's what *we're* saying.'

Hannah wasn't sure about the *we're* part but she remained quiet.

Charlotte continued to stare at their mum with defiance until, in a flash, she was on her feet. 'I've got to get to work,' she said.

It only took seconds. There was the bounding of feet, the slam of a door, and then she was gone.

TWENTY-ONE

ZACK

Zack had never been in a police station before. There was a time in primary school when an officer had come in to warn them about talking to strangers. It was part of a mass assembly and he remembered a general sense of dread, that the world outside the gates was suddenly a terrifying place.

Aside from that, he had never had any contact with the authorities. There were no 999 calls and no particular trouble. He wondered if he'd led a sheltered life because his only knowledge of the police came from the bits and pieces he'd seen through television shows. If everything he'd seen was true, it meant officers were corrupt, drunk, incompetent, or all three.

He waited at the bottom of the steps which led up to a set of double doors and reached into his pocket to grip Katherine's necklace. Nobody knew he had it, which, for now, gave him an advantage over Hannah and any others who were claiming Katherine hadn't arrived at the house. They might think they'd have a story which they'd stick to – but he knew they were lying.

Now he had to convince someone else.

Zack headed up the steps, through the doors, and into a cold reception room. There was a large counter on the far side, with a desk-to-ceiling glass barrier separating that from a grubby waiting area. There were chairs with foam spilling from the sides and a wall decorated with a series of posters showing things like handcuffs and car doors, along with slogans about thefts.

A woman was sitting on one of the chairs, rocking back and forth gently, while muttering to herself. Aside from her, the area was clear.

Zack approached the counter, though there was only an empty office chair on the other side. Through the glass, he could see a computer and a landline phone, two filing cabinets and a security camera that was pointing at him. On the counter, there was what looked like a doorbell next to a taped-down piece of paper that said 'Ring for assistance', so Zack did precisely that.

Nothing happened.

He looked around, wondering if he should have heard something. The woman on the seats was still rocking and hadn't reacted to his presence.

Zack hovered around the counter, wondering if there was something he'd missed until, a short while later, a man emerged from a door behind the counter. He acknowledged Zack with a gentle nod and then slotted onto the office chair before asking if he could help.

There was no particular reason why but Zack was immediately riddled with self-consciousness and nerves. He stammered, 'My girlfriend's missing,' then corrected himself. 'Well, not my girlfriend as such. We're sort of seeing each other but nothing's official and, um...'

The man glanced across to where the woman was still rocking and then focused back on Zack. He had the patient, fixed smile of a man who'd seen and heard all sorts of things like this before.

'What's her name?' he asked.

'Katherine Brown.'

'When did you last see her?'

Zack explained how he'd spent much of Saturday with Katherine before dropping her off for a going-away party. He didn't know the exact address of the house but he knew the street and that it was the house with the steps at the front.

As he spoke, the man behind the counter typed a few things into his computer and continued to ask simple questions, mainly relating to logistics and timings.

Zack said that he'd spoken to the person who was hosting the party. He gave Hannah's name, phone number and address, adding that he knew where Hannah lived because Katherine had pointed it out on the drive to the house. Turned out he and Hannah lived a couple of streets away from one another.

The officer seemed interested when Zack mentioned that she'd told him Katherine had never arrived. His fingers paused over the keyboard and he sat up a little straighter, before turning to look at Zack with narrowing eyes.

'The person who hosted the party said Ms Brown never arrived?'

'Exactly – but I only drove away when she was almost outside. She'd have been at the front door within ten seconds of me leaving.'

That produced a deeper frown from the officer. He turned back to the screen and then re-checked the timeline. He asked about Katherine's family and made a note when he was told that she had none. Zack added that Katherine didn't have any flat-mates, or anything like that. As far as he knew, the people in her life were her colleagues from the coffee shop, a handful of friends, and some sort of charity for which she volunteered on Wednesdays. He didn't know the details for that.

The officer had seemingly finished his questions when he said that he'd get someone to take a proper statement. He started to stand and then seemed to sense there might be more.

He lowered himself back into the chair and Zack felt compelled to speak. 'I went to the party house before coming here,' he said. 'I wasn't sure what to do, whether I had to wait a certain time before reporting someone missing, or whether someone else on the street might have seen her. I found out by accident that the owner lives a few doors down. He let me in to look, just in case there was something of Katherine's there. He'd already cleaned up but I saw something shiny under the edge of the rug...'

Zack reached into his pocket and pulled out the silver pendant. There was a drawer that linked one side of the counter to the other, like one in a bank, and Zack placed the pendant in it, then waited for the officer to pick it up on the other side.

'It's Katherine's,' Zack said. 'She wore it all the time, even to bed.'

He reached into his other pocket and took out his phone, before selecting the photo that showed her balancing all the plates. He pinched the screen to zoom in and then pressed it to the glass for the officer to see.

The officer looked at the pendant in his hand and then up to the photo.

'You found this at the house?' he asked.

'Exactly.'

'The one where her friend said she never arrived?'

'Yes.'

The officer sucked in his cheeks and stared at Zack with a new intensity. 'Wait there,' he said. 'I'm going to get someone – and then we'll see what we can do.'

TWENTY-TWO

HANNAH, TUESDAY

The two police officers sat on the sofa as Hannah's mum fussed around them. She placed two cups of tea on the table, along with a small jug of milk and an eggcup of sugar. There were even saucers, which showed how over the top she was going. Hannah didn't know they even *had* saucers in the house.

While that had been going on, Hannah sat on the chair that she'd dragged away from the dining table. She smiled awkwardly, trying not to appear too fidgety, in case the officers thought it was because of nerves. Then she thought that she might be sitting *too* still, which might seem suspicious the other way.

If they hadn't have introduced themselves as police, Hannah wouldn't have necessarily known. Both were wearing fitted suits and could easily have passed as any other middle manager who worked in the town.

Minutes had passed since her mum had let them in and called Hannah down from her room. While Hannah had been waiting, her mum had been filling the kettle and rattling around the cupboards. Anything to delay what seemed to be inevitable. Perhaps anything to give her, and perhaps Hannah, time to think. They knew this moment was going to come – but Hannah hadn't expected it so quickly.

It had to be because of Zack. He said he was going to the police and she felt certain he had... Not that she blamed him. The more time passed, the more she wished she'd been brave enough to contact them.

The officers waited patiently, occasionally muttering to one another at a level Hannah couldn't make out. They had introduced themselves in the hallway but Hannah had already forgotten their names. The woman was somewhere around Hannah's age, with blonde hair in a tight bun. The man was a little older, with greying tufts around his ears. The sort that could be late-forties and growing old gracefully, or early thirties with a kid or three. Each time Hannah caught either of their eyes, they smiled politely back, though there was steel there. It felt as if they knew something she didn't, perhaps more than one thing. Hannah had to remind herself that this was all to be expected. The normal part of an abnormal situation.

Her mum finally reappeared from the kitchen, this time with a plate stacked with biscuits that had seemingly appeared from nowhere. She placed them next to the cups and saucers on the table and then hovered in the middle of the room.

'Can I get you anything else?' she asked.

The male officer picked up his teacup and shook his head. 'This is great, thank you – though I don't think my wife would approve of the biscuits.'

Hannah's mum plopped into her chair, all smiles and church fete friendliness. Hannah wondered if it was *too* friendly. As if the tea, biscuits and other stuff was overcompensating.

The male officer introduced himself again and Hannah made a point of remembering the name this time. He was Sergeant Peterson and the blonde woman was Constable

Waverly. Peterson sipped his tea and then returned the cup to the saucer.

'As I said at the door, we're following up on a missing woman, Katherine Brown. I understand you're friends...?'

He'd been talking to Hannah's mother but, at the last second, turned his attention to Hannah. She'd been relaxing as much as possible in the situation, figuring the question might be asked to her mum but, from nowhere, she was blinking into the spotlight.

'We've, um...' Hannah didn't know where to look. She glanced to her mum, hoping the words would come before focusing back on Peterson. 'Katherine and me have been friends since school,' she said. '*Primary* school, so twenty years or so. More, I guess.'

'Are you good friends?'

Hannah needed a moment. She had so many regrets about such a short question. 'I suppose we were back then.'

'What about now?'

'We see each other now and then. We had coffee at the shop where she works a bit before Christmas.'

The officer stopped and sipped his tea with an annoying slurp. 'How often do you see each other?'

Hannah found herself trying to count, wanting to keep the lies and misinformation to as much a minimum as she could. Her palms felt slick and she pressed them into her trousers. 'Maybe every other month? We don't usually plan but sometimes we'll forward each other news articles we've seen, or something funny. Then one of us will ask if the other fancies a catch-up. That sort of thing.'

Peterson nodded along as Waverly wrote something in her notepad. Hannah felt her mum watching and wished she wasn't.

'Tell me about Saturday,' Peterson said.

A pause. Such a big question. 'What do you want to know?'

'I gather there was some sort of party on the other side of town...?'

There was every reason for him to know this but it still felt disarmingly real that he did.

'It wasn't really a party,' Hannah said. 'Mum was there. It was more of a get-together.'

'What happened at this *get-together*?'

Peterson emphasised the final two words, as if it was some sort of insult. He seemed like the point-scoring type. Someone who didn't let a lot go.

'Not much,' Hannah said. 'I'm going travelling on Friday, so it was a goodbye meet-up before I go. We played some board games and had a few drinks. We chatted and caught up with each other.'

Peterson took in all of this without the merest hint of movement in his expression. Perhaps he already knew?

'Who was there?' he asked.

Hannah looked to her mother. 'Mum, me, my sisters, my aunt, my friend, Sophie – and her mum.'

Peterson paused, waiting for Waverly to write down the information. He asked for the names of Hannah's sisters and then for Dawn and Janet's. Hannah reeled them off, knowing what was coming. The first time she felt a genuine, deep-down sense of nervousness beyond what she assumed was something normal was when she said Charlotte's name.

Peterson stopped her, checking 'Charlotte Ford' as the full name and waiting for Hannah to confirm. It was unquestionably deliberate and Hannah felt in the middle of a game of second-guessing. Did they already know about Charlotte? And, if so, did they know about her conviction and probation? Should she say something? And, if she didn't, would that seem suspicious?

She reached for the mug of tea her mum had brought for her – no saucers on this side of the table – but she misjudged the distance and nudged the edge, accidentally sending the liquid over the rim and onto the carpet. Her mum sprang up and darted into the kitchen, returning a moment later with a cloth that she used to dab away at the floor. Hannah was close enough that she could have touched her mum's back but, when her mother spoke, it felt distant, as if talking through water. She laughed something about 'always mopping up after your kids' that got a sympathetic smile from the officers, though little more in the way of reaction. Hannah was now trying to stop her palms from sweating by pressing them onto the fabric of the armchair. When she noticed Waverly watching her, she stopped and smiled, as if this was something she did as a matter of course.

By the time the clean-up was done, Peterson had moved on from Charlotte. 'I heard another of your friends, Katherine Brown, was invited...?'

'She was.'

'What time did she arrive?'

Hannah had almost started to reply to a question she hadn't been asked when she realised what actually had been.

'She *didn't* arrive,' Hannah replied.

A millisecond of a pause. *He knew.* 'Are you sure?'

As Hannah went to answer, her mum got in first: 'I think we'd have noticed if she had.'

Hannah bit her tongue gently, willing her mother to stop talking. Either that, or for her to take all the questions. She pushed away the thought. She was almost thirty, for God's sake, she didn't need a parent answering questions for her. Let alone now.

Peterson didn't seem to react to somebody else answering the question. His features were fixed into something close to a smile but not quite. The sort of look somebody had when they were asked a question in school, knew the answer, but didn't want to appear too eager. *He knew. He really knew.*

Unless Hannah was seeing what she wanted.

'Was there any sign of her at all?'

The question was directed at Hannah.

'Like what?'

'Did she text? Call?'

'Nothing.'

'Didn't that surprise you? If I invited someone over to say goodbye, I'd notice if they didn't show up. There were only seven of you, after all.'

Hannah tried not to gulp. 'We were friends but, like I said, we only saw each other now and again. I figured she had something else on.'

'Did you contact her to ask where she was?'

Even though she'd been wishing she could answer her own questions, Hannah risked a glance towards her mother, who was looking at the officers and not her. For whatever reason, she hadn't expected this question. 'No.'

'Why not?'

'I suppose... we were busy. Time went really quickly. I was talking to my aunt, then Sophie, we were playing a game... By the time I thought to check the time, hours had passed. I figured that, if she was going to turn up, she already would have.'

Peterson waited and the only sound was the scratching of Waverly's pen on the pad. She'd barely said a word since they turned up. Peterson reached for his tea and had another sip, drawing out the moment for longer.

Waiting.

Hannah didn't know where to look, or what to do. Her damn palms continued to sweat and, because she'd been caught drying them on the chair, she was back to pushing them into her thighs. She could feel the dampness seeping through her trousers.

'You might not be aware of this,' Peterson said, 'but Ms Brown was dropped off close to the house by one of her friends.

That friend watched her walk along the street and only lost sight when she was more or less directly outside...'

Hannah forced a confidence she didn't feel. 'A guy came round on Sunday and said something like that. It was the first I'd heard of it.'

She was surprised at how steady her voice was.

'Weren't you concerned?' the officer asked.

'On Saturday? I said that I lost track of time and—'

'On Sunday, when you were told that your friend was dropped almost outside the house where you were partying – but she didn't arrive.'

'We weren't partying!' He had her now – and Hannah knew it. There was defensiveness in her tone. She had to stop herself to have a second go. She was quieter next time around: 'Of course I was worried – but what was I supposed to do? I'd never met him before and didn't know who he was. He said Katherine was missing and I didn't know what to tell him. He said he was going to report her missing, so I assumed that would be that.' She paused. 'Actually, I assumed she'd be back before you were involved. I thought it would all be a misunderstanding. She was trying to let him down gently, that sort of thing.'

Peterson nodded, letting his colleague finish writing. He picked up his teacup again and had another gulp. Waverly's remained untouched, as did the biscuits. Hannah thought about taking one, if only to give her time to think while she was eating.

'Do you know about a boyfriend?' he asked.

'There was the guy on Sunday – Zack-something. I've only met him once.'

'Did Katherine ever mention him?'

Hannah was so close to saying that she'd mentioned a date with a work colleague – except that she'd done that on *Saturday* night, at a time when Hannah was claiming she'd never shown up.

'No,' she replied.

'How did you come to invite her? Was it via text, or...?'

'I was in Morrisons on Wednesday. We saw each other as we were checking out and I told her then that I was going away. I mentioned the party and asked if she wanted to come...'

Hannah tailed off, wincing that she'd used the word 'party', having claimed that it wasn't. She was rattled now.

Peterson didn't follow up on this. Instead, he pressed back onto the sofa, still holding his teacup.

Waverly scratched something new onto the pad and then looked up herself. She read out the address of the house where they'd stayed without bothering to check the page. It wasn't a question, more a statement, but then she ended with: 'That's where you were, wasn't it?'

'Yes,' Hannah replied.

'Did you notice a coffee shop at the end of the street?'

Hannah could feel her heart beating, sensing something that she wouldn't like.

'I think so. I didn't pay a lot of attention.'

Another pause. More waiting. More delay. Everyone was looking to her and her mum was annoyingly silent, not that Hannah knew what she wanted her to say.

'There's a security camera at the front of the coffee shop,' Waverly said. 'It points towards the street where you were staying.'

Hannah bit her lip as she tried to keep eye contact with the officer, whose gaze was steady and firm. She knew what would be next. The camera had captured Katherine walking up the stairs and being let into the house. With that, everything was over. The police hadn't come for a concerned chat about a missing woman; they were there so that Hannah could lie to them. They'd set a trap and she'd fallen into it – and now there'd be no easy way of explaining why she'd lied. She could hardly say she'd not seen Katherine if there was footage of her letting her into the house.

Why hadn't any of them thought of this? Why hadn't any of them paid attention?

Except...

If they knew all that, why was this happening in her mum's house? Why wasn't she at the police station, in front of a camera and a two-way mirror?

All those thoughts flowed through Hannah as a lump began to build in her throat. She felt sick and pictured dashing into the kitchen to hunch over the sink.

Hannah's phone started to buzz. It was on the coffee table, close to where she'd spilled her drink and the word 'Unknown' was on the screen as it continued to vibrate. Nobody spoke as she picked it up and pressed the red reject button, before returning it to the table.

'Was that important?' Peterson asked. He was sitting forward on the sofa again, suddenly back in charge.

'No,' Hannah replied.

'You can take it if you want.'

'I said it's fine.'

Peterson leaned back into his seat and she wondered if they had bugged her phone – or, more importantly, if that was even possible. Did the police do that? Her mum had said they should only communicate in person in case anyone checked their messages but why would he encourage her to take a call unless they were listening in somewhere?

Hannah told herself she was being paranoid.

'What was on the camera?'

Everyone turned to look at Hannah's mum and, for once, Hannah was grateful she'd spoken.

'You said it was facing the street,' she added, 'so you must have looked at whatever it filmed...?'

It was framed as an innocent question but Hannah knew her mum well enough to understand there was more under the surface. Sure, these officers might be able to forensically question a person – but Hannah's mum had been doing that for at least a quarter-century. She'd only ask this sort of question if she had some idea of the answer. It was like when she'd ask Hannah or Charlotte who had dropped something, or who'd left the front door unlocked when they were kids. She'd only ask when she knew who'd done it.

The two officers paused for a moment and something passed between them that Hannah felt, rather than saw.

Peterson was the one who finally spoke. 'Are you absolutely certain that neither of you saw Ms Brown on Saturday evening?'

Hannah was already in too deep to back out now. 'She wasn't there.'

Another beat passed and then the officers stood in unison and with an abruptness that made Hannah flinch.

'I think we're done for now,' Waverly said, as she slipped her pad into a pocket.

Hannah stood and so did her mum. Out of nothing, it suddenly felt very crowded in the living room.

'What happens now?' Hannah asked.

Peterson was stony-faced as he replied. 'Let's hope we find her...'

TWENTY-THREE

ZACK

By the time Zack got to The Grind, the morning and lunchtime rushes were over and his manager was in the process of stacking chairs in the back corner. It was the half-hour at the end of the day where clued-up regulars would come in to grab reduced pastries and sandwiches. If it was a slow day, or, as Zack preferred, a *lucky* day, there would be enough left for him to take home a free sandwich or muffin. He and Katherine would sometimes hide the tuna sandwiches behind the egg ones hoping they'd still be there at the close of business.

Thinking of that made him think of Katherine, which was when he noticed Linda staring across the floor towards him. She had a cloth in one hand and a bucket of water at her feet.

'You're late by about eight hours,' she said. 'And that's for today's shift. You're thirty-odd hours late for yesterday's.'

Zack crept across the floor, sticking to the parts that hadn't been washed and then perching on the edge of one of the seats yet to be overturned.

'My niece had to come in to help and I've not heard anything from Katherine at all. It's completely—'

She interrupted herself and then put the cloth down, before

heading across to where Zack was now sitting.

'What's wrong?' she asked.

Linda could flit effortlessly between demanding everyone work as hard as her and then taking a few minutes off to dance around the room at the back because there was a song on the radio she liked. The only reason Zack had remained working at the shop for more than a year was because she was so good to work for. Well, that and Katherine...

'Katherine's missing,' he said. 'I've been trying to find her. I had to go to the police to report her missing.'

Linda stood rigid for a moment and then screeched a chair out from underneath a table, before twisting it to sit on. She stretched across and touched his knee. 'I didn't know,' she said. 'I've been here all day, *both* days, cursing the pair of you, thinking all sorts and...'

'No one's seen her since Saturday,' Zack replied. 'She was supposed to be going to a friend's party. I dropped her off and nobody's seen her since.'

Linda squeezed his knee a tiny amount and then pressed back into her seat.

'How long have you been seeing each other?'

Zack looked up and she gave him a sad, knowing smile. 'How did you know?'

That got a laugh. A *kind* laugh. 'Oh, Zachary. How could I *not* know? It's like *Love, Actually* in here with you two giving each other gooey looks across the counter all day. You both booked off the end of last week. I assumed you were going on holiday together.'

Zack felt his chest tighten, his throat shrink. Linda sounded so happy for them, so excited. 'We're not officially seeing each other,' he said. 'But we spent last week in each other's flats. Just watched TV and...'

He didn't finish the sentence because he couldn't really remember what they'd done with all those hours. The television had been on but it felt as if they'd spent all that time talking to each other. Saying the things that couldn't quite be said while passing across a latte order.

Linda shuffled slightly and he realised she was still holding the cloth. She placed it on one of the already clean tables and then scratched her head. 'What did the police say?'

'Not much – although they seemed to take it seriously. I suppose I'll hear something if they find anything out.' He paused and then: 'Do you know about her family?'

'I know, love. Poor girl. That's why I've not said anything about you two getting all lovey-dovey. I hoped you were having a whale of a time last week. That girl deserves a bit of happiness.'

Zack dipped his head and there was suddenly wetness around the corners of his eyes. He hadn't expected this.

Linda crossed to the counter and then returned with a wodge of napkins that she passed to him wordlessly. She left him to himself as she wiped down a couple more tables and stacked more chairs, before returning to where Zack was sitting.

'Take as long as you need. Don't rush back for this place. My niece loves the extra money.'

He nodded, not quite able to express how grateful he was. 'I was the last to see her,' he said.

Zack felt his manager taking a long breath, understanding what it could mean. 'Look, love, if you need anyone to vouch for you, or anything like that, just give 'em my number. Also, if you need anything, you know where I am. I'm sure it'll all work out. It won't be any time at all and you'll both be back in here, hiding the sandwiches you want to take home.'

If it was any other time, then Zack would have laughed but, instead, he pressed a napkin to his nose and blew. His ears popped and his eyes swam. He couldn't look up from the floor.

'Sorry,' he said.

'Don't be.' Linda stood once more and then picked up the

chair she'd been sitting on, before adding it to the stack. 'You keep me up to date, OK? Call if you need anything – and if you're too busy to eat, or drink, or anything else, make sure you pop by before closing and there'll always be something for you.'

She was behind him now and squeezed his shoulder softly, before removing it.

'C'mon,' she said. 'I've just cleaned that toilet – but you go sort yourself out. Can't go out looking for her like that, can you?'

Mario's Pizza turned out to be a place that Zack had walked and driven past a couple of times a week for at least three years. In all that time, he had barely noticed it and certainly hadn't clocked the name.

The shop was tucked away on a small rank, next to a barber's, something that was boarded up, a bookies, and a Londis on the end. It was on one of the routes that he would take to work if he wasn't in a rush.

As he approached, the smell of cheese left his stomach grumbling. He hadn't eaten all day, although he now had a bag of sandwiches and three muffins in the car.

The inside of the pizza place had a single plastic table with two lawn chairs. A menu was pinned to the window, not that Zack could read it because the glass was steamed with condensation. Another menu was in much bigger letters, high above the counter, and Zack found himself staring up at it, wondering what he should do next.

'Can I help you, mate?'

A young lad was standing at the till and Zack doubted he was out of his teens. He had the air of someone who would much rather be doing anything else, while simultaneously valuing the minimum wage he'd be taking home.

'Do you know who was delivering pizzas on Saturday?' Zack asked.

The guy behind the counter stared at him, clearly expecting a query that was more related to pepperoni.

'We can't do refunds on anything that old,' he replied. 'If there was a problem, you have to call at the time.'

He pointed towards a sign on the wall that probably said precisely that, though Zack paid it no attention.

'I'm not after a refund,' Zack said. 'I was hoping to talk to whoever delivered your pizzas on Saturday.'

The lad behind the counter glanced over his shoulder, likely weighing up if he was dealing with some sort of nutter.

'Look, mate. If you want a pizza, we can do you a pizza. If you fancy the driver, I don't think he's into that. Actually, I know he's not. He's got a girlfriend and they're engaged and—'

'I'll have a small margherita,' Zack said. 'Eat in, if that's OK.'

The lad eyed him with suspicion before tapping something into the till and then naming a price. Zack paid on his debit card and then returned to the table while he waited.

Nothing else was spoken until the pizza was brought out about fifteen minutes later. Zack mumbled a 'thanks' and then sat nibbling away, while pretending to scroll through his phone.

It was probably his mood because it was hard to make a bad pizza... except that it *was* a bad pizza. The crust was too thick and the edges too soft. He ended up leaving more or less all the crust, while eating the rest from the middle out. All the while, he felt the silent, questioning stare of the lad upon him.

A couple of customers came and went and it was soon at the point where Zack couldn't waste any more time. He cleaned his fingers on a napkin and then emptied what was left into the bin, before muttering a 'thanks' and heading back out into the cold.

He was almost at his car when he noticed the small Vauxhall with a peeling sticker of a pizza on the side. It had just pulled into a space and a man was clambering from the driver's seat as steam piled out of the car. He slammed the door and then, despite the cold, he leaned on the top of the car and started to scroll through his phone. He typed out a message with frantic thumbs and then sighed to himself.

Zack edged across, waiting awkwardly near to the car, as if he was waiting to talk to a girl at a bar. The driver soon noticed him and glanced up from his phone.

He sounded sceptical. 'You all right, mate?'

'I was wondering if you delivered pizzas on Saturday?'

The man's eyebrows dipped down from underneath his beanie hat. 'Yeah...'

Zack gave the street name of where Hannah's party had been and then: 'I was wondering if you remember delivering anything in that area? I don't know the exact house number.'

The driver glanced across towards the shop, unsure what was going on. 'Sorry, mate, are you—?'

Zack whipped out his phone and scrolled to the photo of Katherine, which he showed to the driver. 'I'm wondering if you saw her at that house.'

He'd moved so quickly that the driver looked at the photo and replied without questioning. 'I don't think so.' He thought for another moment and then looked towards the photo again. 'I did know the girl who answered the door, though. I went to school with her.'

'What's her name?'

'Beth Ford.' There was a pause as the driver seemingly realised he'd been talking without thinking. 'Do you know her?'

Zack shook his head. 'I think it must be Beth's sister who knows my girlfriend.' He indicated the photo again. 'I'm trying to figure out where she is. She went to that house on Saturday and I've not seen her since.'

'Oh.'

The driver was wearing half-finger gloves and he reached for Zack's phone. He pinched the screen to look properly, no brief glance or hurry to get away. It took a few moments but then he started nodding.

'She might've been there,' the driver said. 'There were two of them who answered the door: Beth and an older one. Might've been her sister. I could see past them, though, and there were definitely other women there.' He passed back the phone. 'One of them might have been her.'

'How certain would you be?'

A shrug: 'Not very.'

It wasn't what Zack wanted to hear – but it could have been worse. 'I've reported her missing to the police,' he replied. 'Do you mind if I pass on your details? They're going to be looking for anyone who might've seen her...'

The driver held up both hands, showing the grubby palms of his woollen gloves. 'I dunno about that. I didn't really see much. Just Beth and the other girl.'

'They'd only be asking you the same as me.'

'Sorry, mate – I'd rather not get involved.'

He opened the back door of the car and grabbed a padded pizza bag from the seat before closing the door again and turning to head towards the shop.

'It could've been someone you know,' Zack said. 'Your mum, or your sister, or your girlfriend. If they'd been missing for almost three days, you'd want someone to help, wouldn't you?'

The driver stopped and turned back to face Zack. 'Look...' he sighed. 'It's just I get money through tips and...' He tailed off and then added: 'I can't really have the police coming round asking about this and that.'

'I don't think they care about any of that. They'd only be asking what you saw at the house. If it wasn't much, then fair enough. I just want to find my girlfriend.'

The driver let out a long, resigned breath that spiralled up into the air.

'Send me that photo,' he said. 'I'll have another look under a proper light.' There was a beat and then he added: 'And, yeah, give my number to the police. I hope you find her.'

TWENTY-FOUR

HANNAH

Hannah waited at the back door of her mum's house, squinting into the darkness. The central heating blazed behind her while, in front, the night offered nothing but icy needles. 'C'mon, c'mon...' she muttered to herself, while simultaneously wondering how she kept ending up doing the things she was told without question. This was yet one more task her mum had asked her do and here she was doing it.

She slipped back into the present as she heard the sound of someone rattling the latch to the back gate. A woman's voice hissed, 'I can't find it' and then another's replied, 'It's right there,' before white light sprang from what was presumably a phone. Moments later, Sophie and her mother hurried along the path towards the house. Janet was blowing into her hands while Sophie rolled her eyes towards Hannah. Even at this age, in these circumstances, they could still find their mums incalculably annoying.

That was emphasised a moment later as Janet half tripped over a large black bin bag that was close to the back door. She scowled at it and then turned to Hannah, muttering that 'someone should move that', before pressing past her into the house. Sophie tutted as she followed and rolled her eyes a second time.

Can't take her anywhere, she didn't say.

As they headed into the kitchen, a flapping mass of scarves, hats and jackets, Hannah locked the door behind them – and then the three of them moved into the living room.

It had been cramped before with the officers, plus Hannah and her mum – but it was far worse now. As well as Hannah, Sophie and Janet, Hannah's mum, Dawn, and Beth were in the room.

Janet squeezed onto the sofa alongside Dawn and Beth. Hannah's mum was in her regular armchair, which left Sophie with the footrest, and Hannah a space on the floor. It felt like getting into a lift that was already full. Limbs stretched across limbs and everyone was sitting with their arms close to their body. With the possible exception of Hannah's mum, nobody looked remotely comfortable.

Then Hannah remembered the other person missing. The one who would never be able to attend anything like this again. She hugged her knees to her chest, looking around the room and taking in the other women. Wondering if they had the same twisting stomach that she'd had since Sunday morning.

Janet had been wriggling, with little apparent realisation of how close her elbows were to Beth. When she finally stopped, she scanned the room and then turned to Hannah's mother. 'Where's Charlotte?'

'We already talked to her, so there's no need for her to be here.'

Hannah knew this was half true. After the argument in this very living room, Charlotte hadn't answered her phone and wasn't replying to text messages – not that she'd have been sent one asking her to come here. As far as Hannah knew none of them had shared anything, except for in person.

'Why are we here?' Janet asked sharply. 'I've not talked to anyone about the weekend.' She paused and then added: 'I was kinda hoping to forget it all...'

It felt heartless but perhaps it was blunt honesty.

Hannah's mum didn't really reply but she turned a little to face as much of the room as she could. With her sitting by herself in the armchair, it was like she was some sort of group godmother.

'Hannah and I were interviewed by the police this morning,' she said. 'It wasn't a formal thing at the police station, it was here. I figured telling you all in person was better than you finding out another way.'

Hannah was watching Janet, whose mouth had slowly dropped open. 'The police...?'

'What we didn't know on Sunday was that Katherine had a boyfriend who dropped her off somewhere on the street. He's reported her missing, so the police came around to ask if we'd seen her.'

'What did you tell them?' Janet asked.

'The exact thing we all agreed on Sunday. That Katherine never turned up and none of us saw her. From what we can gather, her boyfriend didn't actually see her going into the house. There's also a camera outside the coffee shop at the end of the street, which they mentioned. They said it pointed down the street but, again, no mention that it actually filmed her coming into the house.'

This was new information to everyone except Hannah and the change in mood was instant. They all started to turn to one another, wondering what it meant.

As before, it was Janet who asked the question: 'Did they actually *say* what was on the camera?'

Hannah's mum was scolding in her reply: 'Of course not.' She looked towards Hannah. 'They were careful in what they did say but, if the camera showed Katherine going into the house, they'd have already been onto us. *All* of us.'

It was hard for Hannah to describe the sense around the room. Nobody except Janet had been speaking but something fizzed among them. Hannah had once been in a room where a manager announced redundancies and it had felt the same: where everyone was fearing the worst while simultaneously hoping they themselves would be fine.

Her mum waited for the silent din to subside and then continued: 'Chances are, the police are going to talk to everyone by the end of the week. They'll mention that camera and probably the boyfriend. They'll make it sound like they know what happened – but that can't be true. We all need to stick to the story. All it takes is for one person to crack and it's over.'

Hannah shivered. Her mum sounded like a mob boss. It might all be an attempt to keep Charlotte out of trouble but it was so clinical, so calculated, that none of it felt like something of which Hannah could believe her mother capable.

Was this something all mothers somehow knew instinctively? Was it natural, or something she'd learned?

Aunt Dawn was the first to reply. The memory of her rattling around supermarket bags full of booze felt distant – and there was no joy in her now.

'I don't think I can handle the police,' she said. 'I've never been a good liar. You remember what it was like when we were kids. Dad would ask who did something and I'd tell him right away.' A pause and then: 'I'm not like you.'

The 'you' hung and hovered between the women. An accusation thrown into the open, as if it had been thought but unsaid for years. Not that Hannah's mum seemed to notice.

'You've got it easiest,' Hannah's mum replied to her sister. 'You don't know Katherine and you've never met her. You think she's a friend of your niece. That's all you need to say, over and over.'

Dawn pursed her lips as if she was about to say something back to her sister but nothing came out. Nobody spoke for a moment and then Janet started again.

'I *knew* we should've told the truth. It was an accident and look how far it's all blown up now. It's not like *I* gave her the drugs. And none of us made her swing off that chandelier.'

She stared at Hannah's mum, challenging and daring. Despite everything that had happened, first at the house and with the body, then with the police, Hannah suddenly now felt the danger. She tried to catch Beth's eye, hoping for some sort of sisterly camaraderie – but Beth was watching Janet sideways.

It was Sophie who replied. 'It's too late for that, Mum. I'm the one that said I wanted her dead. I didn't but it's out there. People made screengrabs. I told you that. We made the choice on Sunday. If one of us changes our mind, then we're all in trouble for covering it up. If you won't think of me, then think of Trent.'

Janet pushed herself up higher, full of indignation: 'Don't bring my grandson into this.'

'What else can I do, Mum? If this comes out, it's not only Charlotte in trouble. I'm the one who apparently married Katherine's boyfriend. I wrote that I wished she was dead. Then we all covered up what happened. She was covered in bruises from the fall. Nobody will believe I'm innocent if those screengrabs get out.'

Sophie and her mother stared across the room towards one another and it felt as if they'd been talking away from the group. More things felt unsaid.

'Not me,' Janet said coldly. 'I didn't do *anything*.'

'You kept it quiet,' Sophie replied.

'I could tell the truth now. They'd believe me because it's not like I'd want to get my daughter in trouble.'

There was silence again, with menace in the air. As if everything might be falling apart. It was Janet at the house and now her again who felt intent on destroying everything.

Or, perhaps, she was the only one with a conscience.

Hannah's mum shuffled in her seat and sat up straighter. She was glaring fire at her friend. 'What if *I* went first…?' she said. 'What if *I* told the police that I saw Sophie sharing pills with Katherine? *She's* the one who stole her boyfriend and married him. Had a child with him. Said she wanted her dead. *She* had the biggest motive.'

Silence again. Everyone seemed stunned this time, Hannah included.

Janet started to fumble a reply but there was nothing approaching a full sentence.

Hannah's mum wasn't done: 'If you're talking about going first, then any one of us has a lot to lose. I'm going to protect *my* girls – and, if I were you, I wouldn't get in the way.'

That appeared to get the result Hannah's mum was after because Janet shut her mouth and stared at the floor. Alison made a point of glancing towards Sophie and making eye contact for a moment, as if to say that she didn't mean it. That didn't stop it feeling as if things had changed. That whatever pact they had was far more brittle than Hannah believed.

Hannah took a breath, then pinched her left thumbnail and squeezed it into her finger. Took another breath.

What had they done?

Sophie spoke next, her voice croaky and hesitant. 'Do you think we're bad people…? I just… Good people don't do this, do they?'

Hannah had to turn and face the back of the room, where her mum's heavy blackout curtains hung low to the floor across the window. It was one thing for her to *think* it of herself, another for someone to actually say it out loud.

'None of us killed her,' Hannah said quietly, talking to the back of the room. She hated the words, especially from her own mouth, but it was the only way she could get through the days. 'It was one of those things. If she'd got a taxi home, it could've crashed. She might've been in her flat and the roof collapsed.' She took a breath, hating herself. 'Just one of those things...'

The final five words slipped out without thought. As if someone else was saying them. All the memories Hannah had with Katherine growing up and her death was now 'just one of those things'.

It was as she said it that she knew her trip wasn't going to happen. She had been building up to it for months and it had been more or less the only thing she'd thought about. The only reason the party had happened was because of the trip. But there was no way she could fly away and pretend everything was normal. She'd almost forgotten the trip altogether. Her thoughts were only of Katherine and what they'd done.

Nobody spoke for a while but their consciences screamed. Or Hannah's did.

The silence was eventually broken by Hannah's mum. 'This can't affect your college work,' she said, talking to Beth. 'You've got to get your results and go off to uni, like we planned. You're the first in the family. None of this is anything to do with you.'

Beth didn't reply, though Hannah doubted her youngest sister enjoyed having this sort of attention on her in front of others, if at all.

The distraction was welcome as Hannah's phone started to buzz. The screen read 'Unknown' but she wasn't going to miss it this time. Without waiting for anyone's opinion, she pushed herself up and pressed to answer. She told the caller to hang on and then hurried through the house, up the stairs and into her room.

When she put the phone to her ear, there was a man's voice she didn't recognise saying 'Hello? Hello?'

'I'm here,' Hannah said. 'Who's that?'

'Is that Hannah Ford?' the caller asked.

'That depends. Who's this?'

The man coughed as if he hadn't heard either of her replies. 'I think we need to meet,' he said.

TWENTY-FIVE

ZACK

Zack had been driving home from the pizza place when he'd taken the short detour that led him past the house in which Hannah lived. It was barely believable that it was so close to the flat in which he and Katherine had spent the entire day before she had gone missing. They'd have probably driven the same route to the house where she went missing as Hannah and her family.

He parked on the other side of the road from Hannah's house, a little along the street. There were the inevitable curtain twitches that came in this sort of area, though Zack ignored them and continued watching Hannah's place. The curtains in that house definitely weren't twitching. They were pulled at the front, though slim threads of light crept around the edges, showing that someone was in.

Zack didn't know who else lived there, other than Hannah's mum because she had answered the door when he'd knocked. There could be a dad in there, too, plus he knew she had sisters. He assumed Hannah had moved back in with her parents, which wasn't as unheard of as it might have once been. One of his old friends from school had recently gone back into his old bedroom in order to save for a deposit for a house.

Perhaps that's what Hannah was doing? He didn't know much about her, other than she was friends with Katherine. There was something Katherine had said about Hannah going away, which was the entire point of the party. Was it travelling, or a job overseas? Something like that. He couldn't remember.

All that mattered was he knew Hannah was lying.

He'd found Katherine's necklace at the house where Hannah claimed she'd never been. The police were on to her but Zack doubted the necklace would be enough by itself. For one, nobody could vouch for the fact he found it at the house. The owner hadn't seen him snatch it and, even though he knew he was telling the truth, someone else could claim he already had the necklace. Worse still, they could say *he'd* taken it from Katherine. He was the last person to definitely be seen with her, after all.

It didn't look great for him, either.

As Zack continued to watch, the front door was flung open and Hannah strode out of the house with a black bin bag in her hand. She walked underneath an orangey street light which cast its gloomy haze down upon her, then bounded purposefully across the street towards a car. She unlocked it, then tossed the bag into the back. Moments later, she was in the front seat and the lights flared, before she started driving away from the house.

It had all happened so quickly that Zack was left fumbling for his car keys. He tried to pull away so fast that he almost stalled the car, before he caught it on the clutch. There was mist around the edges of his windows and he set the blowers on full before pulling out and setting off in the same direction Hannah had gone.

He caught her around the corner as she waited at a T-junction for a short line of cars. By the time she pulled out, he was directly behind her. All those movies with car chases flitted through his mind, with vague memories of how he should put a couple of cars between him and her. Even if that were true, it wasn't possible in a place where there were no other cars behind which to hide. If she happened to recognise his car, which he doubted, then so what?

Hannah drove past the pizza place where Zack had not long left, and then took the turn onto the main road that linked one side of the town to the other. It was when she was most of the way across town that he realised where she was headed. Or where he *thought* she was headed.

The house.

It had to be the place where she held the party.

Zack was so lost in thoughts of the house that he was driving on autopilot. As Hannah slowed for a roundabout, Zack kept going at the same speed. The rear red lights flared bright through his windscreen and he was almost into the back bumper of her car when he caught himself and stamped on the brake.

She must have noticed the bright white headlights looming down on her but Hannah didn't make any attempt to race away as they pulled off the roundabout. She maintained a pace as Zack eased off and allowed a car to edge in between them.

They were within a couple of minutes of the house when Hannah abruptly pulled over to the side of the road without indicating. Her driving had been predictable until that moment and, if it hadn't been for the car between them, Zack would have passed without having a chance to stop. The gap between them gave him time to pull into one of the spaces outside a dentist's that was closed for the day. He had to crane to the side, straining to look around a parked white van, as he watched Hannah get out of the car. She was parked crookedly, the front further in than the back, and the engine was still idling as the lights burned through the night.

Hannah rounded the car, opened the back, and grabbed the

bin bag. She looked both ways along the road and then crossed, before tossing the bag into a skip that was sitting outside a house with scaffolding attached to the front.

Given the way she'd parked, it felt like an instinctive move – and yet there was something that felt clinical and deliberate.

Hannah checked both ways across the road a second time and then re-crossed to her car. A moment later and she was reversing onto the road, ready to head off again.

Zack only had a moment to make a decision. They were a short distance from the house, where he felt sure she was heading. He could follow her there if he set off now... except...

He watched as Hannah's car disappeared into the distance, before getting out of his car. There was a strange sense of déjà vu as he found himself checking both directions before crossing the road himself.

The house with the scaffolding was missing a roof, as well as any window frames on the upstairs floor. There was a portaloo at the side, plus a small domed cement mixer that was chained and padlocked to the fence. A large sign was attached to the fence, telling trespassers to keep out and saying the site was being watched by a security firm. Zack turned in a circle, taking in the rest of a very normal street. He couldn't see anything or anyone who was specifically monitoring the site.

The skip was mainly full of rubble and dust, with Hannah's black bin bag sitting next to half a dozen others that were caked with sand and muck. Zack moved quickly, snatching the cleanest of the bags from the skip and then spinning to head back the way he'd come. He half expected someone to come after him, to accuse him of stealing from the site, but the street was empty – and it was a bag full of rubbish anyway.

Unless it wasn't.

Unless Hannah was trying to get rid of something incriminating in a place where nobody would think to look.

Zack dropped the bag into the back of his car and then got

into the driver's seat. He was desperate to check the contents but the side of a street didn't feel quite right. Not only that, despite everything, the chances of accidentally tipping bin slime over himself and his car felt uncomfortably high.

He turned the car around and drove back to his flat, all the while feeling the blood pumping. There could be proof of whatever happened to Katherine sitting directly behind him.

Zack could barely contain himself as he parked and then raced up the stairs to his flat. Inside, he cleared space on the kitchen floor, where it would be easiest to clean, and then untied the top of the bag and started to pull it apart.

The smell was instant and unmistakable: rotting, gloopy, disgusting bin juice.

Zack grabbed the rubber gloves from underneath the sink and started to sift through potato peelings, an empty bag of sausages, a squashed tissue box, half a candle, a shattered plant pot... and more of the same.

It was rubbish. All of it. Normal, everyday trash.

There was nothing of Katherine's and not even anything that might have been. At first he thought that Hannah might have known he was waiting on their street and that she'd used this to throw him off the trail of whatever she was doing. Except, even if that were true, there was no guarantee he'd have stopped to grab the bag. And how would she have known specifically that he was parked up the street from the house?

The more realistic explanation, the simpler one, was that she did what many other people in the town did when their bins were full: they chucked a black bag in a skip. People were always complaining about alternate-week bin pick-ups and, though he didn't buy the local paper, he must've seen a front-page headline about it at least five times. They had even had to get a padlock for the bin at The Grind. People really did lose the plot when it came to bins.

Which meant that Zack's kitchen floor was now full of

somebody else's grim rubbish. He was losing it, *really* losing it... Except Katherine's necklace had been at the house.

He was about to start picking the rubbish back up when his phone began to buzz. The caller was 'Unknown' – but he had already been warned at the police station that their calls could show up as this.

Zack pinged off the rubber gloves and pressed to answer. There was a man on the other end, who asked if it was Zack, and then introduced himself as a sergeant.

'I know it's late,' he said, 'but I wondered if you could come to the station.'

Zack was sitting on the floor and he slipped backwards, away from the mess he'd created. 'Have you found her?'

There was a momentary silence, perhaps a glitch in the line, but it was enough to bring something to the back of Zack's throat.

'It's probably best if you come to the station,' the man said. 'We can send a car if you need that.'

'She's not...?'

Another pause. 'It's probably best if we do this in person...'

TWENTY-SIX

HANNAH, WEDNESDAY

It had been a waste of a journey for Hannah the night before. When the call from Unknown came, it had been a blessed relief from the group meeting. She'd told her mum she had something important to check, grabbed the bin bag Janet fell over, and then left in a hurry.

And it had all been for nothing. The paranoia from her mum's living room had affected her more than she'd thought.

Now it was a few minutes after nine in the morning and Hannah was back parked across the road from the house of horrors. The place she would rather never see again. The owner was waiting at the bottom of the steps, tossing those keys from hand to hand, as he had the first time she'd laid eyes on him.

Hannah got out of the car and crossed the road, trying not to wince as she noticed him eyeing her up and down.

'You came then?' he said.

'Why did you call me last night?'

'I think you know...'

Hannah tried not to shiver at this. It was what she feared. It was the reason she'd driven to the house the previous night, even though he'd asked if they could meet at nine the next morning. She'd expected to see police cars and tape. Some sort of cordon and maybe one of those white tents that were sometimes on the news. She'd braced herself for it... but then she'd turned onto the street and there had been nothing. It seemed so nonsensical afterwards. If something had been discovered, it wouldn't have been the house owner calling, it would have been the police – and they wouldn't have phoned, they'd have turned up with handcuffs and a warrant.

She drove away, confused by what he was after, though knowing she'd have to wait until the morning.

And now...

'I don't know what you mean,' Hannah said.

She looked up towards the house but her eyes were drawn to the window next door, where the nosy neighbour from the weekend was staring down upon them.

The owner, Jeff, noticed him too. He huffed with annoyance. 'Let's go inside,' he said, before starting up the steps.

Hannah didn't know if it was a good idea to enter the house with a man who was, essentially, a stranger – but the desire to know why he'd called won out.

She followed him up and into the house, where she was almost immediately struck by how serene everything now seemed. When she'd last been inside, there had been a panicked rush. One half of the group had left noisily out the front to distract from what was going on at the back. After that, people had been lugging bags and cases, silently wondering if they were doing the right thing. It felt such a long way away: as if it had happened to a different person in a different space.

Now, the house was empty and silent, while the endless white felt almost overpowering. Hannah couldn't stop herself from looking towards the spot on the floor where Katherine had fallen after swinging from the chandelier. Another mad, inexplicable moment.

She looked up and realised Jeff was watching her. His keys

were on the counter and he'd closed the door without her realising. Hannah did the only thing she thought she could – and tried to take control.

'Why am I here?' she asked harshly. 'And don't give me any of the cryptic "You know" stuff.'

Jeff craned back his neck a fraction. 'You have some nerve, after what you did.'

Hannah knew she was playing with fire – but she was in too far: 'What did I do?'

Jeff pushed himself up onto tiptoes, making himself fractionally taller than Hannah. 'The cheek on you. Not only do you *steal* my things, you have the *nerve* to act as if you don't know what I'm on about.'

Hannah found herself staring at him and almost asked him to repeat himself. She had no idea what he was talking about. She managed a mumbled 'Huh?' – but Jeff was already ahead of her. He strode around the kitchen counter and started opening cupboards.

'There was a coffee grinder in there,' he said. 'I thought stuff like that would be a draw for guests. Thought it'd be a nice touch. There was a blender, too. State-of-the-art. I thought people might use it for cocktails. I didn't think someone would end up nicking them.'

Hannah was still staring, lost for words.

'It might not have been you,' he added, taking in her puzzled expression. 'But *someone* from your group stole them and I want them back.'

Hannah had lain awake the previous night, dreaming of the owner confronting her with some sort of evidence for what happened to Katherine. She wondered if he'd blackmail her by saying he'd go to the police. Her thoughts had got darker and the scenarios less likely – but, in all that, she'd never once thought he'd been calling to ask about a blender and a coffee grinder.

It seemed so inconsequential... and yet such a relief. It wasn't anything to do with Katherine.

'I, um...'

'Don't you "um" me.' He was scolding her now, like a teacher with a child who'd not handed in their homework. 'They were here on Saturday morning and then gone when I came round to clean up on Sunday night.'

It had taken Hannah a while to catch up but she remembered the appliances now he'd mentioned them.

'Are they definitely missing?' she asked.

'It's not like I'm hiding them.'

'No... sorry.' The apology seemed to placate him somewhat, although everything remained surreal. 'I'll ask around,' Hannah added. 'There weren't many of us here – and I live with about half of them. I'm sure it's just a mistake.'

'Nobody steals kitchen appliances *by mistake*.'

'No...'

Hannah took a step away from the kitchen, somewhat relieved, somewhat bemused. Chances were the items had been cleared away while they were panicking on Sunday morning.

'I *know* they were stolen,' Jeff said. 'I want them back, and there'll be no questions asked. No need for the police.'

Hannah nodded along with this. At least they were united in that the police shouldn't be involved. It felt like something too small for the authorities anyway, not that she was going to argue.

'That blender's a hundred quid online,' he added, still on a roll. 'And the coffee grinder's about seventy.'

'A hundred and seventy pounds?!'

'I can get you printouts if you want?'

Hannah shook her head and told him it wasn't necessary. 'I'll ask around,' she repeated. 'If nobody knows anything, I'll send you the money.'

Jeff was too full of righteous indignation to be put off by

something as simple as this. 'Oh, someone knows something all right,' he said. 'I'm almost certain a bedsheet's missing, too.'

Hannah had taken another half-step away, ready to put this nonsense behind her. She'd been worrying all night because of a *blender*. But then she froze, turning back to the owner once more.

'A sheet...?'

He replied but she wasn't listening. In everything that had happened, she'd somehow missed the obvious fact that Katherine had been wrapped in a sheet. They'd piled up the rest of the used bedding on purpose, making it look as if they were helping the owner with the laundry – but, to anyone paying attention, it would be obvious something was missing.

'...they're good sheets,' he was saying. 'Top-quality stuff from John Lewis. Nothing cheap. That's the whole point of the house. That sheet's worth at least twenty quid.'

It was the mention of the sheet that had Hannah pulling her purse from her bag. She flipped through the pockets, though she hadn't carried more than about ten quid in cash for years. Everything was tap or PIN nowadays. She always felt bad walking past the homeless people asking for change – but none of them had card machines and she didn't know anybody who carried actual money.

'I don't have the cash,' Hannah said. 'If I had it, I'd pay you now.'

The owner seemed surprised by the offer, backtracking enough to say that he didn't mind waiting for her to ask her friends.

By then, Hannah was desperate to leave, not wanting to risk any further questions about where the sheet might have gone. She picked her phone out of her bag and, though there were no notifications, she held it up.

'I've got to get off,' she said. 'I promise I'll ask around and let you know.'

Jeff seemed partially satisfied with this. He stood in the kitchen, arms crossed, mumbling to himself – although he made no more demands.

Hannah headed towards the door and let herself out. She hurried down the steps and back across the road, before getting into her car. It was only then that she risked a peep back towards the other side. It wasn't only the nosy neighbour who continued to watch from his window; Jeff was looking out from the front of the house, too.

Hannah fumbled with her keys, wanting to get away. In her rush, she dropped them in the car's footwell and then had to blunder around trying to find them underneath her seat.

By the time she eventually pulled away, she couldn't figure out whether this was something to worry over. It sounded like the owner would happily take a couple of hundred quid to shut up and forget about it, although the situation felt so odd. Had one of her family or friends *really* stolen those items? Had they taken them during the mass panic immediately after Katherine's body had been found? And, if so, *why*?

Regardless of that, the last thing any of them wanted was the house owner telling the police he was missing a sheet.

Hannah continued to drive across the town, figuring she'd tell her mum she needed two hundred quid to pay off Jeff. She was most of the way there when she remembered she could simply take it out of her own account. It was odd to think of herself as having money. She'd gone her whole adult life living pay cheque to pay cheque – and often her money wouldn't last until the next payday. She'd use her overdraft or a credit card to keep going – but now, thanks to the inheritance, for the first time in her life, there was actually money in her account. Money that wouldn't be eaten up within four weeks, especially now she wasn't travelling.

The nagging voice at the back of her mind told her the planned trip would have been a waste anyway. That she'd be better leaving the money there and using it as a backup fund for the foreseeable future. No more overdrafts, no more credit card fees, no more need to borrow ten quid here and twenty quid there.

Perhaps Beth was right. Perhaps she'd been right all along.

Hannah turned the corner onto the street where her mum lived, figuring she could turn around and go back to a cash machine. There was one inside the Londis, which she had always avoided because it cost three quid to use. She'd usually go ten minutes out of her way to use one of the free ones in the town centre – but she'd rather have this over and done with. She'd turn around, get the money, and drive back to Jeff's place.

She would, except...

Hannah stopped the car in the middle of the street. It was past the time where residents hurried off to work, or to drop their kids at school. There was almost no traffic in the late morning. She watched, blocking the road, as a new sense of unease began creeping through her. It felt like driving into a tunnel and not being able to see light at the other end.

She stared ahead, hoping she was seeing things – except there was no doubt about the empty police car that was parked outside her mum's house.

TWENTY-SEVEN

The car horn hooted loud from behind. Hannah panicked and stamped on the accelerator, before swerving across into a spot on the road outside one of her neighbours' homes. Residents continually lost the plot about people parking outside their houses but, for now, whoever lived at number forty would have to live with it.

She turned off the engine and sat in the car staring along the street towards the unmoving police car. Hannah had been out for around ninety minutes and she wondered how long the police had been there. The curtain twitchers would've noticed, of course. It was the sort of street where nothing of any significance could happen without somebody spotting it. In the old days, which weren't that old, people would only gossip to themselves. Now, Hannah felt certain there'd be a post on the area's Facebook page from Nosy Mrs Witch, or whatever she was called, asking if anyone knew why a police car had been parked in the same place two days running.

Hannah thought about driving away. She wasn't quite in sight of her mum's windows and could easily pull a U-turn and head somewhere else. Except she didn't have anywhere to go.

She found herself daydreaming about driving to the airport and heading off somewhere – starting her trip early, despite the airline fees – but her passport was at the house, along with everything else she owned.

She checked her phone, hoping there'd be something from her mum saying not to worry but that the police were at the house for some trivial reason – except there was nothing. Presumably, her mum was preoccupied by dealing with whatever reason the officers were there. Either that, or she didn't want to send anything that could be read as incriminating if it came down to it.

Hannah thought about calling. She could be breezy – *'Hi, Mum. I'm at Morrisons. Do you need anything?'* – except one of the nosy neighbours could be watching her right now. Hannah could almost imagine the reply to the Facebook post about the police cars.

'Saw the daughter making a run for it. Anyone know what she's up to?'

Hannah thumbed out a message to her mum, asking what was going on, but then she deleted it, not wanting to leave any sort of digital trail.

After sitting for the best part of ten minutes, Hannah got out of the car and walked along the street towards her mum's house. She unlocked the front door and was welcomed by the embracing arms of the central heating. She went through the routine of taking off her coat, hat and gloves as if everything was normal. After that, she headed through to the kitchen, where her mum was standing over the sink, washing out a mug. The water was running unusually hard, the noise ridiculously loud for what it was – although it took Hannah a moment to realise her mum must've heard her come in, and then headed into the kitchen to make a racket.

Hannah's mum left the water running but turned to face her. Her eyes were wide and she nodded through to the living room, where the door was open. 'They won't say why they're here,' she said. It was barely loud enough for Hannah to hear over the din – but she supposed that was the point.

She tried to think of a follow-up but couldn't come up with one. Instead, she headed into the living room, where Sergeant Peterson and Constable Waverly were sitting on the sofa, as if the past twenty-four hours hadn't happened.

There was an untouched cup of tea in front of Waverly but an empty space ahead of Peterson where, presumably, Hannah's mum had decided to take his cup away for cleaning once she heard the door.

Both officers stood when they noticed Hannah, which left her off guard as she hovered in the gap between the armchair and the footrest.

'I didn't think I'd see you again so soon,' Hannah said. She was trying to sound breezy and conversational – but neither of the officers reacted with anything other than stoniness.

Peterson had done much of the speaking the day before but he was silent now as Waverly did the talking. 'I'm afraid we have some bad news,' she said.

There was a gap, with Hannah waiting for either of them to follow up. It felt like when someone might say 'guess what?' and then actually wait for the other person to guess. When neither of them continued, Hannah asked what had happened.

Waverly replied immediately now, calm and clear. 'A body has been found.'

It was only five words but Hannah felt her knees wobble and, without meaning to, she had to clasp the top of the armchair to hold herself up.

'A body...?'

'It was found yesterday and has been identified as that of Katherine Brown.'

Hannah hadn't noticed her mum enter the room – but she

was suddenly there, at her side, a hand touching the lower part of Hannah's back.

'Katherine...'

Hannah whispered her friend's name unwittingly – and then turned to look at her mum, though all she could do was return the shocked stare. Hannah pictured the trees and the dark.

'It was found by a dog walker,' Waverly said, unprompted.

'Dog walker...'

Hannah saw the boggy ground and that pool of water. The body in a sheet. It felt as if they'd walked for ever, into the middle of nowhere and yet... of course a dog would find Katherine's body. The only reason anyone ever went to those places was to walk their dogs.

Hannah hadn't realised she was parroting until the words were already out. She had no idea what to say – but neither of the officers were speaking now and it felt as if she had to come out with something. She looked to her mum again – and then said what she was thinking.

'I don't know what to say. That's... *awful*...'

She felt her mum stirring at her side. 'That poor girl,' she said. 'What happened to her?'

It was such a dangerous question: the sort of thing that Hannah would never have come out with. She found herself holding her breath, waiting and waiting for the reply that seemed to take an age.

It was Peterson this time: 'We're not sure at the moment. The autopsy will happen in due course – but we thought you should know.'

'Autopsy...'

Hannah was parroting again, without meaning to. She tried to figure out if there was an edge in Peterson's tone, something accusatory. If there was then it wasn't obvious. Perhaps they had simply come to let her know?

'I still don't know what to say,' she replied.

She wondered if she should say more. Should she cry? Be more upset? What were people supposed to do in these situations?

The truth was, without needing to act, she was shattered in every sense of the word. They had acted out of preservation for her sister – but Katherine had been a friend for the best part of twenty years. Even though they hadn't been too close recently, there was still that history and connection.

She was horribly, horrifically torn. There was the crushing sense of loss for someone she liked, and who had been a part of her life for as long as she could remember. Of someone with their life ahead of them. She thought of Zack, standing at her door, wondering what had happened to the woman he was seeing. What might have happened to them if Katherine had lived? Whether there was something more than boyfriend-girlfriend there? Perhaps they could have built together? And now... none of that.

But there was also the overwhelming awareness of the panic that was building. They couldn't undo what they'd done. Any of them going to prison wouldn't change what had happened.

The two officers eventually acted in unison as they motioned towards the door.

'We'll stay in touch,' Peterson said.

They were past Hannah and her mum, into the hall, when they both stopped and turned.

'Did you say something about going travelling?' Peterson asked.

Hannah stared at him, off guard at the question from nowhere. 'Yes.'

'When?'

A blink. The trip was so far from her mind that he might as well have been asking about visiting the moon. 'Friday.'

The two officers exchanged a silent glance, although

Hannah had the sense they'd discussed this long before arriving at the house. Neither of them spoke as they turned and headed back towards the door. Waverly opened it and they were about to step through when Hannah stopped them.

'Is that all right?' she said.

Peterson didn't turn all the way back, instead looking to her over his shoulder. 'We'll see,' he said.

TWENTY-EIGHT

Charlotte's voice was a muffled echo as it sounded from the other side of the front door.

'Are you on your own?'

'Who else would be with me?' Hannah replied.

'Is Mum there?'

'She's at home.'

There was a clunk of a lock and the scratch of a latch – then the door swung inwards. Charlotte was in a pair of leggings and the baggiest of baggy jumpers. The sort of thing somebody might wear in the 'before' shot of a massive weight-loss comparison.

'Where'd you get that?' Hannah asked, as she gently pulled on the sleeve of her sister's jumper.

'Three quid at the charity shop downstairs.'

Charlotte lived in a row of flats that was above a flank of shops. The chippy was more than convenient, as was the off-licence. Seemingly, the charity shop was as well.

'You could fit both of us in there.'

Charlotte rolled her eyes and shut the door. 'Have you come round to go through my wardrobe? Anyway, it's got pockets.'

She tucked her hands into the material as if to prove a point. On another day, in another time, they'd have found this funny. Pockets were the holy grail.

'I'm here because you've not replied to any messages in the last day or so,' Hannah replied. 'Plus, you know what Mum said, some things have to be said in person.'

There was another eye roll. 'Mum says a lot of things.' Charlotte nodded towards the kitchen. 'Kettle's full if you fancy it.'

Hannah didn't fancy it and, seemingly, neither did her sister. Charlotte scuffed her feet across the cheap lino floor as she headed for the sliding doors at the back of her flat. Beyond those was a small balcony with barely enough room for two people to stand. That overlooked the alley that ran along the rear of the shops and was home to a collection of large wheelie bins. Hannah followed her out and the reason for her sister's large jumper soon became apparent, given how cold it was. Charlotte picked up a tin from the floor of the balcony and removed a roll-up, which she lit and then held in her mouth as she tucked the other hand into her pocket.

'You want some?' she asked.

The smell of marijuana started to wisp from the end of the cigarette, which wasn't much of a surprise to Hannah.

'That's the last thing I need,' she replied.

'What's going on?'

'Have the police been round yet?'

Charlotte switched hands, taking the cigarette with the one that had been in her pocket and then tucking the other into the warmth of the top. 'Should they?'

'They were round Mum's this morning. They've found a body.' Hannah waited a beat and then corrected herself. 'They found *her* body.'

Hannah swallowed away the small lump that had appeared from nowhere in her throat. In the same moment,

Charlotte took the news with remarkable calm, which Hannah assumed was down to the cannabis. She doubted this was her sister's first of the day. Hannah had spent the six or seven hours since she'd seen the police in a state of growing dread. She wondered if she should take her sister up on the offer, after all.

'They were talking about it at work last night,' Charlotte said. 'One of the customers reckoned they'd had to go the long way round because the police had shut down a road. There are a bunch of photos on Facebook.'

Charlotte continued to smoke as Hannah used her phone to find the photos her sister was talking about. From what she could tell, someone walking through the park had taken a few photos of police tape blocking the trails – though there was little more than that. The police hadn't told her *where* they'd found the body but, if it was on Facebook, the local news website would have it, too.

When she put down her phone, Charlotte turned to her. 'Is that where you and Mum...?'

She didn't ask the full question, so Hannah didn't give the full answer. They both knew anyway. At the time, in the panic of the moment, Hannah thought her mum was being smart by taking them out to the nature park. She thought of it as calculating – but, in retrospect, neither of them knew what they were doing. Why would they? It all felt so naive now. So... disrespectful.

Charlotte finished one roll-up and immediately reached into her tin for a second. Hannah wasn't like their mother in terms of being judgemental – but she still wouldn't usually have approved of chain smoking like this. From the way Charlotte started scratching at her arms, she had the sense it wasn't only weed that her sister was putting into her body.

'None of this would've happened without me,' Charlotte said quietly.

She lit the second rollie and inhaled long and deep, before holding the smoke in her lungs.

Hannah almost replied on instinct, saying that it wasn't Charlotte's fault, except... it kind of was. Whether it was the drugs, or the head injury, Katherine wouldn't have been swinging from the chandelier if it wasn't for what Charlotte had shared with her.

Hannah found herself trying to allay her sister's feelings anyway. 'I probably shouldn't have invited her,' she said. 'I'd already asked Sophie and they obviously had history. If she'd not been there, none of it would have happened.'

Charlotte flicked ash onto the alley below but didn't reply. There was enough guilt for all of them.

They watched as a man exited one of the shops below and stumbled across to one of the large bins. He dumped an armful of cardboard on the ground and then heaved open the lid, before chucking the flattened boxes in one after the other. When he turned, he realised he was being watched, so he doffed an imaginary cap towards the sisters, before heading underneath and out of sight. Moments later, there was a bang of a door.

Charlotte pressed back onto the railing, turning to face Hannah: 'How's Beth?'

'I've not spoken to her much. Mum told her to make sure she kept up with her college work and, if she's not been there, she's been in her room. Can't really blame her.'

Charlotte was near the end of the second roll-up. She squeezed it between her fingers, sucking as much out of it as she could, before mashing the remains into the half-full ashtray on the floor. After that, she reopened the sliding door and headed back into the warmth of the flat, Hannah a step behind. Charlotte crossed the lino and hovered next to a radiator, where the grey paint was flaking and peeling. She held out her hands towards the heat, as Hannah slotted in at her side.

'What did the police say?' Charlotte asked.

'Nothing, except that they'd found Katherine.'

'They'll do the autopsy and find the E in her system.'

Hannah stretched closer to the radiator, enjoying the blaze on her palms. She'd barely been able to feel her fingers outside.

'She still didn't get to the house. If there are drugs in her system then she did them elsewhere.'

'Maybe with her boyfriend...?'

Hannah didn't reply to that. It was one thing for there to be a mystery over what happened with Katherine; a muddying of the waters to help save her sister. Until now, it hadn't occurred to her that somebody else could be implicated. She didn't know Zack but, from the one time he'd shown up at her door, it had been clear that he cared for Katherine. Even though it wasn't how they'd planned it, in their version of events, he was the last person to see her. Assuming the drugs did show up in Katherine's autopsy, perhaps the police would look to him? What would she do then?

Hannah pressed a finger onto the radiator itself, letting the heat burn through her. Would she really go so far as to let someone else take the blame?

'Han...?'

Charlotte grabbed Hannah's wrist and pulled her away from the radiator. She turned her hand over to see the scalding red mark on her sister's finger.

'What did you do that for?' Charlotte asked.

Hannah didn't reply. She pressed her finger hard with her thumb and, though it didn't hurt in the moment, she knew it would.

Charlotte stepped away and headed towards the kitchen, where she flicked on the kettle and, without asking, grabbed two mugs from the cupboard. One was purple, the other mustard yellow, and both had the Cadbury's logo on the side. They'd come with some Easter eggs when they'd both been living at home and must have travelled with Charlotte from flat to flat to flat.

As she reached into another cupboard, Charlotte suddenly stopped. She craned forward to look out of the front window, down towards the street.

'Han...'

Charlotte looked up to Hannah, her eyes wide with alarm.

Hannah was frozen for a second but then she hurried across the room until she was at her sister's side. On the street below, a marked police car had pulled into a spot outside the off-licence. Even from the distance, Hannah recognised Peterson and Waverly as they got out of the car.

Charlotte crouched and reached into the cupboard under the sink. She pulled out an air freshener and sprayed a guff into the air, before hurrying around the flat and spewing more into the air. She spared most of it for the area around the balcony doors. When she was done with that, she rushed back to the kitchen, put the can away, and then took the tobacco tin she'd had outside and hid it behind the rusting tubular vent that snaked up above the cooker.

That done, she reached into a drawer and pulled out a tub of Tic Tacs, from which she clicked a selection into her hand. Once those were in her mouth, she put the tub back in the drawer and then held her hands up to her sister.

What?

Hannah had the sense this wasn't the first time Charlotte had hurried around to cover her tracks. She doubted the police would be fooled, seeing as the flat now smelled like a flower shop on Valentine's Day.

Even though she'd been expecting it, Hannah still jumped when the doorbell rang. Charlotte cupped her palm around her mouth and nose and breathed into it, checking her breath. She rounded the counter and then stepped across to the front door. Hannah didn't know if she should sit on the sofa, out of sight from the front door, and act as if she'd been there all along. The alternative was to stay where she was in the kitchen, near the window, where it might be obvious that she had seen the police coming.

In the end, Hannah had no choice, because Charlotte was already at the door. She pulled it inward and then stepped back to reveal Peterson and Waverly.

Peterson did the taking. 'Are you Charlotte Ford?'

Charlotte was suddenly her old, sarcastic self. The worry and self-pity from moments before was gone as she leant on the door frame.

'I specifically told the agency I wanted *two* male strippers.'

Peterson didn't smile as he introduced himself and Waverly in much the same way he had to Hannah the first time they'd met. Hannah expected them to ask to come in, to ask whether Charlotte had seen Katherine on Saturday night. She figured they'd be making these calls to everyone who'd been at the house.

Instead, as Waverly peered past Charlotte deeper into the flat, Peterson gave the real reason they were there.

'We're actually looking for your sister,' he said.

Charlotte's moment of confidence seeped away like a deflating balloon. Her shoulders dipped and she turned towards Hannah, who was still standing by the kitchen counter.

Peterson took this as an invitation and stepped into the flat, Waverly a pace behind.

'We heard from your mum that you would be here,' he said.

Hannah stared back at him, unsure what was going on. 'I only saw you a few hours ago,' she said.

'New information has come to light.'

'What new information?'

'We were wondering if you might come to the station with us...?'

Hannah looked past Peterson and Waverly towards Charlotte, who was still standing next to the open door. She was frozen, eyes wider than ever, staring back and full of fear.

'Why the station?'

'We've got some results back on Ms Brown's body.'

'What do they say?'

Peterson smiled humourlessly. 'We'd much rather do this at the station. It's better for everyone.'

The burn on Hannah's finger was starting to throb and she had to force herself not to put it in her mouth. She couldn't stop looking at her sister's horrified face. It felt as if she had joined this conversation halfway through and had missed the important information.

'What if I don't want to come?'

Hannah had the sudden sense that she was sounding like a stroppy teenager – but it was already too late. Peterson and Waverly glanced sideways to one another and it was Waverly who spoke. It was like the pair of them were telepathic. 'Are you saying you *won't* cooperate?'

Charlotte let out a quiet 'Han...', though nobody paid her any attention.

'I just want to know what's going on,' Hannah replied.

'We can go through that at the station. It would be better for everyone if you came with us.'

'Better for you?'

'For *everyone*.'

The hairs on the back of Hannah's neck rose and it was as if her entire body was tingling. 'I don't want to go unless you tell me what's going on.'

The officers swapped another glance and then Peterson took a couple of steps towards the kitchen. 'Hannah Ford, I'm arresting you on suspicion of the murder of Katherine Brown...'

TWENTY-NINE

The solicitor scanned the page of the thick hardback journal that sat on the desk between her and Hannah. She had the reassuring air of a headmistress who everyone knew was harsh but fair. The sort who could be heard shouting three classrooms away but who would also remember the names of hundreds of students.

The entire process around checking into the police station had felt like something of a dream. Hannah had been taken through a back entrance and then led into an area where someone had taken her phone, bag, keys and everything else. They'd laid it all out, one item at a time, and catalogued the lot, before reading it all back to make sure she was happy. She'd assumed they were going to question her right away but, instead, she'd been taken into a separate area of the building. There, she had been put in a small room and told that the duty solicitor would be with her soon – if that's what she wanted.

Hannah thought about saying she didn't want the solicitor, because it might make her look guilty if she accepted. Except she *was* guilty – not of murder but guilty nonetheless.

Peterson had specifically arrested her on suspicion of

murder but it had to be a mistake. If they had done tests on Katherine, they'd surely know that there was no murder. She died of some sort of drug poisoning, or injuries from the fall, or... Hannah didn't know.

What she *did* know was that it was too late now to say that they'd simply found Katherine's dead, almost peaceful, body. Especially as she and her mum had then driven that body out to what they thought was the middle of nowhere to get rid of it.

As all that continued to swirl around Hannah's mind, the solicitor looked up from her journal and offered something close to a reassuring smile.

'Why don't you tell me what happened?' she said.

Hannah did... or she told her as much as she'd told the police when they'd visited the first time. She'd invited Katherine to her going-away party, which wasn't a party. Katherine hadn't shown up and, the next thing she knew, here they were.

Hannah wondered if the woman believed her. She was impossible to read because her features didn't change even a little. Was that how she always was? Someone could be confessing to a horrific murder and the lawyer would be straight-faced and professional.

The solicitor asked more questions that mainly related to times and places. The sort of procedural stuff that Hannah had also gone through with the officers before. All the while, she wrote in the journal, presumably scribbling down Hannah's timeline ahead of whatever was to come.

The thing was, everything relating to the timeline was true. Hannah knew the day and time she'd invited Katherine, she knew when her own family arrived at the house and when they'd left. Everything was true – except that none of it was.

When the solicitor was done, she closed her notebook and stood, ready to leave. She quickly slipped back into reassuring mode, telling Hannah the interview would happen in a different room and that they'd catch up then. There was some-body else 'in cells' to whom she needed to speak, but everyone was working as quickly as they could, given the circumstances.

Hannah wondered what she meant by 'circumstances', then she considered whether this meant she was currently in a cell, too. It didn't feel like the sort of cell she'd seen on TV. It was bright, for one, with a sharp overhead strip bulb and calming, beige walls. It wasn't a million miles away from the decor of the house where everything had happened.

Hannah was alone for two or three minutes until somebody came. It was an officer in uniform whom she hadn't met before. He asked if she wanted some water, or 'something from the machine', whatever that meant. He was smiley and chirpy, as if they were friends and he was asking what she wanted from the bar.

After he left, Hannah couldn't remember whether she'd asked for water. She couldn't even remember what he looked like. Her lips were dry, her throat scratchy, and the spot on the finger from where she'd touched the radiator at Charlotte's had turned into pinpricks of white.

More time passed, maybe a few minutes, maybe much longer. Things had moved so quickly and felt so far out of Hannah's control that she'd lost all sense of time. At some point, there was a gentle knock at the door and another officer she didn't recognise appeared. He said, 'They're ready' and then he led Hannah out of the room and along a series of corridors until he motioned for her to go through another door.

This room seemed far more familiar. The walls were a murky grey, with a single bright light overhead which seemed to make the shadows even darker. There was a table in the centre, with two chairs on either side. A tape recorder was fixed to the wall and there was a camera in the top corner, its blinking red light bearing down upon her.

The duty solicitor was sitting in one seat and, as Hannah

entered, she stood and motioned Hannah into the chair at her side. The journal was on the table, closed for now, with an expensive-looking pen sitting next to it.

'Did you have anything to eat or drink?' she asked.

'No.'

'Would you like something?'

Hannah thought for a second. Food was so far from her mind. 'Maybe some water.'

The officer who'd brought her in ducked out of the room and returned less than a minute later with a bottle of water. He unscrewed and removed the cap, then put the bottle onto the table, before exiting and leaving them alone.

'No need to be nervous,' the solicitor said.

It was easy to say.

'Why did he take the lid?' Hannah asked.

The solicitor looked up from her notebook, towards the water bottle. 'That's a good question... I'm not sure.'

Hannah sat, in a daze, staring at the cap-less bottle. If something like this didn't warrant nerves, then what did?

'I'm so sorry,' she said, angling around in her chair slightly, 'I forgot your name.'

The solicitor smiled back kindly and laughed gently. 'It's Marie,' she said. 'Don't worry about forgetting. I'm terrible with names. My husband's even worse. When he's calling the kids, he'll go through all their names until he gets the right one.'

Marie's smile faded slowly but there was something about it that left Hannah yearning for that sort of life. That sort of stability. The kids and the husband who rattled through a series of names. She'd never had that... but then Katherine would never have it either. Not now.

She was lost in her thoughts but not for long as there was a knock on the door and then Peterson and Waverly appeared. They stood tall, smart in their respective suits, Peterson clutching a paper cup which had steam spiralling from the top.

Waverly had a notepad in her hand as well as a large, flat brown envelope. They both stepped across to the table and placed their things on the surface.

For Hannah, the next minute or so felt like she was watching a television show. Peterson checked something on the video camera and then set the tape recorder going. He introduced the four of them as being present and then noted the time. Hannah had seen it all before – but never once thought she might end up on either side of the desk.

After he was done, Peterson listed a set of facts. He said that Katherine's body had been found the evening before by a dog walker and named the park where Hannah knew the body had been left. He'd not said that earlier – but the photos were out there via Facebook and the local news. The only new piece of information came when he said that Katherine's body had been identified by her boyfriend. Zack's name wasn't mentioned but who else could that mean?

Once all that had been logged, presumably for the recordings, the questions began. Hannah had already answered everything in the same way both at the house with Peterson and Waverly – and then again with Marie a corridor or so away. She'd seen Katherine at the checkouts in Morrisons and mentioned the get-together. That was the last time Hannah saw her.

The first part was true and she'd repeated the rest so often that there was a point where it almost felt true. She pictured lie-detector tests she'd seen on trashy talk shows and wondered if this was how people passed them. It wasn't about telling the truth, it was *feeling* like the truth was being told.

She was getting better and better at ignoring the sick feeling in her stomach.

Back in the room, Peterson continued checking more things about timings at the house on Saturday. He pressed forward on the table and picked up his paper cup. He sipped from the top and then put it back down.

'Can you describe the last time you saw Katherine,' Peterson said.

Before Hannah could say anything, Marie cut in: 'I'm pretty sure she already has.'

Peterson looked sideways to Marie and then back to Hannah. 'Just one more time,' he said.

Marie said, 'You don't have to,' but Hannah didn't want to be combative unless she absolutely had to.

'We were on the way out of Morrisons,' Hannah said. 'I saw her at the self-checkouts and we waved at each other and said hello. She asked what I was up to and I told her about my trip. We talked about that for a bit and then I said that we'd hired a house and I was having a few friends round as a going-away thing. I asked if she wanted to come and she said yes.'

That was all true. Hannah caught herself breathing a sigh of relief.

'What happened then?' Peterson asked.

Hannah tried to remember. In all the questioning, nobody had asked what happened in the immediate moment after the checkouts.

'We walked out together,' Hannah said. 'She only had a basket but I redocked my trolley and then we carried our shopping out the main entrance.'

'What then?'

Hannah had a sip of her water and needed the delay to remember. She wondered whether the officers had CCTV from the supermarket and already knew. 'I was parked near the recycling banks at the back of the car park, so I went that way,' she said.

'Where did Katherine go?'

'She went the other way and got into a car.'

There was a second or two of silence, which left Hannah back in that moment. She'd not thought about that actual parting since it had happened. She'd paid very little attention to that car – except, now she thought about it, there was something about it that she couldn't quite get her head around. Something that felt important.

Her clarity was shattered as Peterson continued. 'And that was the last time you saw her…?'

Hannah nodded.

Peterson motioned towards the tape machine. 'Is that a yes?'

'Yes.'

Peterson pressed back in his chair and drained the rest of the drink. Waverly had been quiet until then, scribbling the odd note, although nothing that Hannah could make out upside down. Peterson read out the address of the house where they'd been on Saturday and checked it was correct. Hannah said it was and he nodded along.

'We know Katherine was on that street close to the time you were all due to meet,' he said.

Hannah didn't reply because there was no question.

Peterson left it a moment and then continued. 'She was at the bottom of the steps that led to the front door of number twelve. What do you think happened in between Katherine being there – and then her turning up, covered in bruises, in the woods?'

Marie cut in before Hannah could even think about replying. 'If you want to speculate, you can use your own imaginations, Sergeant. We only want to deal in facts on this side of the table.'

Hannah felt something swelling within her. If she'd been left to her own devices, she would have tried to cobble together an answer.

Peterson didn't acknowledge Marie – although that probably said more than any actual reply. He checked the empty cup before glancing towards Waverly. There were no words spoken between them – and perhaps it was that which felt dangerous.

Waverly picked up the envelope that she'd placed on the table. She reached inside and pulled out a piece of paper, which she flipped around and offered to Hannah. 'Do you recognise this?'

She was solemn, firm and inquisitive: like a teacher asking a question to which every student in the class should know the answer.

Hannah looked to the page, which was a colour printout of a photograph that showed a silver pendant on a silver chain.

'It was found at the house where you stayed overnight,' Waverly said. 'Katherine's boyfriend has identified it as hers.' She paused, letting it sink in and then: 'If Katherine was never in the house with you, then why was her necklace discovered there?'

Hannah put down the paper and Marie reached to pick it up. Suddenly, Waverly caught Hannah's eye and then they were locked together. Hannah couldn't stop staring and neither did Waverly. It was as if they were the only two people in the room – and then Hannah was back in that bedroom, looking down upon Katherine's greying body, knowing that, aside from the obvious, there was something else not quite right. Now it had been brought up, she knew this was it. The heart pendant Katherine had been wearing was no longer around her neck... and now it had been found.

The walls of the interview room started to slide towards Hannah. The ceiling was grinding its way closer as the room shrank.

Tighter.

Smaller.

Hannah was suddenly aware of her breathing. Her chest was tight and her lungs wouldn't fill.

'Who found the necklace?'

It was Marie again, her voice as solemn and firm as Waverly's had been. Air poured into Hannah's lungs and the walls and ceiling raced away. Everything was normal again – and Waverly's stare had left her and was now on her pad.

Neither of the officers answered Marie's question – though Hannah hadn't replied to theirs.

'The question remains,' Waverly said, turning back to Hannah.

'So does mine,' Marie replied, firmer this time. 'Ms Ford says that her friend never arrived at the house. If you want to speculate about anything more than that, you can use your own imaginations. If Ms Brown's body was only discovered yesterday, then I'd be surprised if you had time to get a warrant for that house. You'd then need time to carry out a full search – and then more time to get us all in a room here. More time still to visit Ms Ford's house this morning.' She pushed the photo back across the table. 'From what I can see, this picture has been taken against some sort of table or counter. There's no context of where it was found – so it's a simple question. If you want to bring up the necklace, then *who* found it? And *where* precisely? Because, if it's not an officer in a warranted search...'

Both officers pressed back into their chairs, neither acknowledging Marie, both staring at the desk. Questioning the identity of who found the necklace, let alone the timeline, would never have occurred to Hannah. She could barely believe she'd thought about walking into the room without a solicitor.

Now she was left wondering who found the necklace. If it was the house owner, he'd have surely mentioned it? When she last saw him, he was more concerned about his coffee grinder. If it had been the police, they would have said.

So who had found it?

The officers looked to one another and Peterson raised both eyebrows. Hannah was expecting more questions – but Marie closed the notebook that Hannah hadn't noticed her open.

'Is that everything?' she asked. She shuffled in her chair, as if about to stand, and Hannah couldn't quite believe what was happening.

Except there was one big question that nobody had asked.

'Why murder?' she asked.

Marie stopped moving and both officers turned to take in Hannah. Everyone seemed surprised but nobody answered.

'Why murder?' Hannah repeated. 'At my sister's flat, when you arrested me, you said it was for murder.'

Marie started to speak – but Peterson talked over her.

'Because we got the early results back on her body,' he said. 'Before she was dumped like an old mattress, someone suffocated Katherine Brown until she was no longer breathing.'

PART 3
TRUTH

THIRTY

Marie pulled her coat tight around herself and then fished into the pockets for a pair of slim leather gloves that she battled to stretch onto her hands. Hannah and the duty solicitor were on the police station's car park, where frost was starting to form around the edges, close to the low wall that ringed the tarmac. It was dark and, with only a series of gloomy orange bulbs for light, Hannah would have not felt safe walking if it was anywhere other than directly outside a police station.

Hannah had barely said anything after the interview was over, nor while going through the procedures afterwards. But she finally spoke now.

'I don't know how to thank you,' Hannah said. Her voice was croaky and the cold nipped.

'Just doing my job,' Marie replied. Her gloves were now on and she was back in her pockets, digging for what turned out to be a chunkily knitted hat, which she slipped over her ears.

'What happens now?' Hannah asked. 'I know they said inside but it was all a bit...' Hannah held her hands up, wanting to say it was a bit much but not quite knowing how. Words were an understatement for everything that had happened in the past few hours.

Marie turned from side to side, probably looking for her car and wanting to get away. Hannah didn't blame her. It was comfortably night now.

'They have nothing to keep you in but plenty they're going to go away and investigate. You must know that. You invited Katherine to a place, she was apparently seen on camera very close to that place – and then... who knows? It's not going away.'

Hannah felt a little bit of comfort at the 'nothing to keep you in' part – but Marie was also correct in that this wasn't going away. Hannah suddenly realised her finger was still stinging from where she'd touched the radiator and, when she held it up under the dim light, she could see a small white blister had formed.

'Are you OK?' Marie asked.

'It's hard to answer that.'

A nod. 'The investigation is why you're on bail. You've got the details and you need to be back here next week at noon.'

Hannah clasped her bag tighter to her side. She'd been given a sheet inside that listed her bail conditions.

'I was supposed to be travelling on Friday...'

'That's not happening. If you even get near to an airport, you could be remanded.'

Hannah nodded along. She had already been told it in a more roundabout way inside – but it felt so much more brutal now. She'd spent so long building up to something that wasn't going to happen.

'Are you sure you understand?' Marie asked.

'Yes.' Hannah sighed. 'Will you be here next week?'

Marie took a moment to think. 'We do duty shifts on a rota, so no – but you shouldn't need a solicitor to answer bail. You just go to the counter and say who you are. That's essentially it. It's all on your sheet.'

'What if they want to talk to me again?'

Marie hoisted her own bag higher, making the silent point about wanting to get away. 'You should get someone who specialises in serious cases. Someone who can advise you better on this sort of thing. Someone who's done it before.'

'You were really good.'

Marie didn't react to the compliment. 'I can probably give you some recommendations. I've got your email address on the file but I won't have time till the morning.'

She took another step, angling further away.

'Thank you,' Hannah said again – and this time Marie met it with a slim smile, before she turned and strode away. The shadows soon swallowed her and then there was a growl of an engine with a flare of headlights.

Hannah suddenly realised she didn't know how to get home. Her car was at Charlotte's and there had been nobody waiting for her as she exited the police station. She reached into her bag, fingers trembling from the cold. Her phone was in a ziplock bag and she pulled it out and then turned it back on. She muttered, 'Come on, come on' under her breath, waiting for the home screen to hurry up and load. Her fingers were so cold that she tried and failed four times to type that passcode she hadn't known she shared with Katherine. When it finally unlocked, messages began to ping through, mainly from her mum. There was one from hours before, saying that the police were on their way to Charlotte's – which must have been sent before she was arrested. For whatever reason, Hannah had missed it.

Charlotte had called or texted their mum to say what had happened, because there were lots more messages after that, asking which station she'd been taken to. There were more wondering if Hannah wanted her to come to wherever she was.

Hannah started to type out a message, asking to be picked up. It was like she was fifteen again, out at a friend's house, or some crappy disco in a freezing church hall. If it wasn't her mum they were asking for a lift, then it was Sophie's. Or Katherine's foster parents...

Hannah deleted the message and dispatched the phone back into her bag, before glancing at it again to check the time. She'd been in the police station for nowhere near as long as she thought. She'd have been certain it was close to midnight – but it wasn't even seven.

There were intermittent cars scattered around the largely empty car park, though no actual people in sight. It was so quiet. People would be in their homes, enjoying the central heating, ready for tea.

Not Katherine, of course.

There was no drugs overdose – and neither Peterson nor Waverly had even mentioned the ecstasy that would have been in her system. Either they didn't yet know she'd taken something, or it was irrelevant to their investigation.

That was an uncertainty – but one thing was clear. Katherine had been suffocated or, as the officers later said, she was 'a victim of asphyxiation'. They were both long words to say that someone had killed her.

Murdered her.

And that someone had to be one of the people who'd been in the house that night.

THIRTY-ONE

Hannah started to walk. She wasn't completely sure of the route back to Charlotte's flat – and her car – though she knew the vague direction. The police station was on the edge of a trading estate and, if she could find her way across that, there was a KFC on the other side. After that, she was a housing estate away from Charlotte's.

The cold bit and clawed but Hannah clenched her teeth and continued to put one foot in front of the other.

Hannah knew she hadn't killed Katherine, though she couldn't get her head around the alternative. Of the people closest to her, her blood relatives, her best friend – and her best friend's mother – one of them must have killed Katherine.

There was something not right about the house owner but, if it was him, why would he have bothered with odd tales about stolen appliances? He'd have wanted to distance himself as much as possible.

After that, who was there?

Her hands were buried in her jacket pockets and Hannah rolled her thumb across her blistered finger until she felt a satisfying pop. It wasn't satisfying for long because, a second later, pain started to flow through the rest of her hand.

Hannah ignored it and kept walking. She was glad it hurt.

She couldn't stop thinking about the evening in the house. With the layout, Hannah was relatively sure neither Beth nor Janet had crossed from the side where they were sleeping to the room that contained Katherine. She'd slept in the living room and had been disturbed by a person she felt sure was Sophie. At the time, Hannah thought it might be a dream but it was now horrifyingly real.

Except, despite everything that had happened with Sophie marrying Katherine's ex, Thomas, Hannah simply couldn't picture Sophie holding a pillow or a hand over her friend's nose and mouth.

She also couldn't picture either Charlotte, her mum or Dawn doing it – plus none of them had anything close to a motive.

If anything, Charlotte was the opposite because she'd have been attracting attention to her drug issues.

The people there was her mum, her aunt, her sisters. They'd had issues as a family, they'd fallen out and drifted apart and back together. Hannah simply couldn't believe any of them were killers.

A niggly little voice whispered that it was her mother who'd taken the lead in tidying everything up. It was she who'd done the most to stop them talking. She who had taken Hannah out to that nature park.

She who had made Hannah an... *accessory*.

Hannah breathed in and out, pushing away the voice. Obviously, it wasn't her mum. Her mother was acting out of love for Charlotte.

Except, if it wasn't them, that only left Sophie. A person she'd known for twenty years and more.

Hannah found herself in a dead end, facing a large set of

padlocked gates. She'd been walking without thinking. Beyond the gates was a factory, the windows dark. She turned and headed back the way she'd come. When she reached the junction, she tried the next exit and followed a row of warehouses towards a roundabout, on which someone had stacked a dozen traffic cones in the middle. Headlights flared in the distance and the earth rumbled. Moments later, a long lorry blazed past, coughing bitter exhaust fumes onto the pavement where Hannah walked. She turned her head, trying to avoid the worst, but that didn't stop the taste of diesel filling her nose.

She continued walking, finally seeing the familiar glowing red symbol in the distance. This was the run-down side of town. There were greasy spoons and drive-thru fast-food places here – plus heavy lorries blazing onto the estate from the main road.

Hannah kept going, through to the KFC and the small group of shops on the other side of the road. There were two juice bars, a kebab place, a pizza shop, a regular chippy and a Costa. There was also a Wetherspoons a short distance along the road, with a series of glowing heaters and umbrellas on the pavement outside. None of which was a surprise considering the college campus was around the corner. There was no busier place in town than this area on a weekday lunchtime.

It was quieter now, though pockets of young people still hung around, eating or drinking. The sound of braying laughter drifted along the street from the Spoons, though Hannah was going in the opposite direction. She was almost past the row of shops when she noticed a familiar face sitting at one of the tables in the window of the juice bar.

Beth noticed Hannah at the same time as Hannah spotted her. Beth was with a lad and a couple of girls – and Hannah didn't blame her for staying out with friends after classes. Anything had to be better than returning to their mum's house and sitting in her bedroom with the door closed, attempting to escape the madness.

Hannah half expected her sister to turn away and pretend they hadn't seen each other – but she gave a small wave instead. She said something to her friends and then stood and exited out the door.

'What's happened?' she asked.

Hannah ran a hand through her hair. 'Do I look that bad?'

'You look that cold.'

Hannah laughed a little at that, more on instinct than anything else. 'Has Mum texted you?'

Beth rolled her eyes. 'I've got her on mute. I check it when I'm almost home.'

Another gentle laugh. Mobiles hadn't been anywhere near as pervasive when Hannah was a teenager but, if they were, there was no doubt she'd have had her mum's number muted, too.

'My car's parked outside Charlotte's,' Hannah said. 'Do you fancy a walk?'

Beth pulled her coat tighter and buttoned it, then dug into the pockets for her hat, gloves and scarf. 'As long as we walk quickly.'

She said goodbye to her friends and then the two sisters started walking side by side away from the shops. Before long, they ducked into the alley that would cut through the housing estate at the back of the college.

Neither of them spoke for a while, though Hannah felt comfort in being together.

'How's college?' Hannah asked eventually.

'Y'know...'

Hannah didn't laugh this time but there was the gentlest of smiles. She almost ached for her sister's youth. There was a time in her life when almost every question that came her way would've been met with 'dunno' or 'y'know'.

'Don't let Mum get on to you too much about grades and work,' Hannah said. 'We all want you to go to uni but you shouldn't have to do something just 'cos me and Char failed at it.'

Beth didn't reply at first, though her pace dropped momentarily. 'That's not why I want to go to uni.'

'Good. It shouldn't be. I suppose I never asked if this is what you want. Ever since you got your GCSEs, probably earlier, it was like the rest of us had planned out your life.'

Beth re-upped her pace, which served as a change of subject. 'What's really going on?' she asked.

Hannah snorted at this. Her sister was so much smarter than she'd ever felt. 'I'm not going away on Friday anymore.'

The reply snapped back, higher pitched with surprise: 'What? Why?'

'I was arrested,' Hannah said. 'I've been at the police station all afternoon. They only just let me out.'

Beth stopped and grabbed Hannah's arm, spinning her around. 'What do you mean? Why were you arrested?'

'Murder.'

It sounded so blunt and brutal from Hannah's own mouth. Still not believable.

Beth was suddenly serious. 'Is that a joke?'

Hannah shook her head. 'They found Katherine's body yesterday and say that someone suffocated her. They kept saying "asphyxiation". I don't think I'd ever heard anyone say that in real life until today.'

Beth glanced sideways along the empty alley. Shadows loomed long from the hedges on either side and a hazy orangey glow hovered at the furthest end. Beth turned and took a step, waiting for Hannah to continue.

'I saw something about a body,' Beth said. 'People were talking about it at college. I assumed it was...' She tailed off, not finishing the thought and then adding: 'I don't understand.'

'I'm not sure I do either.'

'Is it some sort of mistake? I thought she died from a reaction to the E? Or from when she hit her head.'

'Those were always guesses. Nobody knew what happened and then Charlotte said we couldn't call an ambulance because there would be drugs in her system. After that, it was kind of irrelevant how she actually died – because things could always be linked back to Charlotte.'

Beth considered that for a second. Her pace was faster again and they exited the alley and headed onto the circle at the end of a cul-de-sac. 'What are they saying happened?'

Hannah didn't reply at first. A man was striding towards them, his jacket collar up high and the glow of his phone illuminating half his face as he mumbled something about telling someone to 'just get on with it'. They passed him in a dark patch between a pair of street lights. Instinctively, the sisters upped their pace a tiny fraction. As they exited the cul-de-sac, they continued into the web of roads with cars parked along either side. They were now deep into the estate, walking along streets lined with a mix of short terraces and semi-detacheds, while cutting through various alleys as shortcuts.

'I'm not sure what they think happened,' Hannah replied eventually. 'I'm guessing they think someone smothered her with a pillow, or their hand. It's not like they'd tell me all of what they know, considering I'm their main suspect.'

It was surreal, walking along in the town they grew up in, casually speaking to her little sister about being a murder suspect. Even more surreal to think that one of them might know the real killer. And that the victim was someone Hannah had known all her life.

They continued walking and it felt as if Beth was trying to absorb the news. It was a good minute until she replied with, 'I don't think I understand.'

'I don't think I do, either. I don't know what to do.' Hannah lowered her voice, probably needlessly. 'If Katherine was killed in the bed, then it means someone in the house...'

She couldn't quite say the words and it was another short while until Beth replied. 'Someone could've broken in.'

'Wouldn't one of us have noticed? Eight of us were staying there.'

'What about the owner? He had keys – and he was a right weirdo.'

'I thought about that – but why would he? What would he get out of it? He's got this big second house that he's spent money to do up. He's probably got a mortgage – and, for no reason, he'd be turning it into a crime scene.'

'But it can't be one of us...'

Hannah and Beth exited a final alley onto one of the roads that led in and out of the centre. There were brighter street lights, with an intermittent stream of traffic heading in both directions. They took the turn towards Charlotte's flat and kept walking.

'I think Sophie was out of bed,' Hannah said. 'I was on the sofa and something woke me up. I thought it was a dream at first but the more I think about it, the more I think it might've been her. I asked her about it the other day and she was a bit funny about it. She changed the subject really quickly.'

A taxi blared past, going significantly over the limit, its exhaust roaring like an injured lion. Hannah suddenly realised she was a couple of paces ahead of her sister. She turned and waited for Beth to catch her and they walked at a slower pace.

'Something woke me up that night,' Beth said. 'Everything was so crazy the next morning and I suppose I didn't think it was worth mentioning – but I'm pretty sure *I* heard someone up and about. Sophie and her mum were in the room next to me and I thought I heard their door open. It must've been a few minutes later that it went again. I figured someone was going to the toilet.'

Hannah let it sit for a moment. She might have been dreaming – but it felt unlikely both she and Beth would've had the same vision.

'Maybe one of them *was* going to the toilet,' she said.

'Maybe…'

Hannah tried to remember what Sophie had said in the park when she'd asked about it. It was something about not hearing anything and her mum not moving. There was also that thing about her mum making loads of noise whenever she got up.

Lights smouldered from the shops ahead and Hannah realised Charlotte's flat was in front of them. Beyond that, Hannah's car was a little further up, precisely where she'd left it.

'Do you remember the ring on the floor?' Beth asked. 'When we were in the bedroom, it was on the floor, remember?'

Hannah had forgotten – but it was suddenly at the front of her mind. Beth had held it up and then Hannah had dropped it into Katherine's bag.

'Do you think it was Katherine's?' Beth asked.

'It wasn't mine. Who else's would it be?'

'I don't know. I suppose that's what I'm saying. If someone else was in the room, maybe it was theirs?'

It was a fair point – although Hannah's mum had dumped that bag, the ring included. There was no way to get it back now.

The sisters passed the shops and then hovered at the back of the car as Hannah tried to get some life into her fingers to hunt for the keys.

'I don't know what to do,' Hannah said.

'I can't drive.'

'Not that. If I tell the police Katherine was there, they can investigate what happened properly – but it puts everyone else in trouble. That's Dawn, Janet, you. People who've done nothing wrong.'

She glanced back towards Charlotte's flat, wondering if their other sister was upstairs, or if she'd made up with their mother and was currently waiting there. The windows were dark.

'Char, too,' Hannah said. 'If it was an actual murder, then all that stuff about the E is irrelevant. Except, if I don't tell them Katherine was there, then someone killed her and might get away with it. Or, worse, someone who didn't do anything gets blamed.'

She thought of the figure crossing the floor in the early hours of the morning. Of Sophie and Katherine and the decade-long feud.

'What do we do?' Beth asked.

'There's no "we".'

'What will *you* do?'

Hannah let out a long breath, knowing her reply would sound ridiculous but not quite knowing what the alternative could be.

'I suppose I try to figure out who killed her.'

Beth drummed her fingers on the back of the car as Hannah finally found the keys and unlocked it.

'There's definitely a "we",' Beth said. 'Sisters united.'

THIRTY-TWO

ZACK

Since identifying Katherine's body the evening before, Zack had felt an emptiness that he couldn't think of a way to describe. It was as if a part of his own body was gone. He had never seen a dead body before – and he would happily go the rest of his life without seeing another. He had driven around much of the previous night before ending up back at his flat. He lived alone and yet, because he'd spent the best part of four days with Katherine the previous week, it felt empty when only he was in it.

Technically, he had slept. It had been twenty minutes here and half an hour there. Perhaps two to three hours in total, although it might as well have been nothing given how he felt.

His phone had buzzed on and off all day, not that he'd looked at any of the messages. Nobody except Linda knew about his relationship with Katherine – but people would know they worked together. The news of what had happened to Katherine was probably out there somewhere – even if via Facebook – but he couldn't face having to reply to anyone. He couldn't face reading or hearing their sympathy. That sort of thing could come after there was justice.

The police had warned him to stay away from Hannah and her family and, for the most part, he'd done exactly that. He'd driven and driven, stopping only to fill up his car and buy awful coffee from the machine in the petrol station.

When he'd got bored of driving, he sat in the back corner of a supermarket car park and people-watched until he was bored of that, too.

And then, eventually, he'd driven to the street where Hannah lived. He parked in more or less the same spot as when he'd ended up following her.

It felt like such a long time ago and he had to remind himself it was one day. At more or less this time twenty-four hours before, he'd been parked there. Shortly after returning to his flat, he'd taken that call from the police that had shattered everything. He'd not heard from them since and he wondered when he would again.

There were lights on in Hannah's house, although that wasn't unusual. There were lights on in most of the houses and Zack felt sure the curtain twitchers would be keeping an eye on him, while he kept an eye on Hannah.

Assuming she was home.

He didn't actually know that she was – but also didn't know what else to do. He didn't want to go home to his flat to be by himself. Technically, he wasn't ignoring what he'd been told by the police. Staying away from a person was surely subjective. He lived a couple of streets from Hannah, so he could never be *that* far from her. Parking on her street wasn't that different. Not really.

He was so tired. The more he sat, the more he felt his eyes starting to close and his thoughts beginning to drift.

Poor Katherine. She had no family, no next of kin. There was nobody to mourn her, except him. Even her friends weren't an option, considering Zack was certain they were lying about what had happened to her. He wondered what would happen with a funeral and who would organise it. Was it him? Who else would go? Their colleagues from the shop? Perhaps a handful of her other friends?

Zack couldn't think about it... except he couldn't think of anything else.

He kept reaching for his phone, wanting to text her and then realising there'd be no point.

Zack unclipped his seatbelt and reclined the chair a fraction. He would go home at some point – just not yet. Sitting here doing very little felt better than sitting in his flat doing nothing.

There seemed to be more cars on the street this evening and they were parked more or less nose to tail the full length of the road. Some houses had driveways, though not many.

A semblance of movement in the side mirror caught his attention as someone took three attempts to parallel park into a space on the other side of the road. He watched in his mirror for a moment and then fought away a yawn as he looked back to Hannah's house. He knew he should go home and try to sleep. The police were presumably doing their jobs.

He almost reached to turn the key – except there was more movement in his mirror. He squinted to see what was happening and then turned to look properly over his shoulder. Hannah and a younger woman were on the other side of the street, walking side by side away from the parked car and towards the house. The girl he didn't recognise said something and Hannah smiled. She might have even laughed.

Zack clenched the steering wheel so hard that he felt his knuckles crack.

Katherine had been in that house on Saturday evening and Hannah had lied to his face about it. She *knew* what happened and now, here she was, a day after Katherine's body had been found, and she was laughing.

Zack continued to watch them, glaring daggers until, almost

through sheer force of will, Hannah stopped. The other woman hadn't noticed and continued moving along the pavement but Hannah turned and looked across the street.

Looked across the street... directly at him.

She squinted, leaned in, as if she couldn't quite believe what she was seeing. Zack didn't flinch, instead meeting her gaze.

I know what you did, he thought.

The younger of the two women suddenly noticed Hannah was no longer at her side. She halted and turned, then Hannah said something to her. The younger one shrugged and then continued along the street, before disappearing into Hannah's house. She must be another of Hannah's sisters.

Once she had gone, Hannah crossed the street towards him. Zack half thought about starting the car and racing away. The police had told him to stay away from her – except she was the one approaching him.

He rolled down the driver's window and Hannah was still in the road when she crouched to look through the now open window. The glass had been steaming with heat before but now the cold singed through.

'Are you watching the house?' Hannah asked. Her voice was croaky, her skin red, as if she'd been out in the cold for some time.

'What's it to you?' Zack replied.

'It's a bit creepy.'

'I'd rather be creepy than lying about a supposed friend of mine.'

She met his eyes and there was something there that he couldn't entirely read. He'd been so furious when he'd seen her laughing a minute or so before but there was no trace of anything close to levity in her stare. She had the dead-eyed blank look of someone who'd spent an afternoon at a funeral.

Hannah shuffled backwards from his window a little,

further into the road. When she sighed, a cloud of air engulfed her face for a moment.

'Did you love her?'

Her question came seemingly out of nothing and felt like a jab to Zack's chest. He was suddenly short of breath, shocked by the bluntness.

'She deserved someone who did,' Hannah added.

Zack tried to say something back but nothing came.

Hannah checked for traffic and then took another step away, further into the road. She was biting her lip and, if he thought more of her, Zack would've felt sure she was about to cry.

Sympathy was one thing he could not bring himself to give her.

Zack spun away and turned the key to start the car. He buzzed his window up and slapped it into gear, before pulling off into the street.

As he sped away, he didn't trust himself to look back.

THIRTY-THREE

HANNAH

Hannah watched Zack's car disappear around the corner at the bottom of the road. When he'd pulled out, there was the smallest of moments where she thought he might slam the car into reverse and swerve towards her. There was no movement to suggest such a thing, though Hannah wouldn't have blamed him. She had lied to him – and they both knew it. He had every right to hate her.

And then, looking at Zack's face, she'd felt so sorry for him. In the time between first meeting him at her door, then seeing him in his car, something in him had broken. There was desolation in his face. There weren't many occasions in which Hannah had seen something similar. There was the time she had told Paul that she was leaving him and she'd watched his eyebrow begin to twitch. After that, it was as if his whole face fell in on itself. She thought he'd have an inkling because they hadn't been getting on for a while – but it had been a total shock. He was crushed and sat on the sofa staring at the floor for the best part of two hours.

Before that, there was the time their mother had told her and Charlotte that she was breaking up with their dad. Hannah had been watching her sister, whose mouth had hung open and stayed there. Charlotte had only been seven or eight at the time and she started to howl to such a degree that their mum said they'd have to go to the hospital if she didn't stop. Hannah hadn't cried, hadn't said very much at all. She couldn't remember how she felt about the separation, she could only picture her bereft sister.

Hannah tried to remember what Katherine had said when they'd been at the back of the house with Charlotte. She couldn't remember the words but Katherine had played down her date with Zack. Hannah had done the same when she'd first started seeing Paul. She'd told people they were 'just friends', when she knew it was more than that.

In other circumstances, she and Zack might be consoling one another for what happened to Katherine. They were on the same side, even though he didn't know it. Or, they would have been if Hannah wasn't caught in the middle.

Hannah crossed the road back to the side of her mother's house. There was always a shortage of parking in the evenings and things were crazier than usual. She walked along the line of vehicles and then looked across, picturing Zack taking that turn in his car.

There was something niggling away in the back of her mind that hadn't quite reached the surface. Like watching a percentage bar on a computer as it installs a program. There was something about his car. Something not right.

Hannah was at the end of the path to her mum's house. The curtains were pulled closed, though light crept around the edges. Beth would be inside, saying that Hannah was out of the police station and safe. Her mum would be worried.

She was at the door, reaching into her bag for her keys, when she stopped because, from nothing, that installation bar hit a hundred per cent.

It wasn't Zack's car that was the problem.

The police had stirred the memories earlier in the day when they'd asked Hannah what Katherine had done after they'd separated at the supermarket. Katherine had headed off towards a car – but it wasn't Zack's. His was blue and scuffed. The sort of thing bought from a second-hand lot and very similar to the one Hannah first owned.

Katherine didn't drive and the car she had got into was red and more or less new, with shiny oversized wheel rims. It was something that Hannah had seen another time recently. A time when she hadn't quite been paying attention.

And then she knew where she'd seen it.

She took out her phone and flipped through the screen until she found Instagram. It was all photos of dogs and cakes – the only reason to ever go online – and she had to search for Sophie's name to find her.

And there it was.

The picture that Sophie had shown Hannah in the kitchen of the house. There was Sophie, her son, Trent, and her husband, Thomas. Hannah had known Sophie and Thomas since they'd been kids. Thomas was Katherine's boyfriend and then, with no warning, he was Sophie's. Then he was her fiancé, her husband, the father to their son. The reason Sophie and Katherine had fallen out so spectacularly.

Thomas was standing next to Sophie and Trent. All three were beaming, although the focus wasn't really on them. It was, instead, on the car that Sophie said he'd got through his garage. The one that was new, red, and had shiny oversized wheel rims.

THIRTY-FOUR

ZACK

Zack wanted to be angry. It was better than feeling sorry for himself, or allowing the bottomless grief to reach up and envelop him. He so wanted to be furious with Hannah – but she'd looked to him with such devastating angst that he couldn't stop wondering whether he'd misjudged her. Perhaps she *had* told the truth on the doorstep. He couldn't explain the necklace but he didn't believe a person could fake that level of sadness.

He *really* wanted to be angry but he couldn't because the grief was impossible to ignore. As he looked around his flat, he could see the spot where, not even a week ago, Katherine had dropped a chocolate digestive. She'd snatched up as much as she could, citing the ten-second rule – and then they'd fake-argued over whether it was the ten- or five-second rule. There was the place on the sofa where she'd fallen asleep as they'd watched the fifth episode in a row of something on Netflix.

He wasn't sure the flat felt like his own any longer.

Unable to face the sofa or his bed, Zack sat on the floor in the corner. There was a series of warm vertical pipes, carrying hot water to the apartment above, and Zack warmed his hands close to them. He took out his phone and, for the first time that day, had a proper look through what he'd been sent. There were messages from his boss, Linda, saying she'd seen the news and hoped he was OK. He didn't know whether the body had been publicly revealed as Katherine's – but it wasn't a stretch for Linda to put the two things together, considering she knew Katherine was missing. Linda didn't mention the shop, or work, only that if he needed someone to talk to, then she was there.

He swiped away from the messages and loaded Facebook, then Katherine's page. She was front and centre with a photo taken by Zack at the end of the previous summer. She was on her way back from the park, wearing huge sunglasses and trying to block the photo being taken. On the one hand, it was an odd picture to use on a profile and yet it summed her up more than words could. There was the want for privacy that came from having her life so open when she'd been young. That was coupled with the smiling joy on her face. It had been the first time she and Zack had spent any time together away from work and he wondered, perhaps hoped, that was the reason why she'd used that picture. It hadn't been a date, as such. There had been seven of them having a few drinks in the park on a boiling Saturday. There were various other friends that they knew from here and there – but Zack only had eyes for Katherine. It had taken months for them to go on a proper date.

Zack wondered what would happen to the page now. There were all those status updates going back years, although they'd been a lot less frequent recently. There were photos dating to when she was a teenager. The history of a person that would, presumably, sit in cyberspace for ever.

He was about to close the page when he noticed Hannah's name on the friends list. He didn't know her, though he'd somehow managed to convince himself she was some sort of monster. Then she'd gone and asked if he loved Katherine, which wasn't the type of thing any monster he'd imagined would do. She'd said that Katherine *deserved* someone to love her. If she'd genuinely been the person to kill Katherine, accidentally or not, is that *really* what she'd do?

Zack clicked through to Hannah's page, though it was hard to tell if he was blocked from seeing anything as he wasn't her friend or if it was simply short of content. There were no cryptic statuses or attention-seeking woe-is-me posts. No dumb memes. No drama.

There were some things he could see, presumably because he was a friend of a friend. Almost all the recent content on Hannah's profile involved her being tagged in other people's photographs. Before that, other people had left messages a few months before saying things like, 'Just heard the news, hope your well' – although Hannah hadn't replied and there was no context. He scrolled through those until he found one where Hannah had changed her relationship status to 'single'. Underneath, there were a handful of comments like 'omg' and 'what happened?', none of which had a reply.

Back further and Zack discovered that Hannah used to be married to someone named Paul Ratcliffe. He clicked the name – but there was no information, other than that he lived in the same town as Zack and Hannah. There was a picture of a man in a too tight suit that had been cropped in a way that made it obvious he'd been standing by somebody else in the original version.

Zack Googled Paul's name, along with that of the town – and got an instant hit. Hannah's ex-husband worked as an estate agent on the other side of town, which left Zack knowing precisely what he would do in the morning. Of anyone, he thought Paul Ratcliffe might have some interesting things to say about his ex-wife.

THIRTY-FIVE

HANNAH, THURSDAY

Hannah hadn't slept well. She dozed on and off – but each period could be measured in minutes, not hours. She eventually gave up and dragged her rucksack out from under her bed. She'd packed more or less everything she was going to take on her trip a couple of weeks back. A weekend had been spent doing laundry, while simultaneously having the clear-out she should have had when she'd left Paul. She'd watched YouTube videos with packing tips about how to fold clothes and what should go in the side pockets of a rucksack.

Back in the present, Hannah spent the early hours of the morning hauling everything out of the bag and stuffing things into the dresser and wardrobe. Assuming she could stay out of the grips of the police – which felt like a large assumption – she didn't think she'd be living anywhere other than her mum's house anytime soon. Ahead of the trip, she'd bought specific items she'd never had before, like hiking pants and a hat with a brim to stop her neck getting burned. They'd be living at the back of her wardrobe for a while before getting dumped at a charity shop.

In an alternate timeline, she'd have spent the day checking

and double-checking everything in her bag. In twenty-four hours, she would been on the way to the airport. It would have been a long day of motorways, queueing, waiting, queueing some more, waiting some more – and then, eventually, soaring up into the air for a new chapter of her life.

That was now such a distant thought that she couldn't remember the person who had been looking forward to it all. There was something so trivial about the idea of travelling, perhaps the overall idea of doing something for herself. Not only was her friend dead, but there was a good chance she had unwittingly helped cover it up for whoever had killed her. It niggled at her how her mum had taken control and yet enrolled Hannah into every part of the cover-up. She'd been there when the body was moved and then when it was dumped.

Hannah was digging out a new, unworn, swimsuit from the bottom of the bag when there was a gentle knock on her bedroom door. She stopped shuffling, hoping her mum would assume she was still asleep and go away. They hadn't talked too much since Hannah had got home from the police station, mainly because Hannah couldn't face running through it again. She also didn't want to explain her growing suspicion around Sophie.

There was a second tap on the door, perhaps a little louder than the first try, and then a hissed whisper of 'it's me'.

Hannah pushed herself up using the bed and then stepped across to the door and opened it. Beth was on the other side, hair ruffled from sleep and wearing her fleecy red pyjamas with stars up and down the sides.

'I heard you moving,' she said quietly.

Hannah edged to the side, allowing Beth to see inside, where the bag was on the floor and small piles of her possessions were dotted around. Beth took it all in and then offered a sad smile.

'Can we talk?'

'Haven't you got college this morning?'

'Not till lunch.' She waited a beat and then added: 'What are you going to do?'

Hannah held the door wider and Beth stepped inside. She trod around a pair of outdoorsy magazines that Hannah had earmarked for the plane, even though she suspected she'd never read them, and then she perched on the corner of the unmade bed. Hannah sat back on the floor, surrounded by the items she had thought would be her life for the coming months.

'Do about what?' she asked.

'About Sophie,' Beth replied.

'You don't need to worry.'

'What else am I supposed to do?'

'Do your college work.'

Beth tilted her head to the side. 'You want me to pretend that what happened on Sunday never happened? I can't unsee it, no matter how much you and Mum want me to. It's not fair that you're trying to keep me away from everything. It's not like I'm a kid.'

Hannah rested her back against her dresser as she slid a pair of new walking boots underneath. She had no idea why she'd assumed so much of her trip would involve walking up, or around, stuff. She *hated* that sort of thing. Perhaps everything with the divorce and her job had driven her mad.

'Han...'

She looked up, to where Beth was watching her, and realised she'd been drifting. Hannah batted away a yawn and then focused back on her sister.

'It *can't* be Sophie,' she said.

'Who else is it? Mum? Aunt Dawn?' A pause. '*Me?*'

'That doesn't mean it's Sophie...'

Hannah tailed off, not knowing what she believed. Even if it had been Sophie she'd seen up and about in the early hours of

Sunday, it didn't necessarily mean anything. She could have simply been using the toilet.

'I still don't understand why they were enemies,' Beth said.

'Sophie and Katherine weren't enemies… not really.'

'Ten years is a long time to argue about something.'

Hannah couldn't dispute that. Katherine and Sophie had been at odds for longer than they'd ever been friends.

'Thomas and Katherine started going out when we were about fifteen or sixteen,' Hannah said. 'We were all the same age, all in the same year at school. We'd go to the cinema in a group with us four, plus a couple of his friends. We'd have pizza after, or go bowling, or skating. Sometimes we'd sit in McDonald's and make a milkshake last two hours. They were going out – but it wasn't serious. They were each other's first boyfriend and girlfriend.'

Hannah allowed her neck to angle backwards, so that her head was resting on the handle of the dresser. She stared up at the dimpled plaster of the ceiling.

'Katherine's parents both died when she was young and she was living with her foster parents. It felt really… *intense.*'

Hannah looked across to see that her sister was still with her. She didn't think she'd get the story out while being watched, so she focused back on the ceiling.

'I'm not saying she was more into him than he was into her… but it felt like there was an imbalance. Katherine would want to hold his hand all the time, or cling onto his arm. She'd always worry if he was off with his friends, instead of with her or us. You couldn't blame her, not after everything she'd been through. It was no wonder she didn't want to be left again.'

Hannah shuffled around the floor, reaching for the glass of water that was on her nightstand. It was warm but she sipped at it anyway and then put the glass on the carpet next to her.

Beth waited until Hannah had stopped drinking and then: 'But he did leave her…?'

'I suppose. They were definitely together until sometime around when we all turned eighteen. It wasn't obvious that there was any sort of overlap between Thomas seeing Katherine and then Thomas seeing Sophie. I had no idea. I remember Katherine not wanting to leave her house for weeks. She sent me a text that said something like "he broke up with me" – and that was it. I'd go round but her foster mum would say she didn't want to see anyone. I gave up after a while.'

Hannah had more of her water, trying to put herself back in the mind of that eighteen-year-old. The truth was, she was caught up in her own life, work and relationships at the time. Their friendship had been drifting before anything happened with Thomas.

'It was probably six or seven weeks until I ran into Katherine in town. We said hello – and then we were friends again. The thing was, at some point in between all that, someone I knew from school said they'd seen Thomas and Sophie out in town. I'm not sure the three of us ever did anything together after that. Not on purpose. There were a couple of weddings where Sophie and Katherine ignored each other. When we were still teenagers, I'd go somewhere with Sophie one weekend and then do something with Katherine the next.'

Hannah looked up to see that Beth was now sitting cross-legged on the bed, with the duvet across her lower half. 'Did they have some sort of argument...?' she asked.

'If they did, then I wasn't there,' Hannah replied. 'Katherine has never been like that. She's not a shouter or a screamer. It's why everything with the chandelier at the house was so weird. I don't even think Sophie is like that...'

'But Sophie and Thomas got married...?'

'Four or five years ago.'

'Why weren't you a bridesmaid?'

Hannah had been staring at a spot on the wall close to the

digital clock that she set to be three minutes fast. It had been a largely failed attempt to help her get up earlier and not be in such a rush to get to her old job. She turned to look at Beth, who was fixed upon her.

'I suppose we weren't really close by then. It was never quite the same after she first got together with Thomas.'

'Because you didn't approve...?'

A shrug. 'It's not that simple.'

Hannah supposed that, deep down, she *didn't* approve. Who would? At the same time, she'd maintained a friendship of sorts with both Sophie and Katherine. She hadn't chosen sides and yet her relationship to both of them had cooled. Perhaps they each wanted her to pick a side and, in choosing both, she had actually gone for neither.

Everything was complicated by the fact that Sophie had a son with Thomas. Trent was seven or eight – and when Sophie had told Hannah she was pregnant, the first thing Hannah had thought was that it meant she and Thomas really were serious. There had been a part of her that expected them to break up in the way Katherine and Thomas had.

Hannah stood and picked up a pile of socks from the floor. She'd seen a YouTube clip that showed a roll and fold technique that would maximise packing space. They were all small palm-sized pockets, which felt ridiculous in retrospect. Hannah picked up as many as she could and dispatched them into her top drawer.

'Why did you invite Katherine if you'd already invited Sophie...?' Beth asked.

Hannah couldn't look at her sister. She stood over the dresser, moving her socks and underwear around for no partic-ular reason. If she was being honest with herself, she probably hoped they could all be friends again. That the evening would act as some sort of reset, where they'd all come together.

With the divorce and her leaving her job, she'd thought a lot about what she'd done with her life – and it was hard not to yearn for that handful of years where their trio of friends had been tight and the world had felt so much kinder and easier.

There weren't the words to say that out loud, though. She could barely let herself admit that all of this was her fault because she'd been focused on some sort of childish reconciliation.

'What are we going to do?' Beth asked when no answer came.

Hannah pictured the car she saw Katherine getting into outside the supermarket. The one she felt sure belonged to Thomas.

'I know you want to help,' she said, finally turning back to her sister, 'but there's something I need to do on my own first.'

THIRTY-SIX

ZACK

A little along the street from The Grind was the estate agent where Hannah's divorced husband, Paul, worked. Zack had walked along this street thousands of time and yet he'd never once paid any attention to the windows that were full of photos of houses. Places like estate agents, solicitors' offices, insurance brokers, and all that sort of thing felt like they belonged to another world of which he wasn't a part.

Zack was on his fourth pass, attempting to summon up the courage to go in, when the door opened and a man in a suit stepped out, phone in hand. He and Zack almost walked into one another but stopped just in time and each stepped backwards. The man was tall, with hints of grey peppering his ears among a largely cropped hairstyle. Paul looked identical to the photo on the estate agency's website and, as they each apologised to one another, he stepped around Zack as if to continue on his way.

'Are you Paul?' Zack asked.

The man looked up from his phone, squinting to Zack and trying to work out if they knew each other.

'I'm Katherine Brown's boyfriend,' Zack said. 'I was—'

He never completed the sentence because Paul cut him off. 'Y'know, I always thought someone like you would end up coming to see me.'

Zack blinked up at the other man, confused; something which Paul seemed to find funny. He snorted with amusement and slipped his phone into the pocket of his wool coat.

'What happened this time? Another fight between them all? I suppose you want the low-down on it all? Honestly, the drama is the biggest reason me and Han are divorced.'

'What do you mean?'

Paul rolled his eyes, though it felt put-on and overly dramatic. 'Katherine and Sophie were going back and forth over Sophie's husband for years. I'd hear all about it through Hannah. How they didn't speak. How all their friends had to tread on eggshells with weddings and that sort of stuff. How Han wished they could all be friends again.' He threw his hands up. 'It was ten years ago!'

'What was ten years ago?'

The next eye roll came with a hint of a smirk. Paul was not only enjoying this, he'd been waiting for it. He nodded along the street towards The Grind. 'You got time for a coffee?'

'I would... but I kinda work there and...'

'I get ya. Don't piss in your own toilet.' Paul turned in a circle and then beckoned towards the estate agent. 'Tell ya what, I'll put the kettle on in here.'

Without waiting for a reply, he reopened the door and held it wide for Zack to head in. Zack found himself obeying – and then he followed Paul through the main part of the office, past a couple of women who were each on a phone, and through a door into a small kitchen. There was a microwave, kettle, half-sized fridge and sink, plus a small table with a chair on either side. Paul motioned towards one of the chairs and, after Zack had sat, he filled the kettle and flicked it on.

He nodded towards the main office on the other side of the

door. 'I told the girls I'd get 'em a posh coffee but this'll have
to do.'

He grabbed four mugs from the draining board, gave them a
cursory wipe with a tea towel and then filled all four with milk,
before dumping a spoonful of instant coffee into each.

When that was done, Paul turned and focused on Zack.
With one of them sitting and the other standing, Zack felt even
smaller than he might do usually against the taller man.

'You from round here?' Paul asked.

'Not really. It's a long story but I've been living here for
about four years.'

Paul nodded along, not really listening. 'If you'd been in our
year at college, you'd know about all the drama. Katherine was
going out with this lad, Thomas. Then Thomas started shagging
Katherine's best friend, Sophie. There was all this fallout and
they didn't talk properly for ages. Anyway, my ex – Han – is
right in the middle of it 'cos she was friends with both of 'em. It
rumbled on for years.'

Zack felt as if Paul was describing another person. Not the
woman with whom he'd worked alongside. Not the one he'd
spent most of the previous week with.

'What was the drama?' Zack asked.

Paul shook his head. 'With your bird? Nothing really.' He
paused for a moment and then added: 'Well, loads actually –
but it was all about Han. I think she wanted things to be as they
were – but Katherine never forgave Sophie and neither of them
would talk to each other. But Han was always about drama.
There's something weird about that family. All those women.
They fall out all the time, make up all the time—'

He cut himself off as the kettle finished boiling and then he
turned to fill up all four mugs. Each got a brief swish of a spoon
and then he plonked a mug on the table in front of Zack,
sending a series of splashes onto the top.

'Be right back,' he said.

Paul snatched two of the other mugs and then disappeared through the door into the office. Zack heard voices from the other side, though couldn't make out anything specific until there was a large bellowed man's laugh. Seconds later and Paul exploded back through the door, where he bumped into the fridge while reaching for his own mug.

'D'you know the middle one?' he asked.

'The middle what?'

Paul went to drink his coffee but somehow sloshed a fair portion onto the floor. He grabbed the tea towel in annoyance and dropped it to the ground, where he wiped up the mess with his foot.

'Charlotte,' he said.

Zack felt as if they were having two separate conversations. 'Who's that?'

'Han's sister.'

It was only at the mention of Hannah's sister that Zack realised what was going on. He'd gone to Paul to ask about the relationship between Katherine and his ex-wife. What he was *actually* going to get was a list of grievances relating to Paul and Hannah's break-up.

It was too late to back out now. He picked up his mug and used the warmth to heat his hands.

'Anyway,' Paul continued, 'Charlotte got done for drug dealing a while back. She tried to keep it quiet but I know some guy at the court who told me.' He shrugged. 'That sums the family up. Always some sort of drama. When Han and I lived together, one of her sisters would always be round. We'd have Charlotte on the sofa, or the younger one, Beth, would've fallen out with her mum or dad, so she'd stay over for the weekend. We never got a minute's peace. Women, eh?'

It was more of a monologue than any sort of conversation but Paul glanced at Zack and might have winked. If he did, then it was there and gone because he was off again.

'I knew then that, whatever happened, those women would stick together. It's the way they are. I was always second to her sisters and her mum. Anyone would be. If Han had to choose between me and her family, she would always go for family. That's why we broke up. I told her I couldn't take all the drama with her sisters any more. It had to be me or them.' He nodded towards the door and, presumably, his colleagues on the other side. 'Besides, it's not as if I don't have options.'

Zack didn't believe much of what Paul had said, certainly not the 'me or them' bit. Paul was all bravado and front – but the line of how the family stuck together was hard to get past given that he believed Katherine had been in the house with them all. And none of them had told the truth about it.

Paul still wasn't paying attention. 'Anyway,' he said, 'if you're with Katherine – but you're here to see me – I'm assuming there's some new drama going on.'

He tutted to himself, amused.

Zack almost told him that Katherine was dead, except it felt as if there might be more to come.

'Something like that,' Zack said.

'Look, mate, if you're after advice, all I can tell you is to keep away from the lot of 'em. Hannah's mum always hated me. I reckon she was trying to break us up the whole time we were together. On the day we got married, Charlotte came up to me and goes, "I don't know why you're marrying her." That's the sort of family it is. You know Hannah's mum? She's been divorced twice. Now Han's divorced. Didn't even want to give it a go. What does that tell you?'

It was almost as if Zack had said he was seeing Hannah, given that every part of the conversation came back to her.

'Did you hear about the inheritance?'

Paul waited this time, wanting Zack's attention. *I know something you don't know* and all that.

Zack played along: 'What inheritance?'

Paul picked up his coffee again, being more careful with it second time around and delaying the reveal. He loved to be centre of attention.

'I heard it came from the grandmother on their first dad's side,' he said. 'Han's dad's mum. She split a hundred grand between the three girls, even though the youngest one isn't related to her.' A pause. 'Doesn't that seem weird to you? Nothing for her son but thirty-odd grand to someone who's not even a blood relation.'

Zack wasn't sure what to say. Perhaps it *was* strange – but it would surely have been odder to give huge lump sums to a pair of sisters and nothing to a third.

'I've never inherited anything,' Zack said.

Paul laughed loudly at this. 'Me, either. We're self-made men, we are. Don't need nobody else's money.' He laughed again, quieter this time. 'You mark my words, there's something fishy there.'

'Like what?'

'I don't really wanna say...'

He looked around conspiratorially, even though there was nobody else in the small kitchen – and he clearly *did* want to say.

'I'm better off out of it,' Paul said, 'but between you and me, I wouldn't be surprised if one or all of that family knocked off that grandma to get her money. She was a real Granny Smith, you know that? That was her name. Like the apple.'

It felt like one piece of nonsense joined to something else that was completely irrelevant, though Zack barely had time to take any of it in because Paul was still talking.

'If you want some advice, then if you're serious about Katherine, you do whatever you can to keep her away from the Ford family. I wish someone had told *me* that, 'cos mark my words, they'll only bring you trouble.'

THIRTY-SEVEN

HANNAH

Hannah pulled into the waiting bays at the side of the garage. There was a scuffed sign with an arrow and the word 'office' pointing back the way she'd come. A grubby air pump was attached to the wall at the back with 'not for customer use' written in big letters above it. Off to the side, in a quiet corner of the yard, was a red sporty-looking car that was, by some way, the cleanest thing in sight.

Instead of heading towards the office, Hannah headed around to the back of the garage, following the sound of tinny music towards a large set of wide open double doors. There was one car tucked in at the side and another up on a ramp above a pit that was cut into the concrete. A radio on a window ledge was covered in dark grease and the music had given way to someone who sounded far too cheery for a morning.

Hannah edged further into the garage, when she realised a man in dark overalls was standing in the pit, looking up to her. 'You've got to go round to the office,' he said. He was wiping his hands on his overalls and, before Hannah could reply, he craned his neck towards her and added: 'Han...?'

She smiled at him, holding her hands wide. 'Hi, Tom.'

Thomas continued wiping his hands as he headed up the steps into the main part of the garage. He grabbed a rag from a counter and touched it to his forehead. 'I didn't know you were booked in for today,' he said. 'Where are you parked?'

'I'm not booked in. I was wondering if you have a minute...?'

Sophie's husband stared at Hannah for a moment, eyes narrowing before he made his decision. He crossed to the sink at the back, where he blasted the taps and squirted some washing-up liquid into his hands, before spending a good minute washing them. When that was done, he headed over to the radio and turned it off, before striding across to a pair of battered leather sofas that sat next to a heater which blazed orange.

'That's the clean one,' he said, pointing to the second of the sofas and then back to his own. 'This one's for overalls, that one's for guests.'

Hannah sat on the sofa he'd indicated and instantly sank into it as a spongy sphere squished its way out of the seat at her side. She'd known Thomas for as long as she'd known Katherine and Sophie, although they'd never specifically been friends with each other. She'd known him first as Katherine's boyfriend and then as Sophie's. Their interactions had always been through or around other people and she struggled to remember a time before this when they'd had a one-on-one conversation.

'What's up with the car?' he asked.

Hannah looked at him blankly for a moment, before realising that he thought she was at the garage because her car was playing up. She hadn't said anything but there must have been something in her face that gave the answer because Thomas quickly added: 'Is it Soph?'

'Is what Soph?'

'It's just...' Thomas angled to look past Hannah towards the rest of the garage, presumably making sure they were alone. 'She's been acting odd since your party. Is that why you're here?' He had leant forward, hands pressed together as if about to pray.

It *was* partly the reason why Hannah was here – but she didn't think he'd know that.

'What do you mean by "odd"?' she asked.

'She's been quiet and seems really distant. I asked if anything happened but she said she didn't want to talk about it. Then she went out the other night to your place. Something's going on...'

He was more focused now, more direct. Not so much a question as a statement of fact, with an implied demand for answers.

Hannah tried to think of how she could explain away her friend's change in behaviour and mood – except it wasn't her job, and that wasn't why she had come to the garage.

Instead, she went for the nuclear option. 'Is something going on with you and Katherine?'

It hadn't been deliberate and Hannah only clocked the present tense after the words were out. The news of a body being found might have filtered around Facebook and local news sites – but the *identity* of that body hadn't yet gone around. If Thomas knew she was dead, he wouldn't have been asking why Sophie was behaving strangely.

She watched as Thomas's eyes widened and narrowed. His body had straightened, arms tense.

'What do you mean?'

'It's a simple question.'

He shook his head quickly, although the glance away felt like a tell. 'Course not. I've not seen her in years. Not properly, anyway. Why would you ask?'

'Because I know you saw her last Wednesday. You picked her up in Morrisons car park.'

Another shake of the head. 'I think you've got—'

Hannah pointed out of the garage, towards the yard at the side. 'I saw her getting into *that* red car. *Your* car.'

Thomas stood and paced back and forth, still shaking his head. 'Not me. Can't have been me.'

'You won't mind me asking Soph about it, then?'

Thomas had been striding the length of the sofas but he continued walking, picking up speed as he crossed the garage and headed to a bench on the far side. He had his back to Hannah, who couldn't spot what he was doing – although she could see his right leg shaking.

She had gone too far in mentioning Sophie and was about to apologise when Thomas turned to face her. He took a step across the floor, then another, slower this time, his gaze steady and unmoving on Hannah.

'I knew I shouldn't have picked her up there,' he said.

Hannah didn't reply – because, in his hand, Thomas was wielding the chunkiest of wrenches.

'Knew it was a mistake,' he added.

'Tom, I—'

He patted his left palm with the flat head of the wrench and continued advancing. 'Soph knows, doesn't she?' he said. 'That's why she's been acting so weird.'

'No, it's—'

Thomas was almost across the room now, a couple of steps from the sofas. He sighed, look down to the wrench in his hand, and then lifted it once more.

THIRTY-EIGHT

ZACK

After the largely one-way conversation with Paul, Zack decided to go to The Grind after all. He wanted to taste something that wasn't bitterly grim instant coffee – and, for the first time since identifying Katherine's body, he felt as if a friendly face might help.

Linda spotted him when he got through the door. She'd been serving drinks to a table and, as soon as they were down, she beckoned him over and put her arms around him. 'I was hoping you'd come by,' she whispered. After pulling away, she smiled sadly to him. 'There's a table free in the corner.'

For the next few minutes, Zack allowed the control he had to slip. He was ushered into the corner and then sat and waited as Linda made him a latte, which she brought across with a tuna sandwich and almond croissant. She pushed both across the table and said he wasn't allowed to leave until everything was gone.

Zack's stomach burbled and, for the first time in a while, he was hungry. One bite of the sandwich quickly led to another and then, in what felt like a few seconds, the first half was gone. Linda watched him eat in the way an approving mother might watch a child empty a plate. Zack had the rest of the sandwich and then a corner of the croissant as he sipped the coffee.

'You're pale,' she said. 'Need a bit of food, you poor thing.' She nodded towards his phone on the table. 'That charged?'

Zack had food in his mouth but Linda didn't wait for the answer as she headed to the counter and returned with a cable, which she connected to the plug socket for him.

'You have to look after yourself,' she said.

Zack nodded past her, towards a short queue that had formed at the counter but Linda batted it away.

'Don't worry about that. Did you ever meet my niece, Cherie? She's fine.'

From the somewhat frazzled hand-flapping going on behind the counter, Cherie didn't *look* fine but Zack didn't want to be left alone quite yet.

'Thank you,' he said.

'Don't mention it. After what you've been through – and that poor girl.' Linda lowered her voice. 'It is her, isn't it? I mean, they've not named her but you said she was missing and then that body was found and I didn't hear back from you. I suppose...'

She tailed off as Zack slowly nodded his head. 'I couldn't face—'

'You don't need to explain yourself.'

Linda pressed back in her chair and watched as Zack forced down a little more of the croissant. He wasn't sure he was hungry any longer. That moment of wanting to see a friendly face had gone now Katherine had been brought up.

Seemingly picking up on this, Linda patted his knee. 'Looks like Cherie needs some help,' she said. 'But don't even think about leaving until you've finished eating, or I'll hunt you down.'

Zack mumbled another 'thank you' as Linda stood and squeezed herself between the customers until she was behind the counter. Zack continued nibbling at the croissant while sipping his coffee.

He also watched the organised chaos unfold.

There was the woman at the front of the line who didn't know what she wanted. She was asking Linda what everything was, even though it was marked on the menu. Behind her, a guy was impatiently tapping his feet. There was the mid-twenties couple pointing towards the menu and whispering to one another about what they wanted. The espresso machine popped and fizzed, while cups clinked on tables. The low hum of chatter was the constant undercurrent.

Zack picked up his phone and loaded the local newspaper's website. It was the first time he'd looked since identifying Katherine's body – and the main story was about the body of a young woman that was so far publicly unidentified. He clicked into the search box and typed 'Smith death', which brought up half a dozen matches, the most recent of which came from around four months before.

There wasn't a lot of information in the obituary but it did say the woman was survived by a son, Richard, plus grand-daughters Hannah, Charlotte and Bethany. According to the snippet, Mrs Smith was almost ninety and died peacefully in her sleep. There was no mention of anything suspicious, an autopsy, or anything that wasn't normal for a person who'd been born in the early part of the twentieth century.

Paul talked about not being surprised if someone from the family had 'knocked off' the grandmother – but he said a lot of things that felt embellished or based on bitterness following his divorce.

Everyone knew a person like Paul. Zack certainly did. No matter what happened, it would never be Paul's fault. He was always one moment from greatness, if he wasn't being kept down by the incompetent clowns around him. A legend in his own imagination.

There was an irony in that, broadly, Paul had told Zack what he wanted to hear. Zack wanted to think Hannah was some sort of monster, capable of doing something to Katherine and then covering it up. Except, even though Paul had more or less said that, Zack hadn't come out of the one-way conversation thinking less of Hannah.

He put his phone back down on the table and looked up just in time to see Linda striding towards him, plate in hand. She put it down next to the croissant that was now three-quarters gone. 'Cheese toastie,' she said. 'Five different cheeses in there, so make sure you get it all down.'

'What are the five?'

The question received a small frown. 'I dunno. Cheddar, mozzarella...' A pause. 'Three of the other ones, I guess.'

Zack let out the tiniest of smiles. 'The *other* ones...?'

That received a much bigger smile. 'Just get on and eat it. I want that plate to be as clean as if it's come out of the dishwasher.'

Zack opened his mouth to protest but there was no point because his boss had already swept past and was on the way to a nearby table, from which a couple had recently left. Zack ate and allowed his mind to wander. Katherine was never far from his thoughts but he watched the customers and made his own judgements about who they were and how their days were going.

Time passed and Zack realised he didn't know what to do next. Engineering a chat with Paul felt pointless in retrospect and, regardless of what might have been said, it wasn't going to bring back Katherine. He had felt such anger the night before but that was fading, which left him with an emptiness that no amount of food would satisfy.

Zack was almost done with the toastie when his phone began to vibrate across the table. He picked it up before it got too close to the edge and the word 'Unknown' was displayed on the front.

Ever since he'd identified Katherine's body, Zack had been waiting for more information from the police – and now, finally, as he answered with a croaky voice, it was time to find out what had happened since.

THIRTY-NINE

HANNAH

Thomas swapped the wrench from one hand to the other and then sank onto the sofa opposite Hannah. He passed it back again and then did a series of small crunches with it, as if lifting a weight. It was like some sort of stress ball as he dipped his head and spoke to the ground.

'Did you tell her?' he asked.

'It was only yesterday that I realised Katherine got into your car.'

Thomas looked up again and blinked. 'Sophie doesn't know...?'

'No.'

He was suddenly energised again, putting down the wrench at his side and drumming his fingers on his leg. 'You can't tell her.'

Hannah hadn't meant to sigh but it happened nonetheless. Thomas misread the action and started to say something along the lines of Sophie not understanding – but he stopped when Hannah held up both her hands.

'This isn't the way you should find out,' she said, 'but I don't know how else to tell you.'

'Tell me what?'

Hannah took a deep breath. 'Katherine's dead.'

Thomas froze, his mouth open, eyes wide. 'She's... what?'

'Katherine is the body they found. The one from the news. I don't think they've named her yet – but it's Katherine.'

Thomas continued staring and the shock on his face was something with which Hannah was becoming all too familiar. It had been a week of things never turning out in a way that could be expected.

'Does Soph know? Is that why she's been weird?'

'Hardly anyone knows,' Hannah replied, aware it wasn't answering his question. 'The police are looking into it.'

'Did something happen to her...?'

That was a question she had no intention of answering. The less she said, the fewer lies needed to be told.

'What's going on with you?' she asked.

If Thomas was annoyed at the lack of an answer, he didn't show it. 'What do you mean?'

'You broke up with Katherine ten years ago – but I watched her get into your car. You're very keen your wife doesn't find out...'

Thomas picked up the wrench again and swiftly passed it back and forth from hand to hand. 'It's not what you think,' he said.

'So what is it?'

He put down the wrench and rubbed his forehead, leaving a small smudge of grease that must have come off the tool. 'Did you tell the police about me and Katherine?'

'I told you – I only realised it was your car yesterday.'

Thomas took a long, deep huff of air. He stood, sat, and then stood again before starting to pace back and forth. 'Soph's gonna kill me,' he said.

'What did you do?'

The pacing continued without reply. There were now a

couple more streaks of oil on Thomas's cheeks from where he was momentarily holding his head in his hands. He stopped eventually and returned to the seat opposite Hannah.

'Up until about six months ago, I'd not spoken to Katherine in years,' he said. 'Since we broke up, basically.' He gulped and then added a needless: 'You remember what happened...?'

'They were my two best friends. How could I forget?'

Thomas nodded along. 'It's not like I ever tried to justify it. I liked one girl and then I fell for another. I didn't plan it. I was a kid.'

He went quiet again, though his foot was now tapping on the hard floor, beating a steady drumbeat.

'Are you going to tell me?' Hannah asked.

Thomas didn't react at first but he slowly started to nod in time with the tapping of his foot. 'I've got a problem,' he said, suddenly looking up and locking onto Hannah. 'I'm not proud of it but—'

He cut himself off because, in a piece of timing worthy of a streaker at a funeral, he was interrupted by the sound of clip-clopping heels that was coming from somewhere out of sight. Seconds later, a woman in a black pencil skirt and white blouse appeared. She started with 'Mrs Green's been on the phone—' but stopped when she noticed Hannah. She frowned slightly until Thomas told her it was fine. The scowl didn't entirely leave her face as she said something about an MOT that Thomas ended up telling her to book. After another disap-proving look towards Hannah, she spun and headed back the way she'd come, the steady *click-click-click* of her heels gradu-ally decreasing in volume until there was the sound of a door opening and closing.

'Don't mind her,' Thomas said. 'She doesn't like it when anyone comes round the back without going through reception.'

Hannah blinked at the unintentional euphemism that she'd have found hilarious a week before.

Thomas stared off into the distance for a moment and then seemed to remember where he was. 'I gamble,' he said. 'It started with football scores. A few quid here, a fiver there. Things like Chelsea to win but the odds were low, so I'd get more specific. I'd have City to win three–one, then it'd be City to win three–one, plus Villa to win one–nil. It would get so specific that the odds would end up being really high. I won a couple early on, fluke I know now, but it was so easy.'

Thomas had been talking to his shoes but he peered up and caught Hannah's eye, making sure she was listening, before turning away once more. Hannah couldn't figure out why any of it mattered.

'It got to the point where I was betting on everything. Which team would have the most throw-ins, or who'd have more than six corners. There was one where I put fifty quid on whether the numbers on the backs of the starting line-up would be higher or lower than three hundred.' He laughed humour- lessly at himself. 'I mean, the goalie wears one and the right- back had two. I was off my head. Then I started betting on games from other countries, where I didn't even know the play- ers. Then games in the middle of the night from Indonesia, where I'd never heard of the teams, let alone the players.' He looked up again and didn't turn away this time. 'I lost a lot of money.'

'How much?'

Thomas sucked on his top lip and breathed in through his nose. His gaze shifted from side to side, as if checking it was only them who could heard. 'Too much,' he said. 'Five figures.'

Hannah couldn't stop herself from letting out a low breath. Gambling and football were two things that had never touched her life – although the endless betting adverts on television were impossible to ignore, let alone the sheer number of bookies that had sprung up around town.

'I went to Gamblers' Anonymous,' Thomas said. 'I knew I

had a problem and I wanted to do something about it. The meetings are held at the church over by the rugby club. D'you know it?'

Hannah nodded that she did. Of course she did. She'd lived in the same town her entire life.

'Anyway, I was there for the first meeting – and guess who's a volunteer? She only does Wednesdays. I could've gone any night, any meeting, but by luck, or fate, or whatever, I went to that one. And there's Katherine helping out with everything.'

Even though Thomas had said it wasn't what Hannah thought, she'd assumed that whatever was going on between Thomas and Katherine probably *was* what she thought. The same that anyone would've done. What she did not expect was something like this. She remembered Katherine mentioning her volunteering in the back garden, when they'd been talking with Charlotte, and this must have been what she meant.

'It was a shock for both of us,' Thomas said, 'but everything's anonymous... I mean that's the name but it's *actually* anonymous. You can talk about your experiences of a session outside of the group – but never anybody specifically. The meetings were helping, so I didn't want to stop, and I suppose, over time, we just started talking.'

'You and Katherine?'

A nod. 'We'd talk about school and college. About her friends and *my* friends. We'd laugh about the old times. Remember when we all went bowling and the boys had one lane and the girls had the one next to it? Then you, or Soph, or someone threw the ball into the wrong lane and it bounced across half the alley and ended up getting a strike on someone else's game?'

He laughed to himself, though it was a memory of which Hannah had no idea. Either she wasn't there, or she had forgotten.

'We talked about stuff like that – but then we started talking about how it is now. She told me about a lad she liked from her work and I'd talk about Soph a bit. About Trent. Nothing weird, nothing out of order. Just old friends...'

He tailed off and Hannah thought back to Katherine at the house, when she'd sniped at Sophie and then when she'd jumped off the counter. It must have been whatever she'd taken that caused the change in behaviour as it didn't sound as if she was particularly bitter about the past any longer.

'I'd had a bad day,' Thomas added.

'When?'

'Last week – when you saw Katherine getting into my car. I'd been in here, listening to the radio and there'd been an advert about a free bet, there was a Champions League game that night and I just...'

He held up his hands and clenched his teeth, flexing his fingers as if squeezing a melon.

'It was a bad day,' he said. 'I ended up calling Katherine and asking if we could have a chat. That's all it was. I picked her up outside Morrisons and we sat at the back of the car park talking until it was time for the GA session. I drove us both over and everything carried on like a normal Wednesday. I think her boyfriend might've picked her up afterwards.' He looked up again, waiting for Hannah to take him in. 'That's all it was. We talked a lot and I'd have probably started betting again if it wasn't for her...' He tailed off and then added a croaky: 'She's dead...?'

Hannah nodded, feeling the back of her own throat starting to tighten. She was unable to actually say the word.

'How?' he asked.

Hannah ignored the question. 'If you called or texted each other, the police will know. They'll have her records. They'll probably come and ask you questions.'

Thomas pressed back onto the sofa and picked up the wrench again. He squeezed the handle and smacked it into his thigh with an uncomfortable *thwack*, which made Hannah wince. 'Soph doesn't know about the gambling,' he said. 'She thinks I go to the gym every Wednesday.'

A wriggling idea had started to worm its way into Hannah's thoughts.

'Could she know that you've been seeing Katherine?'

'I don't see how.'

'*I* saw her getting into your car. How many times might someone else have done? One of her friends, or someone from work? A parent from Trent's school? Anyone might have seen a woman they didn't know getting into your car.'

Thomas was shaking his head, though slowly, as if trying to convince himself it wasn't possible. 'She's not said anything...'

'Would she have?'

More head shaking, which stopped and became half a shrug. 'I think she just feels sad about everything that happened with Katherine and me and her... and you. I caught her looking through old photos a couple of months back, when she was having a clear-out. Then there was this thing on TV that had a group of teenage girls and she said something about the old days.' He stopped and then added: 'Aren't you sad about what happened with us all?'

'I didn't *do* anything. I was the one caught in the middle.'

'I know – but doesn't that make you wish it was all different? We've all lived in this town ever since but we all avoid each other. It's such a shame considering there was a time when we hung out every day.'

Hannah didn't trust herself to reply right away. She'd never quite figured out to what degree she blamed Thomas for shattering her friendship with Katherine *and* Sophie. They were supposed to be a trio, not a pair of duos with Hannah caught in the middle.

'That was a long time ago,' she said eventually.

Thomas didn't reply to that. She wondered if this reckoning

she'd reached, where she wanted to fly away and see something new, was a moment that was affecting them all. They'd been out of school and working for ten years or so. She'd felt a creeping, crushing sense that, if she didn't try something new now, then she never would. That if she didn't leave Paul, they'd end up married, miserable and old, instead of just married and miserable. Looking back to happier, simpler, times was a part of her reckoning – except, perhaps it wasn't only her.

'If Sophie thought you and Katherine had something going on, how would she react?'

Thomas bit his lip again. 'I don't know... not well.'

He eyed her as if he sensed there was more to the question than the obvious. Hannah thought she'd seen Sophie up and about overnight – and Beth had said the same. Now they knew Katherine had actually been suffocated, could it really be as simple as a jealousy thing? Sophie had heard from someone that her husband had been seen with Katherine. And then, from nowhere, she'd been offered the chance to do something about it? Could it *really* be so simple?

From the back of the garage, the door sounded again and there was more clip-clopping of heels. Thomas stood and said he had to get back to work. He yawned and seemed so much more tired than he had when she'd arrived.

'Do you think I should tell Soph?' he asked.

'I don't know – but if you don't, she might find out via the police anyway. Assuming she doesn't already know.'

Thomas stared blankly at her for a second. 'I can't believe Katherine's dead.' He slumped a little, blinked, and then stood, turned, and strode across the hard floor towards the secretary.

Hannah stood as well, unsure if she knew any more than she did when she came in. Perhaps she did – and everything was down to Sophie. Perhaps she was missing something so obvious that it might as well have been in front of her face.

She was out of the garage and almost back to her car when

she realised her phone was vibrating. Hannah dug into her bag – and was more than surprised to see the name on the front.

'Why are you calling?' she said after answering.

'Why wouldn't I?' Beth replied.

'You only ever text. Mum's always going on about it. I don't think I've ever had a phone call from you.'

Hannah's sister ignored this. She spoke quickly, as if the words couldn't come out fast enough. 'I've got something,' she said.

'Something about what?'

There was a pause that almost felt deliberate, as if for effect, and then: 'About who killed Katherine.'

FORTY

ZACK

Zack tripped on the bottom step outside the police station as he headed out. He grabbed the banister to right himself and then stumbled across to the nearby wall, where he sat and stared out towards the car park. He'd been up for hours but it was like he had only now woken up.

The blue stretched far towards the horizon, with only the merest patch of puffy cotton wool blotching the sky. A white dusting clung hard to the shadows around his feet. The frost hadn't cleared over the course of the morning and it felt unlikely to do so later in the afternoon.

The visit to the police station had somehow taken him completely by surprise, while simultaneously being exactly what he expected. Perhaps it was because it all felt so real now. So final.

Katherine had been murdered.

Actually *murdered*. There was no accident, no natural causes. Someone had killed her. Katherine's body had been found in the middle of nowhere, so it was a natural assumption... but the confirmation was still brutal. Still unjust. Still wrong.

The police apparently didn't think of him as a suspect – or, if they did, they hadn't minded sharing large amounts of information. He already knew the vague details – but they told him more about where Katherine had been found. The bog and the mud. How a dog had been off leash and chasing a rabbit when he'd stopped and barked for his owner. They said they weren't yet releasing details publicly because they weren't necessarily after witnesses. Zack had asked what that meant, whether they already had a suspect, but that had gone without an answer. The main point was that they asked him not to share anything they were telling him.

He asked about Katherine's pendant that he'd found but they were only ready to give the information they wanted.

They asked a lot of questions about Hannah and whether he knew her before. He had to say that he'd never heard of her before Katherine told him about the party to which she'd been invited. Perhaps importantly, they wanted to know what they'd spoken about on Hannah's doorstep. He wondered if he'd accidentally tipped her off about something – but they also seemed interested in the precise details of what she'd said.

The police had told him they were working hard and that they hoped to have more news soon – and that was it.

Zack continued to sit on the wall, getting his bearings, not ready to drive. He had a mouthful from the bottle of water the officer on the front desk had given him, wondering what he was going to do next.

It was as he was considering that when he spotted the two men crossing the street and heading towards the police station. One was in a suit, with a brown leather briefcase swinging at his side. Zack didn't know him – though he certainly recognised the man at his side.

Neither of them paid Zack any attention as they bounded quickly up the steps. The second man was scratching his arms, clearly nervous, which left Zack thinking that, if he was the suspect and the man in the suit was his solicitor, then it would explain quite a few things.

FORTY-ONE

HANNAH

Beth was waiting outside the pub a little along the street from the town's college campus. She was standing underneath a tall gas heater lamp, frantically doing something on her phone. Hannah had parked across the street and hurried over, spotting her sister before Beth saw her.

'I thought you had classes at lunchtime?' Hannah said.

Beth didn't jump as she looked up from her phone. 'I do – but some things are more important.'

'You can't skip classes if—'

'Don't turn into Mum.'

Beth's tone was firm enough to let Hannah know this wasn't an issue to push, not now, in any case.

'What have you found?' Hannah asked.

Beth nodded towards the group of three young women who were walking along the street outside the pub. They were each bundled up in big coats and scarves, bounding along as if they had somewhere to go.

'It's quiet inside,' Beth said. 'Let's find a table away from anyone else.'

Hannah followed her sister into the pub, where the wall of

heat walloped her in the face. She started removing her outer layers as Beth led the way across the sticky floor, weaving in between chairs and tables. Some obnoxious music was pounding from the speaker, meaning the chances of a conversation being overheard were close to zero.

Beth found a table in the furthest corner of the pub, well away from the other couples and small groups dotted around the space. It was after the lunch rush and the majority of students had headed back to classes, leaving only the committed drinkers for an afternoon session.

'Do you want something to eat?' Beth asked after they'd sat.

'I want you to tell me why you called – and then you can get back to class.'

Hannah half expected her sister to roll her eyes in the way she did so often – but, instead, she looked past her out towards the rest of the bar, before leaning in and lowering her voice.

'Do you remember that ring we found on the floor?'

'In the bedroom?'

'Right. It seemed out of place, didn't it? Cheap and a bit... rubbish. I've been trying to figure out what it was and where it came from – and I ended up on Insta.'

She tapped something into her phone and then turned it around for Hannah to see. On the screen was a photo of Sophie on a sun lounger with a hazy blue sky behind her. She was sticking her tongue out and there was an orangey cocktail in one hand, with a slice of pineapple hanging from the glass. Her skin was sun-kissed as her legs stretched out in front of her, towards the camera. Hannah stared at it and then turned back to her sister.

'What am I looking at?'

Beth took back her phone and pinched the screen to zoom in. She then handed it back, where the image had focused in on Sophie's feet.

'I think that's what I picked up off Katherine's floor,' Beth said.

It was only as she said it that Hannah noticed the small, plain gold ring that was around Sophie's toe. The image was grainy, the resolution low – and it was impossible to know for sure, though it wasn't dissimilar from the ring Beth had found.

Beth took back her phone and swiped away from the screen, before putting it away.

'It's the same sort of cheap ring. You're not going to wear something like that on your finger, are you? If Sophie was in the room in her bare feet, it could easily have come off.' Beth's nervousness had given way to a burst of harried excitement. 'What happened to the ring?' she added.

Hannah almost didn't want to reply. Any hope they had of comparing to the ring to the photo was gone.

'I put it in Katherine's bag,' she said. 'I thought it was hers.'

'What happened to the bag?'

Hannah could hardly say that their mum had dumped it someone else's bin while they were on the way back from getting rid of Katherine's body.

'It's probably best you don't know,' she said instead. 'Nowhere reachable.'

Beth pressed back onto her seat as she absorbed the news. She didn't know about Katherine and Thomas's recent relationship, no matter how innocent it apparently was. The little bits of circumstantial evidence continued to grow... although Hannah still had a hard time getting over the hurdle of believing someone she'd known for so long could do something so awful.

'Do you think we should tell someone about Sophie's ring?' Beth asked. 'Or do something?'

'Like what?'

'I don't know. Maybe tell the police?'

'But it's a ring we don't have that might look a bit similar to a ring in a grainy photo. Plus, if we tell the police, then we're also telling them Katherine was at the house.'

Beth thought for a moment. 'Not necessarily...'

'You've not been interviewed by the police yet,' Hannah said. 'I told them Katherine wasn't there. Besides, that toe ring could still have been Katherine's, or it could have been left there by whoever stayed in the house before.'

'Or, it could be Sophie's...'

Beth waited for a moment, and, when Hannah didn't reply, she picked up her phone again. Beth stared at the screen for a few seconds, then returned it to the table as a waitress hurried around the nearby tables, clearing glasses. She never queried why Hannah and Beth were sitting there without drinks.

When she left, Beth leaned in, her voice barely more than a whisper. 'What if the police already know Katherine was at the house?' she asked.

Hannah angled towards her sister, copying the whisper. 'How could they? If they knew for sure, I'd never have been released.'

'But she bled after she fell from the chandelier. Maybe they found some dried bits. They'll be testing everything, won't they? The owner would've let them in – or they'll have a warrant.'

'You need to stop worrying about this,' Hannah replied. 'Whatever happens, Mum and me will keep you away from it. Do your work and go to uni.'

Beth picked up her bag and cradled it on her lap. 'I wish you'd all stop saying things like that.'

Hannah started to reply but then realised she'd only be emphasising the pressure Beth had just told her to stop applying.

Instead, they sat in silence for a short while. Beth's mention of the owner had Hannah wondering again if it could all be something to do with him. It felt so unlikely because he'd be an obvious suspect. There was also no way he could've known that everybody in the house would decide to lie about Katherine ever being there.

'You should get off,' Hannah said. 'I'll have a think about that ring and whether we can do anything.'

Beth stood and slung her bag over her back. There was a sulky element to the act, although she sounded pleasant enough as she said she'd catch up with Hannah later. Hannah watched her go and then moved across to the seat that allowed her to have her back to the wall, where nobody could see her phone screen.

She was thinking about the owner now and his reluctance to involve the police the other day.

Hannah scrolled through the various emails she'd had from Luxury Rentals about the house. It was the usual corporate thing. First the 'we noticed you were looking at houses in the area' email, along with a list of options. Then, because she hadn't booked right away, there was an email offering 10 per cent off a booking if she donated a kidney, or something like that. So many emails.

It was in the initial confirmation mail that Luxury Rentals listed the homeowner's first name as Jefferson Johnson. Hannah almost clicked past it – except that, a little further down her list of emails, there was a set of check-in instructions that came from the owner, who called himself 'Geoffrey Johnson'. Curiouser still, when she looked more closely at the second email, it had come from a Gmail address that began with jeff.johnson, before a string of numbers.

She'd never noticed the discrepancies before, though she hadn't paid any of it much attention because she had a mailbox full of bookings for flights, transfers and initial hostel bookings. It had been a mixture of her mum and Beth who'd suggested the night away and found the house; Hannah was simply the one who'd booked.

She double-checked the correspondence – and there was little question that Jefferson, Jeff and Geoff were the same person. The names were spelled with Js and Gs – but all of them used 'Johnson' as a last name.

Hannah's first thought was that he'd spelled his own name wrong. It wouldn't be unusual in the days of predictive text. She'd once called herself 'Banana' in a text to her old boss, which was something she hadn't lived down in the years since.

Her interest was up now, so Hannah typed 'Jefferson Johnson' into Google, along with the name of their town. The top link was a site described as a 'professional property management company'. She clicked onto it but the website was the sort of thing someone knocks together on a web-building platform when they're not sure what they're doing. There was a blocky photo of a house that she initially thought was the one in which they had stayed, though there were no stairs at the front. There was also a photo of Jeff, Geoff, or Jefferson in a suit, with the camera low and angled up, which made him look tall. There was a muddled contact page and a link to the Luxury Rentals website, but it was all a bit of a mess.

Hannah next tried searching for 'Jeff' with a J – but that threw up the same website and little else.

It was Geoffrey with a G that got something different. At the top was a couple of links to the local news website – and, when Hannah clicked them, it quickly became clear why he used three different names. There was a picture of the home-owner in both, with him wearing a suit and holding a hand up to partially block the photographer's view.

Three years before, Geoffrey Johnson had been convicted of breaking and entering – plus sexual assault.

FORTY-TWO

ZACK

Zack sat in his car, opposite the police station, watching the steps. An hour or so had passed since he'd seen the houseowner, Jeff, entering the police station with the suited man who was, presumably, his solicitor. It was cold and Zack didn't want to drain his car battery, so he sat in his coat, with a snood pulled up over his mouth and gloves on his hands.

Each time the double doors opened at the top of the stairs, he readied himself to get out of the car. There was a steady stream of comers and goers until, eventually, the doors opened and the man in the suit stepped out before holding the door open for Jeff. They headed down the steps together as Zack quickly exited the car and hurried across the tarmac. He wasn't sure what he planned to do and he spent more time than anticipated trying to keep his footing on the patches of frost that were hidden in between cars.

Jeff and his solicitor quickly parted, with the man in a suit slipping into a black Audi. By the time Zack had crossed the tarmac, the solicitor's car was already exiting the car park. In the meantime, Jeff was leaning against the parking meter, typing something into his phone with a deep frown on his face.

Zack thought about confronting him. He was surely at the station for questioning around whatever happened to Katherine. Did the police suspect him? Katherine would have walked past his house on the way to the place where the party was happening. If he'd done something to her, he could've ended up with her necklace, which he accidentally dropped while cleaning the house. Hannah and her family would've been telling the truth the entire time.

Zack was around twenty metres from Jeff, ready to barge across and demand to know what was happening – except there was somebody else ahead of him. From the opposite side of the car park, a beefy guy in a padded checked shirt burst from a muddy Land Rover and started a charge. Jeff looked up at the last moment, when it was far too late. The newcomer launched a punch that started from a good metre away and was more of a lunge than anything else. His fist clattered into Jeff's jaw, sending him sprawling to the ground and his phone bouncing away, underneath a car.

Zack was so stunned at the speed with which everything had happened that he hadn't moved. It was as if he was watching something on television. He'd seen the odd scuffle when he used to go out regularly on Fridays and Saturdays – but they were mainly men rolling around with ripped shirts. The brutality of the punch was something else.

Jeff was sprawled on the ground, trying to get himself back onto his feet. There was grit on his palms and he was using a lamp post to try to claw his way upwards. Before he could return fully to his feet, the other man was upon him. He swung his boot like a fly-half with a conversion, smashing his foot into the back of Jeff's knees. Jeff crashed backwards, smacking his head onto the kerb with a *thunk* as the other man loomed over him.

The statue spell had suddenly broken and Zack ran the

final few steps across to where the man was standing astride Jeff, about to batter him once more.

Zack had only ever intervened in a fight once, back in school when he'd been twelve or thirteen. One of his friends had been hit by a wayward football, which led to the two lads throwing a series of punches even more wayward than the football. As the surrounding crowd had started to chant 'fight-fight-fight', Zack had surprised everyone, most of all himself, by getting in the middle and trying to separate the warring parties. For his troubles, he'd been identified as one of the troublemakers by a dinner lady and ended up in detention with the actual fighters.

He thought of that as he dived in front of the man he didn't know, holding his hands wide and stopping him from throwing another punch towards a still scrambling Jeff. The man was panting, his fists clenched tight. They were about the same height and build – although that didn't make Zack feel any less out of his depth.

'Who are you?' the man demanded.

Behind Zack, Jeff was now on his feet. His shoes skidded on the frosty tarmac as he used the lamp post to hold himself up.

'No one,' Zack said, 'but you can't just beat someone up. There's a police station there.'

The man followed Zack's nod towards the police station, which he obviously knew was there.

'Do you know what he did?'

Zack looked between the two men. There was a scuff of dirt across Jeff's chin and he was breathing snottily through his nose. He was trying to back away but he was sandwiched between a car, the wall and Zack.

'Do you know who you're defending?'

The man lunged towards Jeff, angling around Zack, who moved to the side to block it. Jeff was cowering and covering his head, anticipating the blow that didn't come.

'There must be a better way,' Zack said.

He doubted it was the words – but it might have been a mixture of the cold and the location. Either way, the man in the checked jacket stepped backwards, looking over his shoulder towards the Land Rover. He jabbed a finger towards Jeff and growled a dangerous-sounding: 'You should watch yourself.' He then focused on Zack. 'I dunno who you are, mate, but he deserves much more than he got.'

Jeff was still cowering somewhere behind Zack. 'I'm sorry,' he said. 'I've told Tina and—'

The mention of whoever Tina was almost tipped the retreating man over the edge. He stopped moving away and reared high again. 'Don't you *dare* say her name.'

He was filled with such fury that there was a moment in which Zack feared he was going to barrel forward and smash him out of the way. The man bobbed on his heels but then his shoulders dipped.

'What did he do?' Zack asked.

The man didn't need asking twice. 'This sicko videoed himself with my sister. He had a secret camera in their bedroom. She found it and went to the police – and now he's trying to wriggle out of it.' He was huffing like an angry bull about to mow down a cocky matador. 'If those videos *ever* make it online, it'll be the last thing you do.' He poked a thumb towards the station at the side. 'I don't care about that lot. D'you hear me?'

Zack turned to watch Jeff, who was nodding frantically.

'The police have the hard drive,' he said. 'That's the only copy.'

'Oh, I bet they're having a field day with that hard drive. What else is on there?'

'Nothing. It's not like that. I—'

Jeff was cut off as the man feigned a lunge in his direction. 'You better hope you don't see me again.' He took two steps backwards and then pointed a pudgy finger at Zack. 'You should stay away from him,' he snarled.

At that, he stormed back to his Land Rover, almost reversed into a parked car, and then spluttered his way out of the car park in a cloud of exhaust fumes.

Zack could feel his heart pummelling away as he turned. Jeff was straightening his jacket and wiping the grit from his hands. As well as the mud on his chin, there was a crinkle of blood above one of his eyes – which wasn't a bad return considering how hard he'd been hit.

'You all right?' Zack asked.

Jeff was nodding slowly, brow furrowed until he finally realised who Zack was. 'What are you doing here?' he asked.

'You first.'

Jeff had finished righting his clothes and he glanced off towards the road, as if making sure the Land Rover owner had gone. 'You just heard,' he said. 'I'm on bail and have to check in every two weeks.'

'Because you recorded that guy's sister?'

Jeff let out an annoyed *pfft*. 'It wasn't like that,' he said. 'But you can't argue semantics when someone's punching you in the face.'

Zack almost laughed at that. Almost.

'Your turn,' Jeff added.

'They found my girlfriend's body,' Zack replied.

Jeff stared curiously at him for a moment, perhaps wondering if it was some sort of wind-up. 'The girl you talked about the other day at the house?'

'Yes.'

'She's dead...?'

'Haven't the police spoken to you about it?'

Jeff huffed, though it was hard to tell whether it was in annoyance about more police involvement in his life, or because it was cold and he'd just been walloped.

'Not specifically,' he replied. 'They never mentioned a body. I never talk to them directly, only ever through my solicitor. They asked for keys and I assumed it was to do with the missing girl. I didn't know she was, well... dead.'

He was staring up towards the police station and there was something in his tone that didn't sound believable. The news of a young woman's body being found in the woods was out there – and he knew from Zack that someone due to be in his house was missing. Wouldn't he be interested in knowing whether they were linked?

The alternative was that he was one of those people genuinely oblivious to the world around him. Zack once worked with someone who said he didn't believe in Australia. After much pressing, it turned out that he somehow thought Australia was a fictional place 'a bit like Mordor'.

Jeff suddenly started scanning the ground, before he crouched and picked up his phone, which was lodged next to the nearest car's tyre.

'I've gotta go,' he said. 'Thanks for the, um...' He motioned in the vague direction that the Land Rover had headed and then dived into his pockets for car keys. Without another word, he strode quickly off towards a maroon BMW – and then, much like his assailant before him, he roared out of the car park with a guff of exhaust fumes.

Zack was back at his own car when he thought back to viewing the house with Jeff. There'd been something so odd and out of place and yet he'd forgotten about it after finding Katherine's pendant. It had fallen from his mind completely... until the moment he realised what it all meant.

And then he knew *exactly* why Jeff was so keen to avoid the police.

FORTY-THREE

HANNAH

Nobody was answering at Jeff's house. Hannah had knocked on the door, the window, and rung the bell – all of which got no reply. She went through her emails and found his phone number, except he wasn't picking up.

Hannah didn't want to head home but she also wasn't sure what to do considering he either wasn't in, or wasn't answering.

She put her gloves back on and headed to the end of the street, eyeing the camera outside the coffee shop. From the angle at which it was placed, it would have definitely captured Katherine, assuming it was recording. When everything had happened on the Sunday morning, nobody had suggested that a neighbour might have their own security system. It felt like a careless miss considering the number of people with dashcams, fisheye door cams and everything else these days. Even with all that, there would have been a limited number of properties or cars that had an angle which could've shown Katherine specifically entering the house. The police would surely have checked for all that.

Hannah continued around the corner and then entered the gravelly alley that ran the length of the road, along the back of the houses. She counted the properties until she was at the back of Jeff's and looked up to the windows, hoping for a sign that somebody was actually in. She had no idea if he lived alone, or with a wife, or kids. It wasn't based on anything other than her first impressions of him being a bit creepy – but he seemed the sort who lived on his own, with a few kids and failed relationships behind him.

Not that she could talk.

With no sign of movement in Jeff's house, Hannah continued along a few more houses until she was in the place where her mum had parked a few days before and they'd bundled Katherine into the back of the car.

It still didn't feel real. Perhaps it never would. It wasn't easy to think of herself as the sort of person capable of what they'd done. It would have been bad enough to do that to a stranger, let alone a lifelong friend.

Hannah blinked away the guilt and tried the gate, which was unlocked. She edged onto the garden and eyed the spot where she, Charlotte and Katherine had shared a smoke and a gossip in the corner.

Hannah moved deeper into the garden, until she was at the back door. If it was unlocked, it would open directly into the living room. It was the only way into the house from the back and, if someone had opened it while she slept on the sofa, she'd have surely noticed? The only way to the room in which Katherine had slept was past the sofa where Hannah had been sleeping. It felt impossible that it could have happened. If Jeff or someone had entered the house, it would have happened via the front door. They'd have still had to be exceptionally quiet – but they wouldn't have passed Hannah directly.

Except...

It was as Hannah was staring through the glare of the glass, into the living room, that she remembered the chain of events. When Katherine's body was found, they'd all assumed it was a bad reaction to the drug, or because of her injuries from the fall. Everything they'd done was to protect Charlotte. And Sophie, who'd worried it looked like Katherine had been beaten up – and that she would be accused of that too. Nobody thought it was murder – except the person who *actually* killed Katherine.

But, if it was murder, that person would have gone into the bedroom thinking the person sleeping inside was... Hannah.

The last two people awake had been Hannah and Katherine. All the bedroom assignments had been made and it was only at the very end of the night, when Hannah saw how ill Katherine looked, that she forced her to go into the en-suite bedroom.

It would have been dark – and one woman asleep in a darkened room could easily be mistaken for another.

Hannah shivered.

It couldn't be...

She was distracted by the slamming of a car door from somewhere towards the front of the house. Hannah darted out of the garden, closing the gate behind her, and then ran towards the end of the alley. She rounded the pair of corners with her chest thumping. By the time she got to the front of Jeff's house, there was a light on in the hallway beyond the rippled glass of the door.

Hannah wasn't entirely sure why she'd run – and she was certainly regretting it now. Those mad thoughts of trekking up mountains felt even crazier, considering she felt sick having run around a corner.

She wanted to confront Jeff about what she'd read on the news website. Except, now she'd considered everything, it felt less likely he had anything to do with what happened to Katherine.

There was still something not quite right, though. The sexual assault conviction, the multiple names, the leering way he looked at them all on day one.

Hannah knocked on the door and was immediately met by a grumbled 'hang on' from somewhere on the other side. There were a few seconds of someone bumping around, then footsteps, and then the door swung open to reveal a windswept Jeff. There was dirt on his chin and a smear of dried blood above his eye.

He took one look at Hannah and swore under his breath. 'Whatever this is, I don't have time for it,' he said.

Jeff started to close the door but Hannah jammed her elbow in the way. 'Did you do it?' she asked.

'Do what?'

'Kill my friend.'

Jeff's brow furrowed. Hannah was hoping for a reaction, even an angry 'no', but all she got was an annoyed sigh. 'What is it with you lot today?' he replied. 'If it's not you, it's that other lad.'

'What lad?'

Jeff wasn't listening. 'You go into my house, steal my things, have the police round and asking questions – now you're accusing me of God knows what. Weren't you supposed to be paying me back for those things you nicked?'

'I don't know why you're so certain it was us who took those things.'

It was unquestionably the wrong thing to say. Jeff threw a hand up to the sky in annoyance. 'That how you want to play it, is it? I *know* what you lot did – *and* I can prove it.'

Hannah stared at Jeff as he took a half step away. It took a pregnant second for them both to realise what had been said.

'*How* can you prove it?' Hannah asked.

Jeff took another half step backwards and then his gaze flicked past Hannah. There were footsteps and she turned to see Zack racing up the path. He stopped at her side and there was a momentarily triangular stand-off, in which it felt as if none of them trusted any of the others.

'*How* can you prove it?' Zack said.

Hannah turned towards the end of the path and the street beyond. Zack must have been behind the neighbour's bush, out of sight but able to overhear what was being said.

'What are you doing here?' she asked – although Zack's focus was solely on Jeff.

'Go on,' he said. 'How can you prove it?'

'I was, um—'

Zack half turned, pointing towards the street behind them. 'Your girlfriend broke up with you out there. That was Tina, wasn't it?'

'How do you—?'

'That was her brother today, trying to give you a kicking...'

Hannah had no idea what was going on. She looked between the two men – and it was Jeff who was on the back foot. He was shrinking in front of her, stammering the words.

There was no answer forthcoming but then Zack turned sideways to Hannah and fixed her in a confident, knowing stare. 'Was Katherine in the house with you?'

Hannah's heart was thundering like never before, and it was nothing to do with the run. She'd been lying for so long, to so many people, and it was exhausting. Zack was a good guy, she knew that, and it felt as if this was her last chance.

'Yes,' she said.

Zack spun back to Jeff, pointing a finger along the street towards the house in which Hannah had held her gathering.

'You've got hidden cameras in there, haven't you?'

FORTY-FOUR

Jeff wasn't tossing his keys from hand to hand on this trip to the rental house. It was a sombre march as he led Hannah and Zack up the stairs and then unlocked the door. He stepped inside and held it wide for them both to enter and then closed it behind him. There was a laptop under his arm, which he placed on the counter and plugged into the nearest socket.

He'd barely said a word since Zack mentioned the hidden cameras – but that was an answer in itself. Hannah could see from his panicked face that it was true. She wondered how Zack knew – but considering how he was also now aware that she'd spent five days lying about Katherine, she didn't want to risk asking.

Whatever else had happened, Jeff was scared. Zack had demanded to see the footage from Saturday night and Jeff hadn't bothered to argue. He'd picked up his laptop, put on his shoes and, a few minutes later, here they were.

What it *did* mean was that Jeff wasn't involved in whatever happened to Katherine. There's no way he'd have incriminated himself, let alone agreed to show them the footage.

Jeff was fiddling with something on the computer when

Zack spoke. He must've been talking to Hannah, though he wasn't facing her. She didn't blame him if he couldn't bring himself to look at her. She deserved whatever came.

'He's up on a voyeurism charge,' Zack said. 'He filmed his girlfriend and she found out about it. They had a big row on the street and he's on bail. The girlfriend's brother tried to beat him up an hour ago. I was the one who stopped it – but I should've let him get on with it.'

He sounded determined and, though Hannah didn't know Zack, she knew he didn't mean it. What she knew was that Jeff also had a sexual assault conviction from a few years before. With all this, it was no wonder he kept changing his name. Also not a surprise that he didn't want to involve the police when it came to the thefts.

Jeff was tapping away on the keyboard, studiously avoiding anything like eye contact with either of them. 'It was only to prevent thefts,' he said. 'I wasn't doing anything weird. I *never* looked at anything until this lot stole my stuff.'

He poked an angry thumb towards Hannah, which felt more aggrieved teenager than serious businessman.

'Does that mean you've already watched the footage...?' Hannah asked.

Jeff didn't answer – but the dilemma was clear. He'd know for certain that one of their group *had* stolen his items but he couldn't tell anyone, else he'd reveal the existence of the cameras. Given he was already in trouble for apparent voyeurism, he'd have to keep quiet.

And then, if he *had* looked through the footage, he'd know Katherine was there. He must've seen a photograph of her at least once, if not by the police then by Zack.

She wondered if he already knew who killed Katherine. If he cared about her more than he cared about his stupid coffee grinder and blender.

Jeff had finished doing whatever he was doing on his laptop

and he again picked up his keys before crossing to the padlocked cupboard that he'd told Hannah was full of cleaning supplies. He unclicked the lock and opened the door, revealing a stack of toilet rolls and kitchen towels, plus a mop, broom and bucket. He ignored all that, reaching to the highest shelf and unclipping an external hard drive. With that in hand, he returned to the laptop, and plugged in the drive.

All this had happened under the watchful eye of Zack – but now Jeff stepped to the side, holding out his hand towards the computer.

'All yours,' he said.

Zack moved forward, taking control of the laptop. He angled it a little to the side, allowing Hannah the opportunity to see the screen. She knew that, at some point, she'd be there with her mum. They'd be carrying out Katherine's body to the car.

'There are six cameras,' Jeff said. 'Pick whichever you want, plus the day and time. It's all backed up. You can scroll through as far as you want.'

Hannah felt him watching her momentarily – but then he moved quickly away towards the sofas, where he sat and cradled his head in his hands.

There was a brief tremble of Zack's hand as he touched the laptop's tracker pad. It was the first glimmer of nervousness Hannah had seen from him. He clicked a couple of buttons and then the footage started to play. It showed an empty living room from a slightly elevated position. Hannah felt a strange sense of self as she watched the exact spot on which she was standing. She turned and looked up to the wall, wondering where the camera was. She almost laughed when she realised.

It was the ornamental dog.

The camera was hidden in plain, bad-taste ceramic.

On the screen, the front door opened and Jeff entered. Hannah watched herself, Dawn, her mum, Charlotte and Beth all follow him one after the other. She had chills of recognition.

Did she *really* stand with such a stooped back? Did she *really* shrug as often as it seemed?

Jeff pointed towards the supply cupboard and she remembered him saying that it was full of cleaning supplies, which she figured wasn't a complete lie.

From there, Zack scrolled through the night's footage at super speed. They watched Dawn putting her booze on the counter and the three sisters excitedly rushing off to check out the rooms. They watched Sophie and Janet arrive. Zack flipped between the six cameras, following the action, following Hannah.

The first time he slowed everything to regular speed was when Hannah went to the front by herself. The door opened, Hannah stepped back, there was a second that lasted far too long... and then Katherine was there.

Zack had stopped breathing as they watched Katherine move into the house. She looked up and around the room and said something that Hannah couldn't remember. She half thought he'd stop the footage there and contact the police. That he'd leave everything to them.

He didn't.

They watched at regular speed for a minute or two – but then, without a word, without turning away from the screen, he cranked up the pace once more.

They were drinking and eating pizza. They were sitting at the table playing games. Hannah watched Katherine head outside and then she followed. There was no footage from the back and Zack kept everything moving through until they all returned inside. Time passed, both on and off screen – and then Katherine was on the counter, she was swinging from the chandelier that was more or less over their heads – and then she was on the floor.

Zack said nothing but he clicked to pause the video and then scrolled backwards and pressed to re-watch.

The question was unasked but Hannah answered it anyway. 'She was acting strangely.' She pointed to the screen. 'I almost begged her to go to the hospital but she didn't want to.'

'Why was she acting strangely?'

Hannah almost said that she didn't know, except she was so tired of the lies. She wanted to tell the truth – but she didn't want to get her sister into trouble.

Perhaps sensing that he wasn't going to get an answer, Zack turned back to the screen and sped up the footage again.

Hannah watched herself and the others sitting on the sofa. They were talking, and then people starting drifting off to bed one at a time until it was just Katherine and Hannah. Hannah went to the bedroom and then returned a moment later, which was when they had the conversation about swapping beds. Was it really that which cost Katherine her life?

Zack had paused the footage again. 'What did you talk about?'

'I asked if she thought we'd all end up being friends again one day.'

'What did she say?'

'Maybe.'

The word stuck in Hannah's throat and came out with a croak. She wanted that moment so badly that she could barely breathe.

On the screen, the old Hannah picked the bedcovers out of the ottoman and tucked a sheet into the bottom of the sofa. The lights went off and, for a few seconds, everything was dark – then the night-vision kicked in and everything turned a greyish green. The green Hannah tucked herself underneath a quilt and rolled over, then rolled back.

Nothing happened for hours and Hannah could barely stand to watch herself sleep. She threw off the extra blanket at one point, then clawed it back. It was such an invasion – and yet she could hardly ask Zack to stop. She doubted he was getting any pleasure from what they were doing, either.

Green Hannah rolled over once more, then back again. She wondered if she was always this fidgety. If she was, surely Paul would have said something when they were married?

Nothing on the laptop and nobody was moving.

And then they were. Hannah leaned in and felt the tightness in her chest as she'd forgotten to breathe.

Zack slowed the footage to regular speed as Sophie appeared from the corridor and edged across the open-plan room. She stopped for a moment, glancing across to the sofas – which left Hannah remembering that moment when she thought she might have been dreaming. She checked the time in the corner of the screen, which showed that it had been recorded a little after five in the morning.

And Sophie *was* there.

Hannah waited for her to continue moving across the room, to head into the opposite corridor and walk to Katherine's room. She couldn't believe it was going to happen.

And it didn't.

Sophie tiptoed around the kitchen counter and picked up the blender and coffee grinder. She'd first mentioned them when she and Hannah had talked in the kitchen – but Hannah didn't actually think she'd stolen them. She'd largely thought the owner was wrong, or mistaken. But Sophie held onto the items, paused for a moment as she again peered across to the sofas. Then she walked quickly back the way she'd come.

She really was a thief. Like all those years ago when she'd taken those magazines at the newsagent.

But she hadn't gone to Katherine's room... so who had?

Zack kept the footage moving forward as five became six became seven. Hannah watched herself hopping out of bed and then disappearing along the corridor to where Dawn was standing by the bedroom door. Katherine was inside, of course... except, at this point, she was already dead.

Nobody had crossed the living room.

They'd been watching the footage from the main camera in the living room, with the other angles in small windows at the side. Zack had been clicking onto the ones where there'd been movement – but neither of them had seen anything or anyone, except Sophie. She hadn't crossed the floor.

Zack seemed confused. He took a small step away from the laptop and looked towards the other end of the room, where Jeff was still on the sofas.

'What else is there?' he asked.

'You've got everything.'

'There must be something missing.'

Jeff stood and walked across to the counter where they were standing.

'There's a dog outside the bedroom,' Hannah said. 'Check the camera from there.'

Zack clicked a couple of buttons, shrinking the main camera to the smaller window and loading the one outside the bedroom in which Katherine had slept. He clicked the cursor back to the point when the screen turned green and then started to scroll.

It was a few minutes after two when the door to the room where Hannah's mum had slept opened. Hannah held her breath, watching as Dawn emerged. She first walked towards Katherine's room, then stopped and changed her mind, before heading into the bathroom. She was in there for a few minutes and then, when she exited, she returned directly to the bedroom.

There were no detours and Katherine's door remained closed.

Hannah could breathe again as Zack moved the footage forward. Another hour passed and then, at three-fifteen, something impossible happened.

Zack paused the screen and stared. They all did. Jeff craned in and took control of the trackpad, zooming in and then back out.

'I never saw this bit,' he said – and Hannah believed him.

He stepped away and Zack took over the controls once more, rewinding so they could watch again.

The panelled wall at the end of the corridor, adjacent to the en-suite door, slid to the side, like a patio door. Out from the darkness, behind the wall, stepped a crouched, bare-footed figure who quietly opened the door to the room in which Katherine was sleeping.

There was no camera inside, no final proof of the horror within, but five minutes later the door reopened and then the figure ducked back into the secret passage, before sliding the hidden door back into place.

Jeff turned to look towards the corridor that led to the bedrooms. He spun in a circle. 'I don't understand what happened,' he said. 'Where did she come from?'

Except Hannah knew.

It was in the way the silhouette had moved.

Hannah must have tensed because Jeff and Zack were both watching her.

'She came from the other side of the house,' Hannah said. 'One of the other bedrooms.'

'Some sort of passage...?' Jeff sounded disbelieving, even though they'd all watched it. 'How could anyone know it was there? I *didn't* know it was there. It's not on any of the plans.'

Hannah stepped away and the walls were edging towards her again, as they had when she'd been in the police interview room. The ceiling was falling and the world was imploding.

'*How?*' Jeff asked.

'Because,' Hannah replied, 'my little sister had been here before.'

FORTY-FIVE

ELEVEN MONTHS LATER

The ducks had still sodded off somewhere – and Hannah still didn't blame them. The vicious chill blowing across the park reminded Hannah of the last time she'd sat on the bench, when she was waiting for Sophie. It had been a different world then, in more ways than one.

The man slotted in at the other end of the bench, leaving a gap between them. Two metres and all that. Hannah turned to look at him, offering a weak smile that wasn't returned.

'Hi,' she said.

'Hi,' Zack replied.

Since she'd seen him in court, he'd grown out a beard and his hair was down to his shoulders. It wasn't only that but he seemed older than he had then. Something more than physical that she couldn't quite place. She supposed everything that had happened in the past year did that to a person. It had likely done it to her.

'I thought you deserved some answers,' Hannah said. 'I know you heard a lot in court but I wanted to fill some gaps.'

A pause.

'That and I wanted to say sorry.'

Hannah wasn't sure if she expected a reaction but she didn't get one. Zack pressed back onto the bench and stretched his legs out towards the deserted pond.

'It should have been me,' Hannah said. After nearly a year, she could say it without breaking down.

'I know.'

'Beth was trying to kill me. She thought the inheritance would then end up being re-split two ways, instead of three. She thought I was wasting the money by going travelling instead of saving it – or spending it on education, or whatever. She didn't know that I'd told Katherine to take the bedroom. When she did what she did, she thought she was doing it to me.'

Zack still didn't reply. Hannah didn't blame him for being angry. She'd felt all that across what was almost a year. Her own sister had tried to kill her for money. If that wasn't bad enough, which it was, she'd accidentally killed the wrong person.

'Did Beth ever tell you how she did it?'

Hannah didn't know what Zack was asking at first – but then she realised he didn't know what had happened beyond the bedroom door.

'Beth hasn't spoken to me since the moment she was arrested,' Hannah said.

'Did she say anything to anyone else?'

'If she did, then nobody has passed it on. I don't know what happened once the bedroom door closed. You saw the same video as me.'

Zack shuffled at the end of the bench and then stood. He blew into his hands and then delved into his jacket pockets for some gloves. 'Let's walk,' he said. 'It's too cold to sit.'

The déjà vu was strong as Hannah stood and started to follow Zack on a loop around the park. She'd done almost exactly this with Sophie the last time she'd been in the park. There was no man with a dog now, nobody at all. For this moment, it was as if they were the only two people in existence.

Zack led them out towards the pitch and putt in the far corner of the park. Wooden boards were across the windows of the shack from where people hired clubs and balls and the gate at the front was padlocked closed.

'Do you think she planned it?'

Zack's question took Hannah by surprise, partly because neither of them had spoken for a good minute or so – but also because, in what was close to a year since everything had happened, nobody else had asked her this.

'I don't know,' Hannah replied. 'She knew about the passage because it used to be her friend's house. Her friend told the police that she showed Beth the crawl space that linked the two sides of the house when they were younger. Her statement was agreed as fact before it ever got to court. It wasn't presented with her as a witness but the jurors got it in the evidence packs.'

Zack thought on that for a moment and then: 'But how did she get you to go to the house?'

'It wasn't my idea to have the going-away party – and it wasn't me who found the house. Beth picked the location on the Luxury Rentals site – and I wasn't bothered, so went along with it. When we got there, she took over and decided where everyone should sleep. That makes it sound like it was planned – but it didn't *feel* like that at the time.'

'But do you *think* it was planned...?'

It was the same question he'd asked a minute or so before and Hannah needed a moment to think about the answer. It wasn't a simple question.

'Yes and no,' Hannah said eventually. 'I don't think she sat at home in her bedroom coming up with a grand plan. I think she found the house she recognised on the website and so she thought she'd suggest it. If we'd said no, she wouldn't have pushed. Then we got to the house and everyone agreed about where we should sleep. Again, if we'd said no, that would have been that. Then she checked to see if the passage linking the corridors was still there – and it was. I think it's just that things worked out for her. I agreed to have the going-away party, then agreed to the house, then agreed to the bedrooms. After all that, she saw the chance and tried to take it.'

They continued walking, looping around the pitch and putt and on towards the bandstand. A pair of birds were fluttering around the raised bath that sat next to the closed public toilets. Droplets of water splashed over the rim and onto the path below as Zack and Hannah passed. They continued up the ramp that led towards the refreshments stand, which was closed for winter.

'There were a lot of photos of the passage in court,' Zack said.

'Nobody seems to know whether it was built on purpose,' Hannah replied. 'Jeff said it wasn't on the plans – but it kind of was. Nobody could've got through unless they were thin. Someone said it looked like a space where insulation or air conditioning should've gone.'

The two of them neared the refreshments stall and Hannah found herself slowing as they passed the price list that was still stuck to the wall. A coffee would have been ideal in the moment and Zack seemed to read her intention.

'The Grind is round the corner,' he said.

'I heard you left...?'

Zack didn't immediately answer the implied question, not that he held any obligations to her. Hannah was partly surprised when he replied.

'I couldn't go back knowing she wouldn't ever be around again.'

Hannah wanted to say that she felt the same about many things. She hadn't been back to the Morrisons where she'd seen Katherine at the checkouts. She went out of her way to avoid the road on which Jeff's house stood.

'Have you visited her?' Zack asked.

It was another question Hannah hadn't expected.

'No,' she replied. 'I doubt Beth would see me – but I don't think I want to go to prison anyway.'

She only realised what she'd said after it was out. She had been close enough to prison with or without her sister.

The footage of Beth crossing from one corridor to the other had been damning but her defence team had pushed a narrative that nobody knew what happened after she'd entered Katherine's bedroom. From what Hannah could tell, that was more or less the only defence they could offer – and it was no surprise the jury didn't buy it.

Hannah also realised that Beth had tried to push suspicion onto Sophie when things weren't going her way. It was unclear how but she'd stolen the toe ring, planted it in the room, and then pushed Hannah towards that photo of Sophie wearing it.

Given that she thought she was killing Hannah, it was unclear why Beth thought Sophie would be a suspect, other than that it had to be somebody in the house. She was sideswiped by not only the fact that she killed the wrong person – but that the first assumption of everyone was that Katherine had died because of complications around the MDMA she'd taken.

It had been a catalogue of calamities.

Sophie wasn't innocent in that. It turned out that she stole those appliances from the house not to sell or keep – but because she had some sort of compulsion. There was a cupboard in her garage filled with items she'd taken from shops and houses over a lengthy period of time.

As well as all that, Jeff had been prosecuted for two counts of voyeurism.

There had been no winners.

Hannah and Zack continued up the ramp and rounded the corner that would eventually take them back towards the duck pond. There was still nobody in sight.

'What about your mum?' Zack asked.

Hannah thought about not replying, except he'd specifically mentioned it – and she was the one who'd invited him to meet.

'They said that she should be released in six to eight weeks, depending on how many people get sent to prison. I didn't realise but they do a sort of one-in, one-out thing when they're at capacity. Whoever's closest to their release date gets let out early.'

'She must be strong to have carried Katherine's body all by herself...'

Hannah didn't reply to that – and it wasn't quite a question anyway. Hannah's mum had taken full responsibility for removing Katherine's body and dumping it. There would have been footage of Hannah and her mum carrying out the body – except, during the search for Katherine's phone, someone had nudged one of the dogs. Instead of capturing them, it had filmed the wall for almost nine hours until Jeff had righted it. Before they ever went to the police, Hannah had already seen the footage – or lack of it.

Nobody could've truly believed Hannah's mum did it all on her own – but she had confessed, pleaded guilty, and taken the prison sentence that came with it. It looked tidy enough for the prosecution and nobody could prove anything else was true.

Her mum had told Hannah to tell the police that she'd forced her into staying quiet and lying in her statement. That it was only her who'd got rid of the body.

Seven of them had been complicit – but only Beth and their mother had been punished. Well, and Jeff.

The police and the CPS had three high-profile prosecutions so presumably didn't want to push their luck. That was how Hannah's solicitor had framed it. It wasn't worth a bigger prosecution falling apart by going after low-hanging fruit and making a mistake.

Hannah was the fruit. So were Charlotte, Sophie, Dawn and Janet. Beth and Alison were the prizes.

The police knew Hannah had lied while being questioned – but there had been a strong indication that it would be overlooked if she was willing to give evidence for the prosecution at her sister's trial.

Which was what she'd done.

She hadn't exactly faced her sister in court, nor her mother – but she'd told the jurors what they wanted to hear. She'd lied through omission. Another crime for which she hadn't been punished. Something else with which she'd got away.

When Hannah next looked up, they were back at the pond. Zack stopped close to the bench, though didn't sit. They ended up standing a few paces apart, looking across the water.

'Your sister wanted to kill you…?'

Hannah wasn't sure if it was a question. It sounded like it might be. 'Yes,' she said, although it still didn't feel any more real. What a family they were. Their mum was in prison for disposing of a body, Beth was in prison for murder, Charlotte was keeping her head down after avoiding drug-related charges – and Hannah had somehow got away with everything. She didn't feel as if she deserved it – and yet she wasn't brave enough to own up to what she'd done.

Her nights remained largely sleepless, and when she did drift off, everything was haunted by images of Beth and Katherine, their faces blending into one. Her own sister had tried to kill her – and Hannah herself had covered it up, without meaning to. What she *had* meant to do was conceal the death of her old best friend.

Hannah wanted to leave this place behind but she knew she didn't deserve that kind of escape. She'd live in this same town for the rest of her life, tormenting herself because it was the least she deserved.

Zack was bobbing on his heels, probably trying to stay warm. 'Do you remember when I was sitting in the car near your house?' he asked.

'I came across to your window.'

'Do you remember what you asked?'

The moment was entrenched in Hannah's mind because it was then that it felt as if something had changed.

'The answer was yes,' Zack added.

She'd asked Zack if he loved Katherine and, though he hadn't answered, he really had. Now, almost a year on, and he'd left no doubt.

Hannah took a few steps to the side and sat on the bench. Her jeans gave no protection against the cold of the wood but she needed something to steady her.

'I'm so sorry,' she said.

She looked up to Zack, wanting him to respond, though all she got was the merest of nods. Perhaps she didn't even get that and she was seeing what she wanted.

'Do you think there's really only one person for everyone?' Zack asked. 'Just one and that's it?'

Another question Hannah hadn't anticipated. It felt too deep for her to be able to answer – and yet she tried anyway. 'I'd like to think people get second chances,' she said.

'Katherine won't ever get a second chance.'

Hannah bowed her head and stared at the path, wanting it to open up and take her because, for this, there truly was no reply.

THE PARTY AT NUMBER 12 PUBLISHING TEAM

Editorial
Ellen Gleeson

Line edits and copyeditor
Jade Craddock

Proofreader
Liz Hatherell

Production
Alexandra Holmes
Natalie Edwards

Design
Lisa Horton

Marketing
Alex Crow
Melanie Price
Occy Carr
Ciara Rosney

Distribution
Chris Lucraft
Marina Valles

Made in United States
North Haven, CT
18 May 2022

19288642R10188